YOUNGER

YOUNGER

YOUNGER

PAMELA REDMOND

THORNDIKE PRESS
A part of Gale, a Cengage Company

LIBRARY OF CONGRESS CIP DATA ON FILE.
CATALOGUING IN PUBLICATION FOR THIS BOOK
IS AVAILABLE FROM THE LIBRARY OF CONGRESS

ISBN-13: 978-1-4328-8273-0 (hardcover alk. paper)

Published by arrangement with Gallery Books, a division of Simon &
Schuster, Inc.

Printed in Mexico
Print Number: 01   Print Year: 2021

To my daughter, Rory Satran

ACKNOWLEDGMENTS

I'm so grateful to have two of the most brilliant and generous women in publishing on my team, my agent Deborah Schneider and editor Amy Pierpont. Also at Downtown Press, thanks to Louise Burke, Megan McKeever, Hillary Schupf, Anne Dowling, and Danielle Rehfeld, and at Gelfman Schneider, to Cathy Gleason and Britt Carlson. For a key plot twist that bedeviled the rest of the world, thank you to the inspired Leslie Rexach. I'm lucky enough to have close friends who are also smart writers and supportive colleagues: Rita DiMatteo, Alice Elliott Dark, Benilde Little, and Christina Baker Kline. Thank you to the Virginia Center for the Creative Arts and the Geraldine Dodge Foundation for the two most heavenly weeks of my writing life, during which I spun out most of the first draft of this book. For insights into life on the south side of forty, I send thanks and kisses to my cousin's lovely daughters, Kimberly and Katie Kavanagh, and to my own fabulous — okay, awesome — children, Rory, Joe, and Owen Satran. And thank you, always, to Dick.

CHAPTER 1

I almost didn't get on the ferry.

I was scared. And nervous. And over-whelmed by how out of place I felt, in the crowd of young people surging toward the boat bound for New York.

Not just New York, but New York City on New Year's Eve. The mere thought of it made my hands sweat and my feet tingle, the way they did the one time I rode to the top of the Empire State Building and tried to look down. In the immortal words of my daughter Diana, it made my weenie hurt.

I would have turned around and driven right back home to my safe suburban house — *I can see the ball drop better on TV anyway!* — except I couldn't leave Maggie waiting for me on the freezing pier in downtown Manhattan. Maggie, my oldest and still closest friend, didn't believe in cell phones. She also didn't believe in comput-ers, or cars, or staying in New Jersey on

9

New Year's Eve, or for that matter, staying in New Jersey ever. Maggie, who came out as a lesbian to her ultra-Catholic parents at sixteen and made her living as an artist, didn't believe in doing anything the easy way. And so I couldn't cancel our night out, and there was nothing for me to do but keep marching forward to my potential doom.

At least I was first in line for the next boat. It was frigid out that night, but I staked my claim to the prime spot, hanging on to the barricade to keep anybody from cutting in front of me. These kind of suburban yos who were milling around on the dock with me, I knew, majored in line-cutting in kindergarten.

Then a weird thing happened. The longer I stood there, guarding my turf, the more I began to want to go into the city — not just for Maggie, but for myself. Looking out across the dark water at the lights of Manhattan sparkling beyond, I began to think that Maggie had been right, and going into New York on New Year's Eve was exactly what I needed. Shake things up, she said. Do something you've never done before. Hadn't doing everything the way I'd always done it — the cautious way, the theoretically secure way — landed me precisely in the middle of my current mess? It had, and no one wanted that to change more than me.

And so when they opened the gate to the ferry, I sprinted ahead. I was determined to be the first one up the stairs, to beat everybody else to the front of the outside deck, where I could watch New York glide into view. I could hear them all on my heels as I ran, but I was first out the door and to the front of the boat, grabbing the metal rail and hanging on tight as I labored to catch my breath. The ferry's engine roared to life, its diesel smell rising above the saltiness of the harbor, but still I sucked the air deep into my lungs as we chugged away from the dock. Here I am, I thought: alive and moving forward, on a night when anything can happen.

It wasn't until then that I noticed I was the only one standing out there. Everybody else was packed into the glassed-in cabin, their collective breath fogging its windows. Apparently I was the only one who wasn't afraid of a little cold, of a little wind, of a little icy spray — okay, make that a *lot* of icy spray — as the boat bucked like a mechanical bull across the waves. It was worth it, assuming I wasn't hurled into the inky waters, for the incredible view of the glowing green Statue of Liberty and the

11

twinkling skyscrapers up ahead.

As I gripped the rail even tighter, congratulating myself on my amazing bravery, the boat slowed and seemed to stall there in the middle of the harbor, its motor idling loudly. Just as I began to wonder whether we were about to sink, or make a break for the open seas at the hands of a renegade captain running from the law, the boat began to back up. Back up and turn around. Were we returning to New Jersey? Maybe the captain had the same misgivings about Manhattan on New Year's Eve that I did.

But no. Once the boat swung around, it began moving toward the city again. Leaving me facing not the spectacular vista of Manhattan but the big clock and broken-down dock of Hoboken, and darkest New Jersey beyond. Frantically, I looked over my shoulder at the bright, snug cabin, which now had the prime view of New York, but it was so crowded, it would have been impossible to squeeze inside. I was stuck out in the cold facing New Jersey, all alone. The story of my life.

Half an hour later, I was hobbling through the streets of Soho arm in arm with Maggie, cursing the vanity that had led me to wear high heels and fantasizing about grabbing the comfy-looking green lace-up boots off Maggie's feet. Maggie was very sensibly striding along beside me in boot-cut jeans, a downfilled coat as enormous as a sleeping bag, and a leopard-print hunter's cap, with the earflaps down and a velvet bow tied under her chin.

"Are we almost there yet?" I asked, the shoes nipping at my toes.

"Come on," she said, tugging me away from the crowded sidewalk of West Broadway toward a dark, unpopulated side street. "This'll be faster."

I stopped, looking with alarm down the deserted street. "We'll get raped."

"Don't be such a scaredy-cat." Maggie laughed, pulling me forward.

Easy for her to say: Maggie had moved to the Lower East Side at eighteen, back when Ratner's was still serving blintzes and crackheads camped under her stairwell. Now she owned her building, the entire top floor turned into a studio where she lived and worked on her sculptures, larger-than-life leaping, twirling women fashioned from wire and tulle. All those years in New York on her own had made Maggie tough, while I was still the soft suburban mom, protected by my husband's money, or should I say, my soon-to-be-ex-husband's ex-money.

13

My heart hammered in my ears as Maggie dragged me down the black street, slowing only slightly when I focused on the sole beam of light on the entire block, which seemed, for some strange reason, to be pink. When we reached the storefront from which the light was emanating, we saw why: in the window was a bright pink neon sign that read "Madame Aurora." The glow was further enhanced by a curtain of pink and orange glass beads covering the window, filtering the light from inside the shop. Beyond the beads, we could just make out a woman who could only be Madame Aurora herself, a gold turban askew on her gray hair, smoke curling from the cigarette that teetered from her lips. Suddenly, she looked straight at us and beckoned us inside. Taped to the window was a handlettered sign: "New Year's Wishes, $25."

"Let's go in," I said to Maggie. I'd always been a sucker for any kind of wish and any kind of fortune-telling, so the combination of the two was irresistible. Besides, I wanted to get out of the cold and off my feet, however briefly.

Maggie made a face, her "You have got to be out of your fucking mind" face.

"Come on," I said. "It will be fun."

"Eating a fabulous meal is fun," Maggie

14

said. "Kissing someone you have a crush on is fun. Dropping good money on some phony fortune-teller is *not* fun."

"Come on," I wheedled, the way I did when I called to read her a particularly good horoscope, or suggested she join me in wishing on a star. "You're the one who told me I should start taking more risks."

Maggie hesitated just long enough to give me the confidence to step in front of her and push open Madame Aurora's door, giving Maggie no choice but to follow.

It was hot inside the room, and smoky. I waved my hands in front of my face in an attempt to signal my discomfort to Madame Aurora, but this only seemed to provoke her to take a deeper drag on her cigarette and then to emit a plume of smoke aimed directly at my face.

I looked doubtfully at Maggie, who only shrugged and refused to meet my eye. I was the one who'd dragged us in here; she wasn't about to get us out.

"So, darling," said the Madame, finally removing the cigarette from her mouth. "What is your wish?"

What was my *wish*? I wasn't expecting her to pop the big question right out of the gate like that. I figured there'd be some preamble, a few moments examining my palm, shuffling the tarot cards, that kind of thing.

"Well," I stalled. "Do I get only one?"

Madame Aurora shrugged. "You can have as many as you want, for twenty-five dollars a pop."

And no fair, as everybody knows, wishing for more wishes.

Again, I tried to catch Maggie's eye. Again, she looked stubbornly away from me. I closed my eyes and tried to concentrate.

What was the one thing I wanted, above all others? For my daughter Diana to return from Africa? Definitely, I wanted that, but she was scheduled to come home this month anyway, so that seemed like a waste of a wish.

To get a job? Of course. I'd been so determined to support myself when my husband left that I'd negotiated sole title to our house in lieu of long-term alimony. Then I'd spent half the year humiliating myself at interviews at publishing houses. No one, it seemed, wanted to hire a forty-four-year-old woman who'd spent precisely four months in the workforce before becoming a full-time mom. I tried to tell them I'd devoted the past twenty years to reading everything I could get my hands on, and I knew better than anybody what middle-class suburban women in book groups — women exactly like me, who made up the prime novel-buying market — wanted to read.

But nobody cared about my experience in the reading trenches. All they seemed to see was a middle-aged housewife with an ancient English degree and a résumé padded with such "jobs" as co-chair of the book fair at my kid's elementary school. I was unqualified for an editor's position, and though I always told them I would be happy to start as an assistant, I wasn't considered for entry-level jobs. No one put it this way, but they thought I was too old.

"I wish I were younger," I said.

By the looks on Madame Aurora's and Maggie's faces, I must have said that out loud.

The Madame burst out laughing.

"Whaddaya wanna be younger for?" she said. "All that worryin', who am I gonna marry, what am I gonna do with my life. It's for the birds!"

Maggie chimed in. "What are you saying, that you want to go back to all that uncertainty? Now that you finally have a chance to get your life together?"

I couldn't believe they were ganging up on me. "It's just that if I were younger I could do some things a little differently," I tried to explain. "Think about what I want more, take my career more seriously . . ."

But Maggie was already shaking her head. "You are who you are, Alice," she said. "I knew you when you were six, and even back then you always put everybody else first. Before you went out to play, you had to make sure your stuffed animals were comfortable. When we were freshmen in high school, and everybody else was consumed with trying to look cool, you were the one who volunteered to push that crippled girl around in her wheelchair. And once you had Diana, she was always what you cared about above everything else."

I had to admit, she was right. I may have left my job at Gentility Press because I had to, when I started bleeding and almost lost the baby. But once Diana was born, I stayed home because I wanted to. And then, as she got older, I kept telling myself I couldn't go back to work because maybe this was the year I'd finally get pregnant again, but the truth was that Diana herself was all the focus I needed in my life.

So now I wanted to undo that? Now I wished I could go back and put Diana in day care, become a working mom, or even not have Diana at all?

The very idea was enough to send an enormous shiver up my spine, as if even the shadow of the idea could jinx my daughter, my motherhood, the most important thing in my life. I could never wish her out of existence, never dream of wishing away even one of the moments I'd spent with her.

But still, what about me? Had devoting all those years to my child disqualified me from ever claiming a life for myself? The real reason I wished I'd been different back then was so that I could be different now: ballsier, bolder, capable of grabbing the world by the throat and bending it to my will.

"What's it gonna be?" said Madame Aurora.

"I want to be braver," I said. "Plus maybe, if you could do something about my cellulite . . ."

Maggie rolled her eyes and jumped to her feet.

"This is ridiculous," she said, taking hold of my arm. "Come on, Alice. We're leaving."

"But I didn't get my wish," I said.

"I didn't get my money," said Madame Aurora.

"Too bad," said Maggie. "We're out of here."

Now Maggie was walking really fast. I tried asking her to slow down, but instead of listening, she kept forging ahead, expecting me to keep up. Finally, I stopped dead in my tracks so she had to double back and talk to me.

"Give me your boots," I said.

She looked puzzled.

"If you expect me to walk this far and this fast, you're going to have to trade shoes with me."

Maggie looked down at my feet and burst out laughing.

"You need more help than I thought," she said.

"What are you talking about?"

"You'll see." She was already untying her green boots.

"Where are we going?" I always trusted Maggie to be my guide to New York, following unquestioningly, like a little girl, wherever she wanted to take me. Tonight, for instance, I thought she said we were going to a cool new restaurant. But now that I took a moment to look around at the low brick buildings and decidedly uncool neighborhood as I stepped into Maggie's boots, I was starting to wonder.

"We're going to my place," she said.

"Why?"

"You'll see."

Even wearing the heels, she walked faster than me, but at least my feet didn't hurt anymore. And once we passed out of the no-man's-land that still separated Little Italy from Maggie's neighborhood, I began to relax. The blocks around her building used to be terrifying, but had improved considerably in the past few years. Tonight, the streets were full of people, and all the hip restaurants and bars were packed. Every place looked good to me — I was starving, I realized — but Maggie was not to be deterred.

"We'll go out after," she said.

"After *what*?"

She smiled mysteriously and repeated the phrase that was becoming her mantra: "You'll see."

It was a five-flight climb to Maggie's loft, which I used to find daunting but now took with ease, thanks to all the hours I'd logged on the elliptical trainer in the past year. After a lifetime as a dedicated couch potato, I'd started exercising because it was the only thing I could think of, in my past year of horrible events, that would reliably make

21

me feel good. And after a lifetime of dieting, I'd found the pounds disappearing without doing anything at all — anything, that is, except working out for an hour or two every day. I'd even, maybe twice, had a flash of that high you're supposed to get from working out, though I still preferred a Cosmo.

Coming from the suburbs, where Pottery Barn was considered the height of living room fashion, Maggie's loft was always a shock. It was basically one gigantic room that occupied the entire top floor of the building, with windows on all four sides and a bright red silk tent sitting smack in the middle of the three thousand feet of open space — the closet. The only furniture was an enormous iron-framed bed, also bright red, and an ornate purple velvet chaise that provided the place's sole seating, unless you counted the paint-spattered wooden floor. Which I didn't.

"Okay," Maggie said, as soon as she'd triple-bolted the door behind us. "Let me have a look at you."

But I was too distracted by what was different about Maggie's loft to stand still. All her sculptures, all her nine-foot-tall chickenwire women, with their size 62 ZZZ breasts and their ballet skirts as full and frothy as flowering cherry trees, had been shoved into one corner, where they mingled like inmates in some prison for works of art. Now occupying the prime spot in Maggie's work area was a concrete block as big as a refrigerator.

"What on earth is that?" I said.

"Something new I'm trying with my work," said Maggie breezily. "Come on, take off your coat. I want to see what you're wearing."

Now I could finally focus. Maggie wanting to survey my clothes was never a good thing. She was always, from the time we were first able to dress ourselves, trying to make me over, and I was always resisting. Don't get me wrong, I thought Maggie had fantastic style, but fantastic for *her,* not for me. Her hair had turned white when she was still in her twenties, and every year it seemed to get a little shorter and messier, standing up in tufts all over her head. As her hair got more butch, her earrings became more feminine and ornate and numerous. The featured attraction tonight was green-jeweled chandelier earrings. Maggie, whose body was still as slim and limber-looking as a teenager's, also must have had the soul of a French woman. She had that knack for throwing on an odd assortment of

23

clothes — tonight it was the faded jeans she'd had since high school with an antique lace-trimmed cream silk blouse and a long gray-green velvet scarf wound around her neck — that always managed to look enviably perfect.

She walked around me, rubbing her chin and shaking her head. Finally she reached out and grabbed a hank of the oversize beige sweater I was wearing.

"Where'd you get this?" she asked.

"It was Gary's," I admitted. One of the many pieces of clothing he'd left behind when he left me exactly a year ago for his dental hygienist. Clothing I'd kept because, for a long time, I assumed he'd come back. And continued to keep because, for the next few months at least, he was still paying the mortgage on the house where his clothes and I lived together.

"It's a rag," Maggie said. "And what about that skirt?"

The skirt choice I was actually rather pleased with. The same beige as the sweater, it was fitted through the hips and ended above the knee, considerably sexier than the khakis and sweatpants I'd favored for the past two decades.

"It was Diana's," I said proudly. "I couldn't believe it fit me."

"Of course it fits you!" Maggie exclaimed. "You're a stick! Come here."

She spun me around and tried to push me forward.

"Where are you taking me?"

"I want you to look at yourself."

She propelled me across the loft until we were standing in front of an oval mirror with a curlicued gold frame, like the one the Wicked Stepmother communes with in "Snow White."

"Mirror, mirror on the wall," I said, laughing, trying to get Maggie to join in the joke. But she only gazed poker-faced over my shoulder, refusing to so much as crack a smile.

"This is serious," she said, pointing her chin toward the mirror. "Tell me what you see."

It had been a long time since I'd looked in a mirror with much enthusiasm. Sometimes, especially when Diana was small, I'd go for days without checking my reflection. And then through the years, as I got heavier, and my hair started to turn gray, and the lines began to appear around my eyes, I discovered I felt happier when I didn't look at all. In my mind's eye, I was forever some grown-up but neutral age — thirty-threeish — and some womanly but neutral weight

— 133ish — and looked acceptable if not gorgeous or sexy or notable in any way. I was always shocked when I caught sight of my reflection in a shop window or a car door and was forced to see that I was considerably older and heavier than I believed.

But now, compelled to confront my image, really take it in, for the first time in the year my life had been turned upside down and inside out, I had the opposite reaction. I lifted my chin and turned my head to the side; without thinking, I stood up taller and smiled.

"That's right," Maggie said. She gathered the back of my baggy sweater into her hands so the fabric was pulled tight against my newly buff body. "What do you see?"

"I see —," I said, trying to think how to put it. There was me, staring back from the glass, but it was some version of myself before child, before husband, before all the years had clouded my vision. "— myself," I said finally, lamely.

"Yes!" Maggie cried. "It's you! It's the Alice I've known and loved all these years, who was getting buried under a layer of fat and misery."

"I wasn't miserable." I frowned.

"Oh, pooh," Maggie said. "How could you

not have been miserable? Your husband was never around, your daughter was growing up and leaving home, your mother was fading away, you had nothing to do —"

I felt stung. "I had the house to take care of," I said. "My mother to look after. And just because Diana was theoretically grown up and away at college didn't mean she didn't need me anymore."

"I know," Maggie soothed. "I don't mean to denigrate all you did. What I'm trying to get you to see is how much lighter you look now. How much younger."

"Younger?" I said, focusing again on my reflection.

"It's partly the weight," Maggie said meditatively, staring at my image in the mirror, "but it's something else too, some burden that seems to have been lifted. Besides, you always looked a lot younger than you really were. Don't you remember when we were seniors in high school, you were the only one who could still get into the movies for the kids' price? And even when you were in your thirties, long after you had Diana, you'd still get carded in bars."

"I don't think I'd get carded now."

"Maybe not, but you could look a lot younger than you are. A lot younger than

27

you do."

"What do you mean?"

"I mean that with some color in your hair, a little makeup, some clothes that fit, for God's sake, you could still look like you were in your twenties!" Maggie exploded. "That's why I dragged you out of that fucking voodoo parlor! We're the only ones who have the power to turn our dreams into reality."

I smirked at Maggie. She was usually the first one to puncture what she called "that power-of-positive-thinking bullshit." I was the one who made wishes on stars and birthday candles, who believed, as Cinderella said in the Disney movie I'd watched at least two hundred times with Diana nestled into my side, that "if you dream a thing more than once, it's sure to come true." But now instead of smirking back, Maggie only gazed at me with a look of utter conviction.

"So you think," I said finally, "that I have the power to make myself younger just by wishing it were so?"

"Not *just* by wishing," she said. "We're going to need a little help from Lady Clairol. Let's get started."

It was while I was sitting on the purple chaise, munching on a cold slice of pizza that was going to have to count for dinner, with a garbage bag knotted over the chemical glop on my hair, that Maggie told me about her dream. She wanted to have a baby.

"You're kidding," I said, trying to keep my mouth from falling open.

She looked insulted. So insulted that it was clear this was anything but a joke. It was just that I'd known Maggie as long as I could remember, and she'd never had the least interest in children or motherhood. When I was rocking my baby dolls and tucking in my stuffed animals, Maggie was crouched on the floor, trying a new finger-painting technique. When I was eagerly babysitting to earn extra money, Maggie was mowing lawns, helping people clean out their attics — anything to get out of helping take care of her seven younger brothers and sisters. She always said that growing up, she'd changed enough diapers to last a lifetime.

And now here she was, at forty-four, suddenly changing her mind.

"What happened?" I said.

"Nothing happened. I guess I finally decided that I'd been a kid for long enough. I'm ready to grow up and be the parent now."

"But a baby," I said. Living in the suburbs, I was around mothers and babies all the time — the kids in the house behind me, screaming all day and night; the young moms in the supermarket, struggling to keep their squirming toddlers in the grocery carts. After all my years of wishing for and dreaming of having another baby, of looking at pregnant women and mothers with infants with a level of envy and longing that could literally make me double over, I had finally passed into some other stage where I thought babies, like tiger or bear cubs, were adorable but frightening, best viewed from a distance. Through glass.

I struggled for a way to convey my misgivings to Maggie without coming straight out and telling her I thought having a baby at this age, after an entire adulthood of independence, was the worst idea she'd had since shaving her head.

I took Maggie's hand, rough as a carpenter's from years of twisting wire into roundness.

"You know," I said, in the gentlest voice I could summon, "it's so much work having a baby, especially on your own. Waking up in the middle of the night, carrying the stroller up and down the stairs, the diapers, the crying —"

"I grew up with that, remember?" Maggie snapped, snatching back her hand.

"Exactly!" I said. "But you were helping out your mom then; it wasn't all on your shoulders. You live in this neighborhood where almost nobody has kids, none of your friends have kids, your life is in no way set up for it. And it's not just having a baby — you've got the nursery school search ahead, tuition payments, adolescence. When the kid's out of college, you'd be collecting social security."

"That's it, isn't it?" Maggie said stonily. "You think I'm too old."

"You are too old!" I exploded. "We're both too old!"

"I thought that you, of all people, would understand my desire for a child," Maggie said, blinking back tears, "after all you went through to have Diana, after all the years you tried to have another baby."

I softened, remembering how powerful my own yearning had been. But I also remembered how completely a baby, even the quest to have a baby, could take over your life; how exhausting parenthood could be even when you were twenty years younger than Maggie and I were now.

"I do understand," I told her, trying to take her hand again. "But sometimes you

31

reach a point in life where you've just got to leave something behind. When it's just too late."

I knew that was harsh, as Diana would say. But Maggie and I had vowed, way back in fourth grade, to always tell each other the Bottom Line Truth — the BLT — even when we knew the other person didn't want to hear it. She had told me, back when I married Gary four months after meeting him on the sidewalk outside Buckingham Palace on the day Princess Diana married Prince Charles, that I was crazy to get married so young. Then, when I turned up pregnant a few months later, just like the real Princess Diana, Maggie made no secret of being horrified, especially when I was forced to leave my job.

Though Maggie had always adored my daughter, it had been from a distance, sending her outrageously frilly dresses from Paris and taking her, once a year, to art galleries and some wildly unsuitable restaurant, where she would be aghast if Diana gagged on the eel. And she'd been asking me since the day I brought Diana home from the hospital when I was going back to work.

Now she stared at me, with a look I knew only too well. It was the look she got when she was going to say something that she knew I wasn't going to like.

"You mean like it's too late for you to get back into publishing?" she said. "Like it's too late for you to have a career?"

Now I was the one struggling not to cry. And it was Maggie's turn to reach out and squeeze my arm.

"I don't really believe that," she said. "I *don't* think it's too late for you. That's exactly my point. We're not a couple of old ladies who should just fold up our tents and shuffle off to the nursing home. There's still plenty of time for both of us. Come on."

Maggie wouldn't let me look in the mirror again until she was finished. She washed my hair and blow-dried it, spent forever working over me with her makeup brush, buckled me into some very extreme underwear, and zipped me into tight jeans. It was like we were teenagers again, swapping clothes and doing makeovers on each other.

"How come you have all this girlie stuff?" I asked Maggie.

"I'm a lesbian," she said. "Not a man." She spritzed some perfume on my neck and surveyed me.

"Okay," she said, nodding decisively. "I think you're ready."

Once again, she propelled me across the

loft to the mirror.

I swear, at first I didn't recognize myself. I actually swiveled to look behind me, thinking somebody else may have walked into the place when I wasn't looking.

Somebody blond. Somebody hot. And somebody very, very young.

"I can't believe it," I said, blinking hard.

Maggie grinned. "I'd take you for twenty-two!" she crowed.

I couldn't stop staring. Maggie had given me, in its most essential sense, my wish — my wish not merely to be younger but to go back in time and be reinvented as a different person. The woman in the mirror looked like me, sort of, but like a different version of me than had ever existed in real life. When I was really twenty-two, I was finishing up my study of Jane Austen and the Brontës at Mount Holyoke, with my hair scraped back in a ponytail and my body swathed in big baggy sweat clothes and my thick glasses perennially sliding down my unpowdered nose. When I was really twenty-four, I was the mother of a toddler, still wearing the ponytail and the glasses and the sweat clothes, except now they were even bigger and smelled vaguely of spit-up. At twenty-eight, I sometimes made a Big Effort and got myself into leggings and a voluminous sweater to man the kindergarten bake sale.

I had certainly never looked like this: buff and blond, wearing lipstick and baring cleavage and looking smart and a little bit slutty.

"Who is she?" I whispered.

But Maggie, who was busy checking her watch, didn't hear me. "It's almost midnight," she said. "Time to take the new you out for a test run."

CHAPTER 2

The bar on Maggie's corner was packed with people, with more thronged out on the sidewalk, but the tall elegant woman barring the doorway to everyone else waved Maggie and me inside.

"She has a crush on me," Maggie shouted in my ear.

"I hope my being here doesn't give her the impression that you're taken."

"She knows you're straight."

I looked quizzically at Maggie. "How does she know that?"

"She's psychic," Maggie said, with a poker face. And then, "No, really, sweetheart. You could be wearing motorcycle boots and a Melissa Etheridge T-shirt, and you'd still look straight. It's just something about the vibe."

Maggie began maneuvering us forward toward the bar, craning her neck to survey the room as we wound our way through all the people.

"Who do you want?" she said.

"Want?"

I must have looked even more alarmed than I felt, because Maggie burst out laughing. "To kiss!" she cried. "Do you see anybody you want to kiss at midnight?"

I'd been married so long that I couldn't remember ever considering this question. Last New Year's Eve, I had still been with Gary, at our friends Marty and Kathy's annual New Year's dinner party, and as always it had been Gary I'd turned to first. I'd had no idea that in twelve hours he'd tell me he wanted a divorce; never in a trillion years would have guessed that the next New Year's Eve, I'd be surveying the throng at a downtown Manhattan restaurant in search of a stranger to kiss.

And then I saw him. He was standing at the bar, half listening to a skinny redheaded guy talking on the stool beside him, but focusing more on looking around the room, a little half smile on his lips. His hair was long and dark, his skin pale. He looked to be medium height and medium build, but with extraordinarily broad shoulders, shoulders wide enough to ride on. His eyes seemed to be dancing, as if he'd just remembered a really good joke and couldn't wait

37

to tell someone.

It was at that moment that he turned, as if I'd shouted that he could tell the joke to me, and looked directly into my eyes. His face broke into a grin, leaving me no choice but to smile back. It was like we were old friends, ex-lovers who'd parted on the friendliest of terms, recognizing each other in the crowd.

Then the redheaded man said something more insistent, and my man looked away.

"I'd kiss him," I said to Maggie.

"Who?"

"At the bar," I said. "Next to the red-headed guy. The one with the artsy hair."

He looked at me again then, and Maggie started nudging me forward. Then, all at once, a shout went up and two televisions mounted above the bar flickered on. It was the Times Square ball, with an onscreen clock showing the minutes left until the new year: just under five.

"Perfect!" Maggie shouted in my ear as she propelled me along. "He's a baby!"

I stopped. "What do you mean?" Now I was trying to look at him without him seeing me. I hadn't exactly pegged him as middle-aged, but neither did he look like a college kid.

"He's definitely in his twenties," Maggie

said, poking me in the back.

I frowned. "I'd say thirties."

"No way. Come on. We have to see if you pass."

Move forward? Or run shrieking into the night? Maggie made the decision for me by giving me a major shove, practically right into Mr. Dancing Eyes' arms.

"Oh," I said, my breasts jammed against the starched cotton of his shirt, the soapy smell of his neck filling my nose. "Sorry. My friend —"

"It's all right," he said. "I was wondering whether I was going to be able to get close enough to talk to you. You look so familiar. Don't I know you from somewhere?"

Not unless you've been loitering at the Lady Fitness near my house in New Jersey, I wanted to say. Or attending meetings of the Homewood Garden Club.

Then again, he couldn't possibly know me from anywhere, because I'd never *been* anywhere — not the me that was standing in front of him, anyway.

"Ten," the crowd started to chant. "Nine. Eight —"

"Oh, no," I said.

"No?" He looked surprised.

"It's just —"

It was just that I could feel Maggie mere

inches behind me, awaiting our kiss like some pimp with an overdue car payment. And I wanted to kiss him, but I was scared.

"Five. Four —"

Scared of kissing someone new, I mean *really* kissing someone *really* new, for the first time in twenty-three years. Scared I wouldn't remember how. Scared because it was clear, now that I was so close, that this guy had probably been a toddler the last time I'd done this. Scared that I didn't care.

There was shouting. There was cheering. I stared at him, feeling like a rabbit who'd come face-to-face with the fox. And also, a little bit like the fox. He looked back, his eyes sparkling with that joke again.

And then I realized something that, in my terror about going into the city and in my focus on making the right wish and throughout my overhaul by Maggie, had eluded me. The year was over. This moment marked the end of the worst year of my entire life — the year my husband left me and my mother died and my only child moved half the world away. It was done now, and it seemed as irrefutable as a law of the universe that the year that had just started could only be better.

I was filled with such a sense of joy and relief that I let out an enormous sigh and smiled at him, which was all the encouragement he needed to lean in and touch his lips to mine. The thing was, they fit so perfectly, his curved upper lip notching exactly into the space between my two, his lower lip landing neatly below my own. He tasted of sugar; I could feel the actual little grains.

When we finally pulled apart, I said the first thing that came to my mind: "Thank you."

He burst out laughing. "You're very welcome, but let me tell you, that took a lot of effort."

I felt my face begin to burn. "It's only —," I said. "It's just that I mean —"

"That's okay," he said softly, bringing his finger to my lips.

And then he moved as if to kiss me again.

"No!" I cried, springing backward.

He looked confused. "No?"

"I'm not interested in a relationship."

He laughed again. "I'm not interested in a relationship either," he said.

"You're not?"

"No," he said. "I just broke off my engagement."

"Just . . . ," I said, ". . . now?"

He smiled. He was big on eye contact, which was very nice but, in my experience, unusual in a man.

"Well, last June," he said. "I realized I didn't want to get married, not yet, anyway. I'm not in any hurry to step onto that whole fast-track-career, mortgage, babies thing."

"That's great," I said.

All around us, people were cheering and throwing their arms around each other.

The dark-haired man leaned in closer to me, boring into me with those brown eyes. "You're serious? Because most girls I meet, I tell them that and they walk away. They're totally turned off."

"No, I think that's really smart," I said. "This is the one time in your life when you can be free, experiment, do whatever you want to do, and you should take advantage of that. Don't be in any rush to settle down."

It was the same thing I'd told my daughter Diana, who'd taken my advice so seriously she'd moved five thousand miles away from me. Now he was talking to me again, but I'd become so lost in my thoughts of Diana that I seemed to have missed what he was saying. The only word I heard was "Williamsburg," but he was obviously waiting for a response.

"All those weird costumes," I said, remembering Diana's eighth-grade trip.

He looked at me strangely. "I know a great

club there that should be quieter than this. I wondered whether you'd like to go."

I couldn't believe it. "Go all the way to Virginia?" I said. "Tonight?"

A smile came over his face, and he shook his head. "I mean Williamsburg, Brooklyn. I live there."

"Ohhhh," I said, suddenly feeling as out of it as if I'd been wearing a flax apron and a mobcap.

"So what about it? Want to go?"

Did I want to go? Well, of course I'd want to go, if I was really the person that it apparently looked like I was. But in fact, I might as well have been this guy's mom. I didn't have the heart to tell him that, though, and ruin his year when it was only a few minutes old.

Where was Maggie when I needed her? I'd felt her hovering at my shoulder until the midnight kiss. Now, though, she was nowhere to be seen. Finally, I spotted her way over near the door, whispering in the ear of the lovely female bouncer. She was clearly going to be no help.

"I thought you didn't want to get into a relationship," I said.

"This isn't a relationship," he said. "It's just a . . . just a . . ."

"One-night stand?" I said. "Because I'm

not interested in that either."

I wasn't, was I?

"No," he said. "I mean, if we wanted to hook up . . ."

His shoulders sagged, and he stared at the floor. Then he beamed in on me again.

"Listen," he said. "I like you. That's all. I'd like to know you better."

I hesitated. "I don't think you'd be happy with what you discovered."

He moved a tiny bit closer, just enough to make me uncomfortable. "Why don't you let me decide that?"

I could feel something fluttering in my chest again, dangerously close to my heart. When I broke his gaze, I looked at his lips, and when I averted my eyes from his lips, they fixed on his shoulders, which were all too easy to envision naked. A year without any kind of sex, a year during which I'd finally made very good friends with the vibrator Maggie had long ago foisted upon me, had sent my fantasy life into high gear. Now that I'd become an expert at having an electronically fueled orgasm whenever I wanted — something I'd never accomplished with a real live human being — I thought I might have one right there on the spot.

I felt his hand on my hip. His hip pressed

gently against mine.

But then the big steel clock above the bar gonged once — 12:15 — bringing me back to my senses.

I remembered something a few guys had said to me, something I'd always wanted to say to someone, except no one would ever have believed it. Now, though, I felt as if it might even be true. "Believe me," I said, suddenly feeling cooler than I'd ever felt in my life. "I'm trouble."

Rather than making him back off, however, my warning only seemed to pique his interest. Come to think of it, it had always had the same effect on me.

"Let me see your cell phone," he said.

"I'm not going to give you my number."

"Just let me see the phone."

He held out his hand. I'd slipped the phone into the front pocket of the tight jeans Maggie had dressed me in, and I could feel it pressing against my thigh. Reluctantly, I took it out of my pocket and handed it to him.

"Wow," he said, when he had flipped it open. "You have Tetris."

That sounded like a disease. A disease of the cell phone.

He must have noticed the puzzled look on my face, because he explained, "It's one of the oldest video games. That's what I do. I'm a game designer. Or at least I'm learning to be."

"Oh," I said, feeling even more alarmed than I already had been. "You're still in . . . college?"

"I'm heading to Tokyo this spring for game design school," he said. "But actually, I already have my MBA. Along with not getting married, I decided I didn't want to get a job in the corporate world. What about you?"

"What about me?"

"What do you do?"

"Uhhhh," I said, wondering if laundry, dusting, or unloading the dishwasher were worth mentioning. "Not much of anything, at the moment."

"So you're in school?"

"Oh, no," I said. "I've been out of school for a long time." I kept telling myself that as long as I didn't tell him a direct lie, I wasn't doing anything wrong.

"So you've been . . . traveling?"

That was, if not exactly true, true-ish. I nodded. "I've been away."

"In, like, France?"

"Somewhere like that." Well, I told myself, there must be *someone* out there who thinks New Jersey is like France.

He began pressing the keys on my phone.

"What are you doing?"

"I'm putting my number into your phone book," he said. "My name's Josh, by the way."

"Alice," I said.

"Ali?"

"No. Alice."

"Okay, Alice, pick a number between one and thirty-one."

The number that popped into my head was what I guessed his age to be. "Twenty-five," I said.

He sighed. "Couldn't you pick a lower number?"

Oh, God, I hoped not. "No," I told him.

"All right." More punching of buttons. "We have a date on January twenty-fifth."

"We do?"

"Yes. I set your phone alarm to remind you. We're going to have a drink at . . . name a bar."

"What if I don't want to have a drink with you?"

"You have twenty-five days to think about it. If you decide you don't want to do it, you can always cancel. Now pick a bar."

The only bar I could think of was the famous place, Gilberto's, around the corner from the office of my one and only long-ago employer, Gentility Press. That was the last time I had any real occasion to go out for a drink in the city. I had a moment of panic wondering whether Gilberto's was even still there, but Josh told me he knew exactly where it was, and noted the name and address in my phone before handing it back to me.

"I don't know how to use that phone alarm," I warned him.

"You don't have to do anything," he said. "At four o'clock on the twenty-fifth you'll hear the alarm go off, and the phone will tell you everything you need to know. I'll see you then."

CHAPTER 3

The ringing of my cell phone jarred me out of a deep sleep. The first thing I thought, still in a fog after the late night, and in the unfamiliar light of Maggie's loft, was that it was the alarm going off for my date with Josh. I'd been dreaming about him, something vaguely erotic that was hurtling out of my reach as the phone kept up its insistent trilling.

I finally managed to wake up — my neck was stiff from sleeping on the purple chaise — and find the phone still lodged in the pocket of the jeans I'd worn, crumpled on the floor. After I said hello, there was only crackling on the line, crackling and silence, and I was about to hang up except finally, tinny and far away, I heard my daughter Diana's voice.

"Mom?" she said. "Mommy? Is that you?"

"It's me, sweetheart," I said, at once fully awake. Diana wasn't able to call often. The

49

nearest phone was a ten-mile hike from the village where she was working as a Peace Corps volunteer. Contrary to popular belief, there still were some places — make that many places — where cell phones and the Internet didn't reach.

"It doesn't sound like you," Diana said.

I ran my hand over my hair, remembering as I did everything that had happened last night, my transformation at Maggie's hand, the encounter in the bar. Getting up off the chaise, I walked over to the oval mirror and looked at myself. With the makeup washed off, I looked more like the old Alice. But my newly pale hair and the choppy cut Maggie had given me had done wonders. Even in this early-morning raw state, I looked like a young woman.

But not a young woman that my daughter was ever going to encounter. Like my pot-smoking days and a few drunken and semi-anonymous sexual adventures, this was not something I was ever going to tell Diana. "It's me," I assured her. "Are you all right?"

"I'm fine, Mom," she said, with that edge to her voice that let me know she thought I shouldn't be questioning her fineness. Of course she was fine. She was a grown-up and didn't need me to take care of her.

"Good," I said. "Are you in town just for

the day?"

There was a silence so long I thought we may have lost our connection, but then Diana said, "No, I actually went to Morocco for a few days with a couple of the other volunteers. I thought I told you."

It was as if she had slapped me. She definitely had not told me, and I knew she knew it. I had wanted Diana to come home for Christmas, and she had raged at me that since her tour of duty was almost over, there was no way she could possibly leave her village, that just because it was a holiday in the United States didn't mean anything where she was, that poverty and need didn't *take* any holidays, and so on until I was apologizing for being so selfish as to have offered to buy her a ticket home.

Don't start a fight with her, I told myself. It's not worth it, she'll be home soon, none of this will matter.

"I didn't remember that," I said. "How was it?"

"You never remember anything I tell you," she said. "I don't know why I even call."

Oh, Lord. It had been like this for the past year, ever since her father and I had broken up. Even though he'd been the one who'd left, it was me Diana had been furious with, maybe because I was safer, maybe for the

51

very reason that I was the one she was clos-est to, who wouldn't abandon her. Last January, two weeks after Gary left, Diana announced that instead of returning to NYU to finish her senior year, she had joined the Peace Corps and was leaving for a year's posting to Africa. Now, after a lifetime of affection and closeness — Diana had not even gone through an adolescent period of testiness — she called me from five thousand miles away to pick a fight.

"I'm glad you called," I reassured her. "I can't wait until I see you again."

More silence. I guess she needed a few minutes to find something wrong with my having said that.

"Well, you're going to have to wait a little longer," Diana said finally. "I've decided to extend my stay here another couple of months."

My breath caught in my throat. I'd man-aged to suspend everything — my fear; my anxiety; my overwhelming desire to be close to her, physically and emotionally, again — by telling myself she'd be back in January. And now all those feelings I'd kept dammed up came flooding through me, and I let out a cry that was much louder than I'd in-tended. Across the room in the red iron bed, Maggie's eyes popped open, and on the other end of the phone line, Diana was squawking.

"How dare you give me a hard time about this?" she said. "I have my own life to live. Just because all you want to do is sit in that house in New Jersey doesn't mean it's enough for me."

I felt myself go very still. Maggie was sitting up in bed now, staring across the room at me with a look of concern on her face. She raised her hands and her shoulders as if to ask, What's going on? and I had to turn my back to her to keep from bursting into tears.

"Mom?" Diana said. "Are you still there?"

"I'm here."

"I know you don't just sit around. You have your garden club or whatever. But now that I'm here, I just want to stay a little longer. You can understand that, can't you?"

Of course I could understand that. What I couldn't understand was why she had to be so hurtful to me.

"Diana," I said. "If you want to stay, of course you should stay. I'm just a little disappointed, that's all."

"See, that's the problem," my daughter said. "I don't think you have a right to be disappointed. Instead of sitting around waiting for me to come back, it's time to get your own life together."

Now I could barely breathe. And definitely couldn't speak.

"Listen," she said. "This call is costing you — or Daddy or whoever — a million dollars. I'm still not sure how much longer I'm staying, at least a couple more months. I hope you're going to be okay with this."

"Mmmmm-hmmmm," I managed to say.

"All right. I'll call you again as soon as I can. I love you."

I was about to say I loved her too, but the line went dead. I stood there for a moment breathing, and then turned around to face Maggie, who took one look at me and leaped out of bed and crossed the room to take me in her arms. Now I let myself go, sobbing against her shoulder. It wasn't that Diana was staying that left me so shattered. Sure, I felt let down, but I could certainly survive for a few more months, for however long she decided to stay away. What was intolerable was how distant we'd become in every other way, and how impossible it felt for me to reach her.

"That's all right," Maggie soothed, patting my back. She hugged me and reassured me as I told her what was happening, what Diana had said, how I felt.

Finally, when I calmed down, she stepped

back and forced me to look her in the eye. "You know," she said, "this might be a blessing in disguise."

"What do you mean?"

"What you started last night," Maggie said. "It gives you a chance to see it through."

"With that guy?" I said. "I'm not really —"

"I'm not talking about the guy," Maggie interrupted, "though he could be part of it. What I mean is with the looking-younger stuff. You could play it out, see what happens."

"You mean see how many twenty-five-year-old guys I can hoodwink into kissing me?"

"If you're going to pretend to be younger," said Maggie, "you're going to have to stop using words like *hoodwink*."

"What's wrong with *hoodwink*?"

"It's antiquated. It's the *beau* or *nylons* of tomorrow."

"Wait a minute," I said. "Who says I want to pretend I'm younger?"

"Listen to me," Maggie said. "What happened in the bar last night, that wasn't a fluke. Since I've had my way with you, you look fantastic. And now Diana calls and says she's not coming home for a while. It's your

55

opening! There's nothing stopping you now from putting yourself out there, applying for a few jobs, and why not, maybe going out with a few guys —"

"This is outrageous."

"What's outrageous? You said yourself, you wish you were younger. You've got to get a job, whether you want one or not."

"I want one," I assured her.

"Okay, then. It's got to be easier going in there as a woman who's twenty-eight than one who's forty-four."

"I don't like lying," I said. "I may be wearing tight clothes and a bunch of makeup, but I'm still just myself. Why do I have to be any age?"

"Exactly," Maggie said. "Why do you have to say you're forty-four or twenty-eight or whatever? You don't have to tell the truth or lie."

I nodded. "Right."

"So if you look younger, and people assume you're younger, why not just let them believe it?"

I kept nodding, but we were veering back into problem territory.

"I mean," said Maggie, leading me over to the minuscule kitchen setup, where she started making coffee in her teeny-tiny pot, "when you go to a job interview and tell them you're forty-four, that makes them assume all kinds of things about you that aren't necessarily true, right? Like you're middle-aged, you're out of it, you're too old for an entry-level job."

I had to admit, she was right.

"And so if they believe you're somewhere in your twenties," Maggie continued, "they'll be more likely to think what you want them to think: that you're eager to learn, that you're happy to get a starting position, that you'd have no problem working for some whippersnapper of a department manager."

"But I'm not in my twenties."

"But they don't have to know that," said Maggie. "In fact, they're not allowed to ask. Discrimination law."

"Don't you remember what Sister Miriam Gervase taught us?" I said. "That's a sin of omission."

" 'Don't ask, don't tell.' "

"Sin, sin. Sin, sin."

"Oh, come on, Alice. You stopped being a Catholic when you got married under a huppah."

She had me there. Despite my unbroken years of Catholic school education, I'd given up going to church when I went away to college, and completely surrendered my

57

status with the pope when I married a Jew. But though Gary rediscovered his religion after Diana was born, and even tried to get me to convert so Diana would be considered thoroughly Jewish, I had resisted. I couldn't say I believed Jesus was God. But neither could I bring myself to say I didn't.

Over the past year, I'd even tried going back to church, feeling the need for spiritual sustenance, seeking some sense of community. The problem was, the Protestant congregations I visited seemed like toy churches, with ministers who were not only married but female — moms! — and bare-walled sanctuaries, devoid of mystery and majesty. But while I didn't feel like a Unitarian or a Congregationalist or a Presbyterian, I couldn't make myself reclaim my Catholicism either, given the church's denial of everything that had been most important in my life: my marriage, my daughter's legitimacy, even my divorce.

And that was what was really bothering me about Maggie's idea that I pretend to be younger, I realized now. It wasn't mainly the lying or the ethical implications that disturbed me, but the idea that, by erasing all those years from my age, I'd also be wiping out everyone and everything that I loved.

"So I'm supposed to pretend that my

daughter never existed?" I said, plopping onto the chaise and wrapping the red satin quilt around my shoulders. "That I was never married, that I never lived in my house?"

"You don't have to pretend anything," Maggie said. "It isn't like you're going to be going home to Diana and Gary every night, leading this double life. In fact, you don't have to go back to New Jersey and pretend anything to your old friends and neighbors at all. You can sublet your house for a couple of months, move in here with me —"

"Whoa whoa whoa," I said. "I thought you said you could only fly solo." Maggie had been involved in some extended romances over the years, but she'd never allowed any of her girlfriends to move in with her. When she traveled, she didn't even like to share a hotel room.

Maggie grinned. "That's something I'm going to have to change," she said, "now that I'm becoming a mom."

"And you're going to practice on me."

"It could be good for both of us."

God knew Maggie would benefit from learning to share her space and her life with another human before her theoretical child came into her world. And come to think of it, maybe I could use some taking care of, too.

"So you think I should become a totally different person?" I asked her.

"Think of it as a performance piece. You ride it as far as you can — get yourself some new clothes, see if you can land a job — and let it end when it ends."

"And what if I do get a job? Then this so-called performance piece will be my real life."

"I thought you said if you were younger you'd take more risks and be more selfish," said Maggie, as the espresso began to percolate. "See, I knew you couldn't do it."

"I could do it."

"Then do it," said Maggie. "Go ahead. I dare you."

CHAPTER 4

I stood in the lineup of young women — I mean, genuinely young women — all of us holding our résumés and waiting our turn to speak with the baby-faced owner of the supposedly hippest new restaurant-to-be in Manhattan, Ici. There must have been fifty of us, all vying for the coveted position of waitress, and as far as I could see, I didn't stand a chance.

I may have been blond, I may have been thin, I may even have passed successfully — and no one had batted an eyelash — for young. But these other women were from some different planet than me, some land where big boobs and boyish hips coexisted on the same body, where teeth were white as paper and feet felt as comfortable in four-inch heels as they did in nothing at all.

I, mere mortal, could have sat down right there on the poured concrete floor. I could smile, I could enthuse, I could even swing my hips with the youngest of them. But I just couldn't train my old feet to like wearing high heels.

"Ms. Green?" the baby restaurateur called. "Ali Green?"

I hobbled his way, trying to make it look as if I was gliding. This was my fourth interview of the day. My first week out, I'd dispensed with all the book-publishing companies — all except my old employer Gentility Press, where I'd been turned down not once but twice last year. Although Gentility was still the company where I'd most like to work — it published all my favorite books, and its founder Mrs. Whitney was one of my idols — I was afraid that either they'd recognize me if I showed up again, or turn me down a third time. Or both.

After striking out with the book publishers, I'd moved on to the national magazines, then the trade magazines, then the public relations and advertising firms, on down to such deathless publications as *Drugstore Coupons Today.*

Everywhere, the story was the same. There were so few entry-level positions, and the ones that existed were mostly claimed by interns, not actual paid help. I'd been offered a few work-for-experience-not-money positions, but I couldn't afford to do that.

This week, I'd started looking for a waitressing job. Next would be bagger at the supermarket — but if I had to do that, I was going to go back to being forty-four, when at least I'd get to wear comfortable shoes and no one would stare at my chest.

"Alice," I said, handing him my résumé. "My name is Alice."

He looked at me as if he'd never heard the name before.

"You know," I tried to help him. "As in *Wonderland*."

He didn't so much as crack a smile.

"Would you consider a name change?" he asked me.

Maybe if he were offering me the lead role in an Oscarworthy movie. But to sling Cosmos in some Tribeca dump?

Still, this was too intriguing to shoot down without first stringing him along.

"What would you suggest I change my name to?" I asked. "Ali?"

"Or Alex," he said. "Or maybe Alexa. Or, I know: Alexis!"

"Like on *Dynasty*," I said.

"Alexis is hot," he insisted, ignoring my analogy. Or more likely, not getting it.

"Is this like the Mayflower Madam?" I asked him. "You know, she had lists of alternate names for the girls, names she considered hot. Or maybe they didn't say 'hot' back then. They probably just said 'sexy.' "

He looked blank, and I tried to look just as blank back. The truth was, I really couldn't take much more of this crap. This guy — I'd actually Googled him before I came, on the mistaken belief that doing my homework mattered more than the hotness of my name — considered himself some kind of culinary genius. But what, I wondered, could some infant in size 26 jeans possibly know about cooking? So, he put pepper in his ice cream. It was different, but was it edible?

I missed cooking. Despite being alone, despite losing weight, I still cooked all my favorite recipes, getting out my best china and my grandmother's silver that she'd carried over from Italy, lighting candles and putting on a nice CD. In the few weeks I'd been camping at Maggie's, seeing whether I could even find a job before I took the leap of renting out my house, I tried to cook for her, but she was usually deep in her work by dinnertime, slurping ramen noodles from a coffee mug and staring at her gargantuan block of cement.

"I'm very interested in food," I told the

baby genius, in an attempt to steer the interview back to Planet Earth.

He yawned. "That's nice. Are you an actress?"

"No," I said.

That got his attention. He studied me, his eyebrows raised. "You don't want to work in the kitchen, do you?" he said. "Because I can't have girls in my kitchen."

Talk about illegal! I shook my head no, but this kind of blatant discrimination made me feel better about my age fibs.

As if he were reading my mind, he asked, "How old are you, Alexis?"

With someone else, I might have fudged this question. Or even, in the face of such a flat-out question, told the truth. But I looked him straight in the eye and said, "Sixteen."

Finally, a laugh. "Oh, a comic. I get it. All right. Show me your tits."

I looked for another laugh, but none was forthcoming. Instead, he sat there waiting.

"You have got to be kidding," I said.

He kept sitting there, obviously not kidding.

I reminded myself that I needed, really needed this job. If I were really twenty-two or twenty-seven, I wondered, what would I do? Make a joke of it? Maybe even show him, and cringe whenever I thought of it for the rest of my life? Or maybe, like the young women in the MTV videos that Diana watched or on the covers of the outrageous new men's magazines I saw on the newsstand, I'd do it and think nothing of it.

But that wasn't me. No matter how much makeup I put on, I'd never be that young or have the mind-set of that generation. And I was becoming more assertive, wasn't I?

"What do my tits, as you call them, have to do with my ability to be a good waitress?" I asked him.

His answer: "Everything."

I was about to argue back, but then I thought, He's right. All it takes to get hired and be a good waitress and make good tips here is to be gorgeous and sexy. This is going to be one of those fake hip places where I couldn't even get a table. He isn't going to give me a job, whether I show him my breasts or not. He doesn't even have the slightest interest in seeing my breasts; he just wants to humiliate me. Well, I'm done.

I snatched back my résumé. I wouldn't leave even a piece of paper in his custody.

"I don't want to work for you," I said. "And my name is Alice."

Out on the street, my feet didn't hurt anymore. I was walking too fast, too driven

66

by the pounding of my heart. I couldn't keep doing this, keep competing for jobs I didn't want and pretending to be someone I didn't even like. If looking younger could help me get a great job, the kind of job I dreamed of when I first started applying last year, the kind of job I'd had at Gentility Press so long ago, then I was willing to go forward with the masquerade. But so far, being young was even worse than being old.

As I walked, I started thinking that maybe it was time to give this up. I was exhausted from sleeping on Maggie's chaise, with the covers over my head to block out the lights and noise from her working late into the night. I had spent money I didn't really have on work clothes I couldn't wear. Now I just wanted to go home.

Except.

Except there was still Gentility. My choices, as I saw them, were to go to Gentility and risk probable failure, or head back to New Jersey and certain failure.

Looking at it that way, it was clear I had to head back to Gentility. At the very least, I'd show Maggie that I could be bold and assertive. In fact, I felt bold and assertive, marching toward Gentility's offices. True, I was wearing an outfit chosen to apply for a cocktail waitress's job — a red silk blouse and black-and-white-checked mini, plus full makeup. Maybe I should go back to Maggie's and change. Oh, screw it. It was a bold and assertive look in perfect harmony with my mood.

Half an hour later, cheeks flushed from my speed walk uptown, I was sitting in the office of Gentility's Human Resources Department, filling out the very familiar-looking application form. Good thing I had an ordinary name. My résumé was nearly the same as it had always been, but without any dates or mention of my twenty years of volunteer work. I used Maggie's address instead of my New Jersey one, and my cell phone number instead of my home phone, and prayed I'd be interviewed by the assistant rather than by Sarah Chan, the head of HR.

No luck. I wanted to melt into the floor as the all-too-familiar Ms. Chan, thirtyish and lovely and completely humorless, came striding across the gray-carpeted room toward me, manicured hand outstretched.

I stood up and braced myself for the look of recognition to cross her face. Sarah Chan was way too young to have been working at Gentility when I was. The first time we met was last February, right after I got done dry-ing my tears from the breakup with Gary and Diana's departure for Africa. I'd walked into Gentility, in the size 14 suit I'd bought to accept my Parent of the Year award from Diana's middle school seven years before, assuming they were automatically going to rehire me for the job I'd left when I was pregnant. Even when the interview was over twenty minutes after it started, even as Ms. Chan, as she introduced herself, suggested I "keep in touch" rather than talking salary and title, I still expected she'd be calling me any day.

By June, when I hadn't heard from her, I'd gone back in, wearing the same suit — a little baggy by then — and carrying a handkerchief because my hands were sweating. Maybe I hadn't made myself clear the last time, I told her. I hadn't been stopping into Gentility just for a visit, for old time's sake. I was there because I wanted an editorial job, *needed* a job. I knew it *looked* like I hadn't been working, but I'd been doing many things that demanded all my organizational and managerial skills. And books, especially women's classics like the ones Gentility published, hadn't changed, had they?

That time, Sarah Chan was more direct. She had understood before that I was applying for a job. Sadly, all the editorial positions were filled. There might be something in publicity, if I . . . ? But as recently as June, I wouldn't consider anything in publicity, anything except editing. Editing, working with writers, with words, was where my interest and talent lay. Anything else was a waste of time, I foolishly thought just a few months ago.

Now Sarah Chan poised in the middle of our handshake and looked at me curiously, her head tilted to one side.

"Have we met?" she asked.

I could confess all, say I'd moved, I was back for a third go, obviously not having learned the meaning of no.

Or I could think of it, as Maggie had coached, as a performance piece. Not lie, exactly, but play things out as far as I could.

"I don't know," I said, tilting my head to match Sarah Chan's and looking her straight in the eye. "Have we?"

I'd had the feeling, when I was here before, that she wasn't really seeing me. That she, like so many young professional women, saw me and registered: old, fat, housewife. And instantly the curtain slammed down.

Now she pressed her lips together and shook her head and looked puzzled. "You

70

look awfully familiar."

"So do you," I said, mimicking her mystified expression.

"Oh, well," she said, giving up with a more vigorous shake of the head. "Come in and tell me about yourself."

This time, it seemed as if she really wanted to hear. She asked me about the literature classes I'd taken at Mount Holyoke, about my interest in Gentility. Although what I told her was virtually the same as what I'd said — twice — last year, this time she seemed to really be listening. And I'd gotten smarter in the intervening months as well. Rather than insisting that the only kind of job I was open to was editorial, I now claimed I was interested in all phases of the publishing business.

Ms. Chan tapped her pencil against my résumé and said there was something in marketing that might be right for me. Marketing? Of course! I *loved* marketing, or at least I thought I might, if I had any idea (this part I didn't say out loud) what it was. Absolutely, I had time to talk with Teri Jordan, the director of marketing.

Walking along the halls, wending my way behind Sarah Chan through the cubicles, I was struck by how much the same the offices looked after all these years — the same, but not as prosperous. I'd been there when the company was flush from the feminist fever of the 1970s, when women were buying feminist tracts and classics by the great female writers as fast as Gentility could print them. Now, nobody read as much of anything, and Gentility was clearly feeling the pinch.

Scuff-marked paint and worn carpets aside, Gentility looked just as it had when I'd worked there last time, only all the people were different. Not only different, but *younger,* though I suppose we were all young when I worked there too. The only exception was the towering white-haired founder of the company, Florence Whitney, whom I glimpsed now only from afar. Mrs. Whitney was still a goddess to me, a decisive visionary who'd been a huge inspiration to all the women who worked for her, and I was glad not to be allowed to get too close. I might have knelt in adoration at her feet, and thoroughly given myself away.

The assistant's station outside marketing director Teri Jordan's office looked very empty. The chair had evidently been used as a dumping station for books, and the desk was dusty. That was the good news: This woman was almost certainly desperate for an assistant.

The bad news was Teri Jordan herself. It seemed clear to me even as we shook hands why this woman had had so much trouble hiring an assistant, why it was that I was able to walk in off the street and get an interview with her, right on the spot. Everything about her was severe, from her short slicked-back hair to her black suit to her grim line of a mouth. Ms. Chan, for one, couldn't get out of there fast enough, as if she were throwing me into a tiger's cage like so much raw meat.

I heard Maggie's voice in my head — "Don't let her intimidate you" — but it was too late, I was already intimidated. I'd been intimidated as soon as her handshake crushed the bones in my hand, intimidated as I surveyed the photographs of her three small children atop her completely cleared desk, which held only three perfectly sharpened pencils, all pointing directly at me.

"What makes you think you can work for me?" Teri snapped.

I felt my mouth go dry. Because no matter how nasty you get, you're probably not going to ask me to show you my tits? Because this job is my best chance to get the life I most want?

Be bold, I heard Maggie urge me. Speak from your gut.

73

But my gut was responding as if she were Gary, home from a long day of drilling root canals. When he was stressed, he'd go on the offense, just as Teri was, and my cowed response had always been to speak in a soothing voice and try to get him to talk about what was really on his mind.

"What do you think it takes to work successfully for you?" I asked.

"Well," said Teri, "the person has to be thoroughly reliable. I can't take any more of these girls calling in sick every time they get cramps or a sniffle."

"I haven't been sick in twenty years," I assured her.

She looked at me strangely. "You're not allowed to be late, either," she continued. "I'm here by eight, and while I don't expect you to do the same, I'd still want you to be in every day well before nine."

"I'm up most mornings by six," I said. "Ever since —"

I'd been about to say that ever since Diana was born, I'd found it impossible to sleep late. But that probably wouldn't be a good idea.

"I'm always up by four-thirty," she informed me, just in case I should be feeling any sense of superiority about my six A.M. wakeups. "That's when I exercise, then I get my house organized before waking up the kids to say good-bye."

I eyed the pictures of the children — a girl who looked to be about six, with her front teeth missing and a long brown ponytail; a boy of three or four with severely parted hair, looking like a little political candidate; and a round-faced infant of indeterminate gender. It was hard to believe that Teri's knife-thin body had produced these three soft little creatures.

"I work at home in Long Island on Fridays," Teri was telling me, "but make no mistake, I'm not playing with my kids and checking my e-mail every few hours. I'm really working."

I imagined her master bedroom with a huge desk and a full array of electrical equipment whirring and beeping, something like a command station. Did her husband stay home with the kids? I wondered. Or maybe she was the general to an army of nannies and housekeepers. It was hard to imagine Teri Jordan scraping by with a quasi-efficient au pair or day-care center and letting the housework slide.

"So part of your job," she said, "will be to function as my ears and eyes and hands in the office on the days when I'm interfacing from home. Is that understood?"

75

She'd said "my job." Did that mean I was hired?

"Now," she said, "tell me your ideas about marketing the Gentility line."

Uh-oh, apparently she wanted to know whether I was actually qualified before she hired me. Slight catch there. My only publishing experience, at Gentility itself, was inadmissible evidence. Plus, I still didn't have a clue what marketing *was*.

But I did know Gentility's books, as well, I'd wager, as Florence Whitney herself. I'd followed the company all these years, keeping track of the imprint and trying to read everything it published. Plus, as longtime director of Diana's school book fairs, as a member of my library board and two local reading groups, I knew a lot about how books were packaged and sold.

"Gentility publishes some of the best books by women ever written," I began cautiously. "There's always a market" — I silently congratulated myself on finding a way to use the word — "for Jane Austen and the Brontës."

"Yes, yes," Teri said, waving her hand dismissively. "But it's a smaller market, and we want a bigger share of it. What do we do?"

"Uhhhhhh . . ." I was terrified of saying

the wrong thing, for fear of blowing my chances at the job and also of Teri Jordan leaping across the desk and sinking her sharp little teeth into my throat. But saying nothing was *definitely* wrong. At least if I said what I really thought, as a devoted reader if not a professional marketer, I'd have some minuscule chance of being right.

"There are so many more factors vying for our attention now," I said, "and the popular images of women are so much sexier and more idealized. The clothes, the bodies — young women feel like they have to look like Paris Hilton or they're nothing."

Even I, in the past few weeks, had found myself trying to measure up in ways that had never entered my mind before. Shopping for my new younger wardrobe with Maggie, I'd encountered clothes that were both narrower — were these clothes made for thirteen-year-olds? for *men*? — and more revealing than anything I'd ever owned. I'd felt like I was supposed to be both more feminine and more professional, less threatening as well as more ambitious, and I had to spend a lot more money in order to earn less. And no matter how well I fielded those conflicting pressures, I couldn't even get a job.

Teri shook her head. "What does this have to do with marketing books?"

I'd gotten so worked up, I wasn't sure I remembered my point myself.

"I just think you can't sell the classics any longer with classic covers," I said. "You know, the same old watercolors and portraits of nineteenth-century ladies. To get young women's attention, you have to key into contemporary ideals of women's lives, play with that in terms of bright colors, more exciting ads —"

Now Teri was shaking her head so hard that her hair was actually moving, which I would have thought to be a physical impossibility.

"I want you to understand," Teri said, "that I'm the only idea person in this department. Are you going to be comfortable with that?"

I nodded, my mouth firmly shut.

"Are you going to be happy xeroxing and FedExing and keeping coffee — black, no sugar — running through my veins?"

Again, I nodded.

"All right," Teri said, rising and — praise the Lord — not extending her hand and subjecting me to another bone-crushing handshake. "I'll see you bright and early Monday morning."

I didn't let go until I was alone in Gentility's ladies' room. To anyone else, that place might not have felt like a temple of emotional expressiveness, but I'd gone through such big-time emotional events there that the mere sight of its peach tile walls set my heart on fire. I'd come here directly from the lunch when Gary asked me to marry him. Found out I was pregnant with Diana in one of these stalls. And right here, I discovered I was spotting and in danger of losing the pregnancy.

Now, though, it was joy that surged through me, elation and excitement that I'd actually landed this job. "Yes," I whispered, pumping my hands. That gave way to a full-out chuckle, and then I let out a whoop, complete with arms stretched into the air.

That felt so good, I began to dance. I'd done this after Gary proposed, pranced around this very bathroom to the inner tune of our song: Elvis Costello's "Red Shoes." I had always remembered that as one of the highest moments of my life, and now I felt almost that good again. I closed my eyes as I swung into a real dance, hearing Elvis the Second's voice in my head: "Red shoes, the angels wanna wear my red . . . RED SHOES . . ."

And I guess I was letting myself sing a little bit out loud, because when I opened my eyes and looked into the mirror, there was someone behind me, watching me with an enormous grin on her face.

"Good day?" she asked, still smiling as she moved to wash her hands.

She was so ethereal-looking, she might have been a ghost, with her pale red hair, nearly the pastel of the bathroom walls, and her alabaster skin, which looked even whiter contrasted against her all-black clothing.

"I just got a job here," I told her.

"Really," she said, arching her delicate eyebrows. Her eyes were the pale green of jade. "What are you going to be doing?"

"I'm going to be an assistant in the marketing department," I breathed.

She stared at me for a minute, all traces of a smile now vanished from her face.

Finally she said, "You're not going to work for Teri Jordan, are you?"

"Yes," I said.

"Oh." She'd uttered only that one noncommittal syllable, but she looked like she was holding back volumes.

My heart lurched. "What's wrong?"

"Nothing," she said. "You'll probably be fine."

"What?" I insisted.

She studied me, seemingly trying to determine whether I could handle the news she was about to deliver. "Well," she finally said, looking around the bathroom, as I should have done, and lowering her voice almost to a whisper, "she fired the last three girls who worked for her."

"Really?" I said. While I'd experienced a range of emotions in this room, I'd never swung through the whole range in such a short time.

"I don't think the last one made it through a day."

"Really." I felt my shoulders sag as my heart dropped toward the floor. "What's the problem?"

"Mrs. Whitney — you know, she's the head of the company — is apparently convinced that Teri Jordan is brilliant and wonderful. But that's not what the people who work for her think. She's apparently very demanding and not so scrupulous."

"Not so scrupulous?" I said, thinking guiltily of my own dodgy scruples. "What do you mean?"

"I don't know the specifics," she shrugged. "I'm in editorial."

81

"Editorial," I breathed. "That's where I really wanted to be."

"You can move up a lot faster on the business side," she said, "if you can manage to survive Teri Jordan."

I let out a sigh so deep, it seemed to have been trapped inside for years. In the past year, I had survived my separation, my only child's departure, and my mother's death. I'd grown both more brave and more afraid, more confident in my ability to deal with pain and more reluctant to open the door to any more of it.

"I don't know," was all I could manage to say.

"Don't worry," said the redheaded young woman, laying her hand on my shoulder. "I'll take care of you."

This waif was going to take care of me? I smiled weakly.

"I'm Lindsay, by the way."

"Alice."

"Ah," she said. "As in Munro. Or Walker."

I could have kissed her. "Everyone says 'as in *Wonderland,*' " I told her.

"I'm not everyone," she said. "But I'll still be your White Rabbit." And with that she vanished down the maze of corridors of Gentility Press, leaving me more nervous than ever about the coming week — and more excited.

CHAPTER 5

My house in New Jersey looked as strange and distant as if I'd been gone for years, not a mere few weeks. I stood on the sidewalk — mine was the only one on the block that was slick with ice and tamped-down snow — gazing at it as if I were coming home after a long journey. Everything about the place — the towering trees, the broad yard edged with its split-rail fence, the black shutters against the crisp white of the window frames and the warm beige of the painted brick — seemed quiet and peaceful, like a drawing in an old-time romantic novel, captioned "Home."

Old Mr. Radek from next door edged down his driveway, using his snow shovel like a crutch, and when he caught sight of me he stopped and waved. This is why I'd avoided coming back these past weeks: I didn't want to explain my new hair, my new clothes, what I'd been doing in the city,

84

whether I'd be coming back for good. But Mr. Radek just waved at me, looking sublimely uncurious.

"Hello, Diana," he called.

Diana. He thought I was my own daughter. Younger neighbors with sharper eyesight would not be so easily fooled. And if one of my two close friends from the neighborhood had been in town, I would have had a lot of explaining to do. But Elaine Petrocelli and her husband Jim, now that their kids were all out of the house, had fulfilled a lifelong dream and were spending a year living in Italy, and my friend Lori, inspired in a kind of backward way by my divorce from Gary, had finally gotten out of her long-unhappy marriage and moved back to Little Rock, her hometown.

Rather than enlightening Mr. Radek, I gave him a friendly wave and headed up my walk. It was almost impossible to open the door because of all the mail littering the hallway, and the place was freezing because I'd turned the heat down before I left for what turned into my endless New Year's weekend at Maggie's.

Now the plan was that I would spend a whirlwind weekend getting the house ready to put on the rental market. The real estate agent I'd called assured me there was high demand for month-to-month rentals to people moving to Homewood or having work done on their own houses who needed a temporary furnished place to stay. That way I could store my things in the attic, even stow my car in the garage, and spend every month until Diana's return at Maggie's.

But standing there in my front hallway, my eyes lighting on one thing after another that I loved — the dented pewter pitcher I'd rescued from Mr. Radek's garbage, the watercolor of the Irish hills done by a book group friend who'd died of breast cancer, the first note Diana had written from camp ("I love you like pancakes love syrup"), which I'd framed and hung on the wall — all I wanted to do was hurl myself on the ground and hang on so tight nothing could make me let go. How could I dream, even for an instant, of camping out in Maggie's drafty loft, of wandering alone through the frigid (in every sense of the word) city streets, when I could be in this wonderful home?

The idea was so overwhelming that I pushed it aside by busying myself the way I always had on coming into the house: hanging up my coat, turning up the heat, sorting the mail, putting on the kettle for tea, building a fire with the wood that had dried out nicely in the big basket beside the living room fireplace.

Maggie had her sculptures, but this — these stenciled walls, these blue-and-white dishes arranged behind glass-fronted cupboard doors, this rich collection of books, and these dark waxed floors — was my work of art. Gary's parents had helped us buy this house right after Diana was born. It was part of the deal: I had to quit my job and lie in bed for the duration of my pregnancy, so Gary, who'd been working at becoming a great poet, needed a more lucrative career. Gary's parents offered to buy us the house and pay all our bills *if* Gary went to dental school, as they'd always dreamed. Though he'd been accepted to dental school at Rutgers before he went off to Oxford to study and write poetry, he'd had no intention of actually going. But now he changed his mind. I didn't want him to sacrifice his poetry for dentistry, but in the end I had to agree that we had no choice.

For a long while, Gary continued writing while he went to school and started practicing, and then he got so involved in dentistry — his specialty was endodontics; root canals — that he stopped. He used to say that doing a really good root canal was like writing a really good poem: a concentrated endeavor

87

in which the tiniest detail could make the difference between pleasure and pain. Maybe that was the problem; he embraced too wholeheartedly the art of the dentist. I admired him for finding a way to love it, but he was also deluding himself and was resentful, I think, deep inside, of me, of his parents, even of Diana, for foisting this lesser life upon him.

And I embraced housewifery and motherhood as enthusiastically as Gary did dentistry, and in much, I see now, the same spirit. Given the threatened miscarriage, Diana's premature birth and delicate health, my repeated and failed attempts to have another child, it had ended up being the best life available to me, and I'd relished it with the same fervor I'd once reserved for dissections of *Jane Eyre.*

I'd even loved the hard work of fixing up the house: ripping the old linoleum up from the wide-board floors, patching and painting the cracked plaster, sewing curtains for the windows made of wavy antique glass. Later, when we had more money, I designed a new kitchen that looked as if it might have been original to the house and put in a perennial garden, now blanketed with snow.

The house, along with Diana's upbringing, was my domain. Gary worked long hours and left all decorating and contracting — as well as parenting — decisions to me, which I'd considered a plus, until I realized it was a symbol of how separate our lives had become. We shared perfectly civil evenings in the same house, but we might as well have been living on different planets.

The heart of the problem was that Gary and I mistook our very romantic meeting in London and ecstatic first weeks together as a sign that we should spend the rest of our lives together. The Royal Wedding did that to a lot of people.

I knew I wasn't happy, but I thought that was just the way marriage was, after twenty years. That's the way many of my friends' marriages were. We rarely had sex, we even more rarely told the truth about anything meaningful, but neither did we fight. It was acceptable; I liked my life, and I certainly wasn't going to leave him, having no confidence there was anything better out there.

But Gary did find something better, in the person of Gina, his dental hygienist. I know, I know, it's a cliché, but where are you going to meet someone new, if not at work (and if you don't have a job, like me, where are you going to meet anyone at all)? I was shattered, humiliated, jealous, furious — but I was also, deep down, relieved. Gary had on some level done me a favor by forcing my life to change, when I was too wimpy to change it myself.

I'd been more genuinely shaken by Diana's flight to Africa, and then, last summer, by my mother's death. My mother had suffered from Alzheimer's for several years, and in the end didn't know me, but there's no finality like death, and once she was gone, I felt, for the first time in my life, truly alone.

I sat now, as I'd sat for so many months, in front of the fire, indulging in my solitary pleasures, a glass of white wine beside my empty mug of tea, a pile of magazines warming my lap. To the world, apparently, I looked like someone new, but sitting here I felt like my same old self: comfortable, frightened of leaving this cozy nest.

And yet the very act of stepping back into a younger life required a spirit of adventure and a belief in the future, in the possibility of possibilities, that I was going to have to revive. Revive and cultivate, as if I were a vampire, and it were my fresh blood.

It wasn't until I got to Maggie's, late the next afternoon, exhausted from all the work I'd done and from hauling my suitcases onto the bus and into the subway and through the freezing streets, that I burst into tears. Maggie had been working with wet concrete for a new cube, but she stopped when she saw me, peeling off her elbow-length rubber gloves and rushing to my side.

"What's wrong?" she said.

"I just don't think I can do it."

"What happened?"

"I miss my house. I miss my daughter. I want my mommy, for Christ's sake."

I really started blubbering then, and Maggie pulled me to her and held me, patting my back like an infant, while I wept and drooled against her shoulder. It occurred to me, even as I was besmirching her shirt, that she was the only one who'd held me, really held me, in a whole year.

"I'm okay," I said finally. "I'm just having" — here I paused for a major sigh — "doubts."

"Doubts?" she said.

"Fears."

Maggie hesitated. "Which is it, fears or doubts?"

"Fears *and* doubts."

"Tell me," she said.

"I'm worried about pulling off this younger act. I mean, maybe I *look* younger, but can I really *be* younger?"

"You don't need to be younger," Maggie

said. "That's the beauty of the new you: you've got the bod of a babe and the mind of a mature adult. You're the perfect woman."

"But what if I get caught?" I said.

Maggie blew air out through her lips in the universal language for "You're an idiot." "Who's going to catch you?" she said. "And so what if they do? This is a lark, right?"

"Not totally," I said. "I really need that job. I really need that money. If this doesn't work out, I might lose the house."

"So what if you lose the house?" Maggie said.

That felt like a slap. "Maggie, you may have been done with New Jersey a long time ago," I said, "but it's still my home. I love that house."

"Okay, okay," Maggie soothed. "But for now, this is your home."

I looked around. I'd been camping out on the velvet chaise, but now that I was really moving in, I needed something a tad more permanent. If I kept sleeping on that chaise, pretty soon my neck was going to be frozen in a painful crick, and no amount of hair dye would make me look younger than a hundred and three.

"I think I need a real bed," I said, thinking of my own top-grade king-size mattress, with its down mattress pad and Egyptian cotton sheets and feather comforter.

A pleased look stole across Maggie's face. Beckoning me to follow her, she led me across the room to the red silk tent that functioned as her closet. She pulled back the fabric that stood in for a door. There, in the red glow inside the tent, instead of racks and shelves full of Maggie's clothes, stood a narrow bed covered with a red satin quilt, and an even narrower dresser.

"What's this?" I asked.

"It's your room," Maggie beamed.

"I thought it was your closet."

"Right. But I cleared it out and ran a cord under the door so you could have a little light."

For Maggie, this was *huge,* not only inviting me to move in with her, but making me my very own space. Once she'd fought her way out of her overcrowded childhood home, she'd never seemed willing to let anyone invade her hard-won privacy. But now she seemed to be welcoming me in. I just had to be sure she was doing it with a full heart.

"Maggie," I said, sitting on the bed and bouncing a little. "Are you sure you really want me here? I'm afraid I'm going to cramp your style."

"I want you," she said firmly. "Plus now that you're in the red tent, it should be easier to stay out of each other's way at night. I'm really on a roll with this new work."

"You still haven't told me what's with the concrete," I said. The block she'd been working on when I came in wasn't really a block yet, just a basketball-sized lump that she would add on to until it was the size of a washing machine.

"I'm experimenting," she said.

"With what?" I insisted.

She let out a big sigh and looked toward the roof of the tent. "Cow hearts," she said finally.

"Excuse me?"

"I was afraid you'd be grossed out. The idea is to encase a cow heart in concrete, and then to build this block around it, which of course just looks like a block, but contains this secret — this heart, literally. You know, like Chopin's heart is entombed in that pillar in Warsaw."

"I didn't know that."

"Of course, Chopin's heart isn't secret," Maggie went on, caught up now in talking about her art. "But the notion here is that my concrete blocks will emanate this power. You might not know what it's from, but that organic matter hidden inside will give the block this mysterious aura of life."

I must have looked as clueless as I felt, because Maggie finally looked at me and said, "It's about pregnancy. About how a woman can have a new life growing invisibly inside her, and how that will change her ineffably."

I was the English major, so I wasn't going to admit I wasn't totally sure what ineffably meant. But suddenly I thought Maggie might be talking about herself.

"Are you telling me," I said, my heart starting to beat faster, "that you —"

"No no," she said, her face turning even redder than it already looked thanks to the light shining through the fabric of the tent. "No no no no no no no. But that reminds me of something I need you to do for me. I'm going for my first insemination this week, and I need you to be my partner."

"You mean you told your doctor," I said, "that I was your —"

"No," she said. "No no no. It's just that my doctor believes insemination has a better chance of taking if you have a loved one with you to, like, commune with in a soothing way afterward. And right now, you're the closest thing I have to a loved one."

"Oh," I said, picturing us sipping champagne and laughing — gently, of course — in a dimly lit examining room. "Okay, sure. When is it?"

"Ten on Tuesday morning."

"Tuesday morning! That's my second day at work. Teri Jordan wouldn't let me take off if it was my own insemination. Can't we do it in the evening? Or at lunch hour, even?"

"I don't schedule it, my body does," Maggie said. "That's what my doctor says. It's got to be the morning."

"Oh, Maggie," I said, taking her hand in my sweaty one. The mere idea of telling Teri Jordan I needed a morning off summoned a vision of her looming over me, wielding a whip. Or more likely, coolly firing me as she had done to so many before. "Isn't there any other way?"

Maggie shook her head. "This is it. And depending on my hormones, it may be my only chance."

All this year, I'd been the one who'd needed Maggie. All this year, she'd been there for me, taking my midnight phone calls about Gary, holding me upright at my mother's funeral. And now she was asking for something, the first thing, back.

"Of course," I said, squeezing her hand. As the vision of the whip-cracking Teri rose

96

up again, I whipped her back. "Don't worry; I'll figure something out."

CHAPTER 6

"Alice!"

My bottom had just touched the seat, but already Teri was calling me back into her office. It had been like this all morning.

I rushed to her deskside.

"My coffee's cold," she said, without looking up.

"But I just poured you a fresh cup." As in, 1.5 seconds ago. "I even put it in the microwave, to be sure it would be superhot, like you like it."

The woman drank her coffee so hot, her mouth must be lined with asbestos.

"Microwave hot is not the same thing as real hot," Teri said. Still without looking at me, she lifted her cup and dropped it into her wire mesh wastebasket — I mean a real cup, not paper, full of hot coffee, which was even now seeping onto the floor.

"You'll have to clear this away," Teri said. "And bring me a new cup of coffee."

As I carried the dripping wastebasket from the office, I told myself that if I wanted a young person's job, I had to be willing to be servile, obedient — to act, in other words, like a young person. An extremely meek, self-effacing young person, much like the young person, in fact, I'd actually been.

Except now I was determined to be different — and the fact was, I actually was different. All those years of life had made me more self-possessed, better able to know what I thought and more willing to say it out loud. That was the spirit with which I wanted to invest my new young self.

But my new boss would have none of it, I could tell. She wanted an employee even quieter and more frightened than the real entry-level Alice Green had been.

I could do it, I told myself. If I could bring my smarts to bear to get myself this job, I could put them to work keeping it, whatever that involved. Teri Jordan might act like a terror, but the truth was she was younger, more overwhelmed, and a way bigger jerk than me. I could definitely handle her.

I brewed a new pot of coffee, adding an extra scoop of coffee to the filter, running the water until it was really cold, waiting until the entire pot had dripped through so that Teri's cup would be of maximum strength. Then, arranging a smile on my face, I carried it to her.

"Fuck," she muttered.

"I made a whole new pot," I said, wondering what I'd done wrong this time.

"No, it's this report," she said. "Like every other publisher, we want to market to the book group ladies, and like every other publisher, we have no fucking idea what they want."

This was funny to me, because Teri Jordan could very easily be one of the "book group ladies" herself. She was a mom, she lived in the suburbs, she was balancing job and home and marriage. And, presumably, she liked books. But for some reason, she saw the women in the book groups as "them," very different creatures from "us" here in our bastion of publishing know-how.

"I think they want what we all want," I said, "a book that's going to keep them awake beyond half a page at the end of a long involved day. A book that's going to feel like it was worth the fifteen or twenty bucks they might have spent on a new top or a nice lunch with a girlfriend because it lifts them out of their lives for a few hours. A book that's rich enough to make that book group night — which might be the only night they get out without their husband or kids — one of the most stimulating, fun nights of the month."

I hadn't realized I had so much to say on this subject, but I guess after a couple of decades of book group attendance, my thoughts were pretty well honed. I was certainly holding forth, and Teri was sitting there staring at me, her mouth slightly open, exposing the points of her sharp little teeth.

"We're not editors," she said. "We have nothing to do with the quality of the books."

I felt myself color. I guessed what I'd been talking about did have to do with editorial, not marketing.

"Our job," Teri said, pronouncing very clearly as if I was hard of hearing, not hard of marketing, "is to get the books in the hands of the book groups. And no one has figured out an effective way to do that: not via the Internet, not through display techniques, not in the books themselves."

"Maybe we could give special discounts," I blurted.

Teri looked at me as if I'd spoken Croatian.

"You know, for volume. If a book retails, with discounts, for eighteen dollars, offer it to book groups who order eight or more for fifteen dollars a copy."

Teri looked away

101

"My book group was always very price-conscious," I tried to explain. "We wanted new books, but we didn't want to pay hardback or even full trade paper prices."

Now she was shaking her head. "I'm not interested in what some impoverished assistants' or college girls' book club is doing," she said. "We're marketing to grown-up women with families and houses and professional jobs."

I opened my mouth to explain, but then realized I couldn't without incriminating myself.

"I thought I made it clear that I was the only idea person in this department," she said. "I thought you said you were comfortable with that. Have you changed your mind?"

I pressed my lips together and shook my head no, keeping myself from welling up by focusing on the photos of the angel-faced children smiling in their picture frames, my sole piece of evidence that Teri Jordan was human.

"Good, then," she said. "Mrs. Whitney has called a staff meeting for three thirty this afternoon. I can't imagine why she wants assistants there, but she does. Your function will be to occupy a chair."

She lifted the new cup of coffee I'd made

her and took a sip.

"Ugh," she said, spitting it back into the cup. "This is horrible. You're going to have to learn to make a decent cup of coffee if you're going to last in this job."

When I filed into Mrs. Whitney's huge corner office for the staff meeting along with, it seemed, virtually everyone else who worked at the company — there were more than fifty people filling the big beige and gold room — I tried to hide behind one of the other assistants and chose a seat in the far corner of the room, as far as possible from where Mrs. Whitney sat near the door. I took out my notebook and kept my head down, relieved I'd let Maggie talk me into cutting long bangs that, if necessary, would cover half my face. I bent my head and let them hang down now, but even so, when everyone was seated and quiet and the meeting finally came to order, I looked up only to find Mrs. Whitney staring hard at me.

Mrs. Whitney looked exactly the same as I remembered her, impressively tall and erect even sitting down in her office chair. Her hair was short and white, and her dimples showed even as she sat with her lips pressed together. She seemed if anything younger than she had when I worked here more than twenty years ago. She was even wearing the same clothes — possibly the exact same clothes — as she'd worn when I last attended a meeting in this office: black patent leather Ferragamos, pearls, and a burgundy wool dress that might have dated from any time in the past forty years.

The fact that she was so unchanged made me feel exposed, as if I too must look utterly as I'd always looked, must be completely recognizable. She kept staring at me, and finally I could no longer stop myself from smiling at her, suddenly wanting only to be myself, hoping for a nod of recognition in return. I idolized Florence Whitney, and I had been one of her favorites, an editorial assistant she'd believed would rise to the top. I'd always dreamed of one day getting the chance to restore her early faith in me, to show her I hadn't failed but had just taken an extended time-out.

But Mrs. Whitney only looked confused and looked away. Unsure of whether I felt disappointed or relieved, I turned toward the door just in time to see Lindsay, the young editor I'd met in the ladies' room the day I got the job. She looked even paler than I remembered, again dressed all in black, and she flashed me a big smile as she took the last chair in the room.

"By now you've all seen the new sales figures," Mrs. Whitney began abruptly. "They're abysmal."

People shifted in their seats.

"Who can help me with this?" she said, impatience tingeing her voice.

One of the only men in the room ventured, "The economy —"

"Yes, yes, the economy," said Mrs. Whitney dismissively, waving a hand as if to shoo a fly. "Of course that's the problem. What are we going to do about it?"

Bring her solutions, not problems: I remembered that as the mantra from the last time I worked at Mrs. Whitney's publishing house, founded with the proceeds from her own best-selling feminist tract, *Why Men Must Die.* Instead of dwelling on setbacks or mistakes, the entire staff was trained to think in terms of solutions, an approach I'd found as useful when dealing with a tantruming toddler or an incompetent roofer as with a manuscript that was two years late.

Emboldened by both our eye contact and Mrs. Whitney's failure to recognize me, I raised my hand. "We might do some special marketing to book clubs," I said.

Everyone in the room turned to stare. Teri was glaring.

"What Alice means," Teri interrupted, "is that book clubs are very price-conscious these days. They want new books, but they don't want to pay full price, even for trade paper."

Mrs. Whitney was nodding. I felt the color creep into my face as I heard Teri parroting my words, but giving me no credit.

"My idea," said Teri, "is that we offer book groups a discount for volume — say two or three dollars off if they buy eight copies or more. We could start a special Web site for book groups, outlining the discounted titles each month."

At least that part was her own idea.

"That's very interesting," Mrs. Whitney says. "But I don't know if it really addresses the problem with our classics, which as you know still make up the bulk of our business."

Again, I raised my hand, but this time Teri simply started talking.

"We have to work harder than ever to get young women's attention these days," Teri said. "Plus the popular images of women have become so sexy and idealized — think Paris Hilton. I think we have to revisit our cover look —"

That's when the song started. The loud digital rendition of "Here Comes the Bride."

All talk ceased as everyone looked around the room for the perpetrator. There was confusion at first over where the sound was coming from — Was there a radio somewhere? Was someone playing a joke? — until the man who had blamed the economy for Gentility's woes said, "That's somebody's cell phone."

Everyone looked around the room. Who would bring a cell phone into a meeting? A cell phone that was turned on? A few women rummaged through bags and men reached into their jacket pockets, only to find their phones silent. I knew it couldn't be mine because mine rang like a normal phone. And stopped ringing, going over to voice mail, if I didn't pick it up after four rings.

But when the song kept playing, louder and louder, and all the people who'd already checked their phones had come up with nothing, I took my phone out of my bag, simply to declare my innocence.

My phone was flashing. It was vibrating. And, now that it was literally out of the bag, it was playing "Here Comes the Bride" loudly enough to waltz to.

"Oh, God," I said, feeling as if I could drive the phone, like a stake, through my own heart. "I'm so sorry."

I pressed the button on the back of the phone to turn it off. Nothing. Again. It kept playing.

Finally, in desperation, I flipped it open and tried to press the Off button, not caring if I hung up on the caller before we even spoke.

The song played on.

As the whole room watched, I brought the phone to my ear.

"Hello?" I said tentatively, expecting to hear Diana's faraway voice, or maybe Maggie's.

But there was no one there. The phone was now blasting the wedding march.

"Hello?" I said, jamming my finger down on the Talk button. "Hello?"

"Oh, for God's sake!" Teri cried. "Get out of here! Get out of here right now."

Did she mean leave the room, or leave the company? Was I about to set the world record for marketing assistant fired in the shortest time ever?

My face flaming, I stood up and began to push my way across the entire length of the room, like a bride making her way down the aisle. When I reached the door, Lindsay leaped to her feet and followed me out into the hallway.

"Oh, God," I said. "I'm so embarrassed."

She reached for the phone. "I know what it is," she said. "I have this same phone."

Expertly, her fingers played across the keys until the music finally, thankfully stopped.

"It was your alarm. Apparently you're supposed to have drinks tonight with someone named" — she peered at the phone — "Josh?"

Josh. It all came flooding back to me. New Year's Eve. The guy I kissed. Him programming my phone for our date on the twenty-fifth at Gilberto's. Which was right downstairs.

"So who's Josh?" Lindsay asked. "Your boyfriend?"

"Oh, no," I said. "No, not at all."

"Just some guy you have a date with."

"Not really," I said. "I didn't even remember about tonight. Obviously."

"Oh," Lindsay said. "Well, good. I mean, because I was going to ask you to come out for a drink with me and my boyfriend tonight, to celebrate the first day of your new job."

"I'd love to," I said. "But after that episode with the phone, I'm worried today may also be my last. Especially when I break it to Teri that I have to take off tomorrow morning for this medical thing that was scheduled

109

before I knew I was going to be working here."

"Don't worry," said Lindsay. "I'll tell my boyfriend, who I really want you to meet, to fix everything with Teri."

"What's he going to do?" I joked. "Threaten to beat her up?"

"No, silly," said Lindsay. "He's *her* boss. Thad is the publisher of our division. But don't tell anybody we're going out. Our relationship's supposed to be this big secret."

"Oh, okay," I said.

"So you'll come out for a drink with us?"

"Sure." How could I refuse, in the face of Lindsay's connections as well as her kindness? Though I couldn't help but wonder exactly why she was being so sweet and welcoming to me.

"Great. Don't give Teri another thought. Thad and I will make sure she doesn't give you a hard time, about today or tomorrow morning or anything else."

Nearly two hours later, when Teri finally went home — without firing or indeed even speaking to me — I felt free at last to leave my desk. It was time to go meet Lindsay and the mysterious and all-powerful Thad at a bar a few blocks away.

110

I had genuinely forgotten about my theoretical date with Josh; I'd nearly forgotten about Josh completely in the life-capsizing events of the past weeks. Even if I had remembered I was supposed to meet him, even if I felt vaguely prepared to embark on a relationship with a guy twenty years younger than me, I was far too late.

Still, I couldn't resist stopping and peering in the window of Gilberto's, where I was stunned to see Josh sitting at the bar, his hand cupped around a glass that seemed to hold only ice. I hadn't really expected to see him there, had guessed I might not recognize him in any case, but he looked more familiar and more appealing than I thought he would, like an old friend that I was dying to see, and I nearly went through the door, if only to apologize and talk to him for a moment. Without the hubbub of New Year's all around, he looked older somehow, and more serious.

But he's not older, I told myself. At least, he's not old enough for you. A spontaneous kiss with a stranger on New Year's Eve was one thing; a deliberate meeting held a different level of intent, one I was afraid wasn't fair to either of us. Before Josh could see me, I reeled around and hurried away, darting around the corner to the bar where I

111

was meeting Lindsay and Thad.

I had noticed Thad in the meeting in Mrs. Whitney's office — it was impossible not to notice any man in that sea of women — but I never would have picked him out as someone Lindsay would go out with. I had imagined, I realized, that he would look something like Josh — maybe like Josh if he were putting his MBA to use.

But this guy looked more like my ex-husband, more like all the boring husbands, the tedious men, I'd known in Homewood, the men who talked only to each other and then only about themselves. It wasn't that he was middle-aged, just that he aspired to be, with his clipped hair and his tightly knotted tie and his eyes full of judgment, as he looked me over and deemed me, I could tell, not worthy of his serious consideration. But this guy was my boss, I reminded myself; he was even *Teri's* boss. And he was the boyfriend of the only friend I had at Gentility.

"So, Alice," he said. "Lindsay tells me this is your first publishing job."

"I've never worked anywhere but Gentility," I said.

"Really?" said Thad, assessing me. "Where did you go to school?"

He was the kind of guy, I knew, who if

you asked him the same question, would say "Cambridge" or "New Haven," wanting you to think he was modest because he hadn't said Harvard or Yale.

Try to like him, I told myself. At least, try to handle him. God knew after twenty years of practice at the swim club and on the suburban fund-raising circuit, I should know how to do that.

"I went to Mount Holyoke," I said, reminding myself that Thad's favorite subject would almost certainly be Thad. "And what about you?"

"Cambridge," he said.

"Oh." I couldn't resist a dig. "MIT?"

He narrowed his eyes at me, obviously deciding, I was gratified to see, that maybe he'd underestimated me after all.

"No," he said shortly. "I once dated a girl from Mount Holyoke, Hilary Davis. Maybe you knew her?"

"No," I said, suddenly enormously thirsty. "What are you drinking, Lindsay?"

"Bombay Sapphire martini, extra dry, straight up with olives," she said. "I used to drink mojitos, but Thad's converting me. Isn't that right, sweetie?"

"So what years were you at Mount Holyoke?" he persisted, ignoring Lindsay. "You must have crossed paths with Hilary at least part of the time."

Maybe I'd underestimated Thad, too. He seemed to have a greater capability to focus outside himself than I'd given him credit for. I was obviously going to have to try harder.

"That's ancient history," I said. "I'd love to hear about you, your thoughts about the line. Lindsay tells me you're the hottest publisher in the business."

Lindsay, of course, had said no such thing, but she was pleased that he thought she had, and I'd finally diverted his attention away from me and when I had or hadn't gone to college.

"Suppose I am," he said. "Rooster in the henhouse, and all that."

Oh, yuck. Still, if I was going to be smart about my career, I should keep feeding Thad the flattery he so obviously relished, rather than treating him like the jerk he was.

"I hear you're the kind of publisher who's open to new ideas," I told him, "who can recognize a real innovation when it comes along."

"Well," he said, swallowing the bait, "I definitely believe Gentility could use some changes."

"You'll see," said Lindsay, leaning in close to him, "Alice is just the person you need on your team. She has all these fabulous new ideas that are really going to shake up that marketing department."

The memory of Teri Jordan's stony face across Mrs. Whitney's office when I'd dared to open my mouth was enough to make me want to divert Lindsay from that path.

"I'd love to do a good job for you," I told Thad, "but I'm really just a beginner."

"Don't worry. I'll break you in," said Thad. "What was your major?"

"English," I said.

"I knew it!" Lindsay cried. "You're really a writer!"

I had tried writing a novel when Diana was little, laboring under some vision of myself spinning out great prose while my child gamboled at my feet. The reality was that I had to stop so often to tend to my little girl's needs that I got very little written — or very little that was decent, anyway. When I'd finally, after months, finished a handful of pages, I'd given them to Gary to read. He was sorry to tell me, he said, that they weren't really very good. I'd put them away, mostly relieved not to have to push myself anymore.

"I used to want to write, but I gave it up," I told Lindsay.

"What kind of stuff?" Thad asked. "Children's books?"

Apparently he considered me incapable of stringing together more than five words at a time.

"No, women's fiction."

"Oh," he said dismissively. "Romance."

"If you ever want to show me anything you've written," said Lindsay, "I'll be delighted to look at it."

"Thank you," I said. "Right now, I think I'm more interested in the kind of career that makes money."

"That's cool," said Lindsay, turning to Thad. "Didn't I tell you she was great, Thad? We should introduce her to Porter Fitch, don't you think? He likes to make money."

"My college roommate," explained Thad. "Big Wall Street job now. Never had a lick of an urge to give back, the way I did."

So working in publishing was "giving back"? Maybe because it was women's publishing. I wanted to tell Thad that we women would probably be able to muddle along without his charity.

"We could have a real dinner party," Lindsay said, growing more excited, "just like you've been wanting to, sweetie! I could even cook!"

I smiled weakly. Lindsay was so sweet, she

116

reminded me so much of my own daughter, I found her utterly irresistible. Thad was another story, but he had a lot of power over me — and he was the first person I'd encountered who seemed not to automatically accept my age story.

"What do you think, Alice?" Lindsay said, eyes shining. "How's Saturday night?"

"Uh . . . ," I said. "Uh . . ."

The only thing I could do was nod, and figure I had five days to find a way out of it.

CHAPTER 7

I stood at the head of the examination table, gripping Maggie's hand. The doctor had just completed the procedure and left the room, and Maggie lay there with her bottom half draped in a sheet, her knees up, following instructions to lie as still as possible. The doctor had used a spotlight when he was working, but he'd turned it off and left us in the twilight of the candles Maggie had brought along.

"Very romantic," I said.

"Try to play along."

"Okay," I said. "Darling, I'm so thrilled that you're having our baby."

"My baby," Maggie said. "I'm having *my* baby, I hope." She made a face. "I don't know how you straight girls stand it, lying around with all this goop between your legs."

I suddenly remembered something from the recesses of our childhood. "Remember when we used to kiss our arms?"

The summer we were ten or eleven, Maggie and I had spent days mashing our lips against our own forearms, trying to simulate the experience of making out with a guy. Or maybe, in Maggie's case, a girl. I remember, when she first came out to me, questioning for about a minute and a half whether I might be gay, too, since I'd been the one lying beside her while we dreamed about and practiced for love. But then I thought about Jimmy Schloerb, my crush du jour, and how he was only the latest in a long line of boys who'd set my heart aflutter since kindergarten, and realized I was straight as a needle.

"Oh, God," Maggie said. "I'm not supposed to laugh."

"I'm sorry," I said. "Maybe if we visualize the sperm and the egg meeting and dividing, we'll help make it happen."

Maggie looked at me as if I were insane. "Who told you that? Madame Aurora?"

I was stung. "It can't hurt to be optimistic."

"Except when it blinds you to the reality of your situation," said Maggie. "The doc told me that if this one doesn't take, he's only going to give me one more chance."

"What about a donor egg?" I asked. "I'd give you one."

"You may be looking pretty hot these days, sweetie," said Maggie, "but your eggs are as old as mine."

"Oh," I said. "I forgot."

"Plus it's not only your eggs that go, but this hormone that needs to be at a certain level to sustain a pregnancy," Maggie said. "Mine's borderline right now, and the doctor said if it dips any lower, he wouldn't even attempt an insemination. So I've put my name in for a Vietnamese adoption."

"Maggie, that's awesome!"

"Don't use that word around me, okay? I just felt I should cover all my bases. Plus, it seems even harder to adopt than to get pregnant. They do all these elaborate character checks."

"I guess they want to be sure you'll be a good parent."

"It's so ridiculous," Maggie said, "that poor teenagers and alcoholics and child abusers can have babies whenever they feel like it, and someone like me, with money and love and attention to give, has to be monitored by teams of people who might decide I'm just not going to get a baby, and that will be it."

I didn't think it necessary to point out that some of those people might sooner give a baby to a crack-smoking stripper than a lesbian. And that nature seemed out of step with modern society to make it easier for a fourteen-year-old to get pregnant than a forty-four-year-old. Instead, I smiled and squeezed her hand.

"I only wish I'd started this long ago," Maggie said. "Did you know that fertility declines at thirty-five, not forty or forty-five, the way they told us when we were young?"

In fact, I did know that because Lindsay had told me so at the bar last night, when Thad went to find the men's room and she informed me that she was dying to marry him, the sooner the better.

When I asked Lindsay what her big rush was, she fed me the fertility and age statistics and said that if I were smart, I'd get busy looking for a husband and starting a family too.

"Otherwise you could find yourself forty-five and all alone," she informed me.

"That could happen anyway," I said.

She looked at me strangely. "Not if you play your cards right."

That was an aspect of youth I didn't think, no matter how good my makeup or my acting skills, I'd be able to reclaim: the belief that if you were smart or ambitious or beautiful or together enough, you could make your life turn out exactly as you wanted.

"I saw that guy last night," I told Maggie suddenly. Coming home from drinks, I'd told her all about Lindsay and Thad and Teri and my first day at work. But I'd forgotten to tell her about Josh. "You know, the guy from New Year's Eve."

"Ohhhh," Maggie said, remembering. "The kiss guy. Where did you see him?"

I realized I'd never told Maggie about the theoretical date, not having had any intention of keeping it. Now I told her about how he'd set my phone alarm and how the arrangement had totally slipped my mind. But also about how attractive he'd looked, sitting on the bar stool at Gilberto's.

"So why didn't you go in?" Maggie asked me.

"I was on my way to meet Lindsay and Thad. Plus, what would I have said? Hi, I wasn't going to come meet you, and I'm never going to see you again, but you looked so cute I just had to say hello?"

"How can you be so sure you never would have wanted to see him again?"

"Oh, come on, Mags. You said it yourself: He's a baby. I can't date a twenty-five-year-old."

"Why not? I hear the older woman/

122

younger man thing is very cool right now. You're both at your sexual peaks. Plus, no one needs to know you're older, not even him."

I felt myself blush. "It makes me uncomfortable," I said, "all this lying."

Maggie raised her eyebrows. "It seems to me," she said, "that you're wasting an opportunity if you don't at least carry this a little bit further. I mean, what can it hurt? You said you wanted to be younger, and now you got your wish. Make the most of it."

"Lindsay wants to fix me up with some friend of her boring boyfriend's," I said miserably.

"And you're going to let her do that?"

"They're really in a position to help me at work. They're why I get to be here this morning instead of acting as Teri Jordan's full-time barista."

Last night, Lindsay had made Thad promise to tell Teri that he was sending me to a corporate orientation session.

"That doesn't mean you have to be their ho," said Maggie. "Stand up for yourself! I thought that was what this whole younger thing was about!"

She was really agitated now, up on her elbows, wagging her head as she talked. Her earrings, a row of silver hoops getting bigger and bigger as they worked their way down to her shoulders, shimmied in the candlelight.

"Calm down," I said, putting my hand on her arm and trying to ease her back onto the table. "Remember, you have to create a peaceful environment for the sperm and egg to meet."

That, at least, persuaded Maggie to flop back down.

"I just think you have to be more assertive and do what you want, right from the beginning," she said, staring at the ceiling. "How are you going to become a brand-new person if you keep acting like your same old self?"

It wasn't until Thursday and what I've come to think of as the Bikini Wax Incident, after the Krav Maga — a form of Israeli martial arts — class Lindsay dragged me to, that I got up the nerve to tell her I didn't want to go to the dinner at Thad's with Porter Swift. It all started when I asked Lindsay whether she knew of a gym near the office that I might join. I'd gone for nearly a month without following my daily Lady Fitness routine, and I was afraid that any minute all the muscles in my new killer bod were going to give way, totally blowing my cover. In just four days of working for Teri Jordan, I'd found myself reverting to some of my old comfort-eating habits, hiding a bag of Hershey's Kisses in my desk drawer and whipping up a pot of creamy mashed potatoes before bedtime every night, spooning out a crater that I filled with molten butter and salt and then savoring the concoction under the covers in my tent.

Lindsay asked what kind of exercise I liked to do, and when I mentioned the elliptical trainer and hand weights, she looked at me as if I had said I did calisthenics under the tutelage of Jack LaLanne.

"That's kind of retro," she said, giving the word a twist that made it impossible for me to tell whether she considered that a good or a bad thing. "Why don't you come with me Thursday night to my Krav Maga class? It's awesome."

In the class, I felt as if I burned off the entire week's intake of chocolate kisses, along with learning to disable any terrorists I might encounter on the way home. In the plush locker room, I tried to follow Lady Fitness etiquette and keep my eyes averted, which was difficult, as Lindsay was standing beside me holding forth on the menu for her upcoming dinner party while completely and unself-consciously naked.

It was further difficult not to look because Lindsay's severe black clothing had been hiding several remarkable physical attributes. Her breasts, for instance, were so high that there was far more square inchage on the part below the nipple than above it. Was that normal for women in their twenties, I wondered — I mean for women in their twenties who weren't featured in the magazines I sometimes found when I cleaned under Gary's side of the bed? I couldn't remember, though the contrast with my own breasts, which until now I'd considered one of my best unclothed features, made me hunch over in shame.

Lindsay also sported several startling tattoos — a dragonfly on her shoulder, a snake at her hip, and what looked like a USDA symbol perched atop the crack of her butt — made all the more vivid by the contrast of their inkiness against her ethereally pale skin. And the color of the tattoos seemed to provide the only variation in the expanse of paleness: Lindsay's nipples were the faintest blush of pink, her pubic hair a thin strip of peach fuzz.

"Alice," she said.

"Hmmmm?" I feigned nonchalance as I trained my eyes on my locker, pretending to

126

rummage around for my bra, which I knew was hanging beside my sweater.

"What do you think I should make for dessert Saturday night? I was thinking about trying to do this amazing pear crostada that Thad had the other night at Craft."

I pulled my bra out of the locker and fumbled to slip it on while keeping my body angled away from Lindsay's gaze, without making it seem like I was trying to keep it angled away.

"But then I was thinking," Lindsay said, propping her hand on her hip, right beside the indigo snake, "that maybe I should just go with something simple, like a crème brûlée."

I was about to answer that making crème brûlée was anything but simple when Lindsay let out a little scream and, pointing directly at my crotch, cried, "Ew! What is that?"

I looked down. Had my period started? Had she spotted a stretch mark? Had all those mashed potatoes waited until this moment to deposit themselves as a pad of fat atop my belly? But no, despite all the eating I'd done the past few days, my stomach was still taut from my year of exercising compulsively.

"That jungle of pubic hair!" she squealed.

"It's practically down to your knees!"

"Oh," I said. "Well . . ."

"Is that what they do where you were?"

"Where I was?"

"Wherever it was you were traveling," she said. "Like you told Thad the other night."

"Oh," I said. "Right."

"So they just went all natural there?" Lindsay pressed. "Were you in, like, the Third World?"

"Sort of," I said. Well, some Manhattanites consider New Jersey the Third World.

"We're going to have to do something about that," Lindsay said, "before you hook up with Porter."

"Do something?" I said.

I must have made a terrible face and cringed away from her, because she laughed and said, "Don't worry, I'm not going to whip out a straight razor. But tomorrow after work, I'm taking you to my waxing person, Yolanda, for a Brazilian."

"A Brazilian?"

I tried to imagine it, but never having been to Brazil or known a Brazilian person, never mind glimpsed its native pubic hairstyle, all I came up with was something vaguely bikini shaped. Which is what I believed mine was to begin with.

"Like mine!" Lindsay cried, presenting the

look with a flourish of her hands that reminded me of Vanna White directing the television viewers' attention to a new Buick.

"Oh," I said, eyeing Lindsay's narrow strip of hair. "I don't know."

"You have to!" Lindsay said. "None of the girls in New York go natural anymore. Porter would be shocked."

Thad's friend. Saturday night. Dressed or undressed, hairy or plucked, I couldn't let this go on a minute longer.

"Lindsay," I said. "You and Thad have been great to me, and I'm really glad we're becoming friends, but I'm not interested in hooking up with Porter."

Lindsay looked at me, both hands now on her hips, as if I had told her I'd recently landed from the planet Xenon.

"But Porter is the perfect catch," she said finally.

"I can't do it," I told her, my mind churning in search of an argument-proof excuse. Because . . . we Xenonians are forbidden to consort with earthlings? "In fact, I have a confession to make. There's another guy."

"You said you didn't have a boyfriend."

Now even the truth was getting me in trouble. "He's not really my boyfriend. Just somebody I'm . . . hooking up with. You know, the alarm guy. Josh."

Lindsay shook her head, worked her lips. Finally she said, "I don't believe you."

Without even trying, I'd convinced her I was twenty-whatever years old. That I'd never done anything more involved in my life than backpack through Bulgaria or some similarly unwaxed place. But I couldn't convince her of this.

"It's true," I said.

She looked at me for a few moments, and then finally she nodded and said, "Okay, prove it."

"Prove it?" I gave up a forced little laugh. "How am I supposed to prove it?"

She reached into her locker, took out her bag, extracted her phone, and handed it to me.

"Call him," she said. "Right now. Go ahead."

I didn't take the phone. "What am I supposed to say?"

"Invite him to dinner on Saturday. At Thad's. That is, if you're really hooking up with him."

I hesitated, partly because I realized I wasn't really sure what hooking up meant. Dating? Having sex? Pledging eternal conjoinment? Whatever, I decided, if it meant getting out of a blind date with a friend of Thad's.

"All right," I said finally. "But I have to call him on my phone."

"Why do you have to call him on your phone?"

Because I don't know his phone number. Because, under the circumstances, it's lucky I remember that at least he programmed his number into my phone, which I retrieved from my bag, trying to think.

"He won't answer if he doesn't know the incoming number," I told Lindsay, finding Josh in my phone book, holding my breath as I pushed Send. Lindsay stood above me, still naked, her arms crossed over her high little breasts. I listened to the phone ring, and prayed for voice mail.

Instead I heard Josh's voice. "Okay, I understand," he said.

"This is Alice," I said. It sounded as if he'd been expecting someone else.

"I know," he said. "I'm telling you I understand why you blew me off the other night."

"I couldn't —," I began.

"I know," he said.

"I thought about it," I said truthfully. There was something about him that made me want to tell the truth.

"Favorably?"

I laughed. "At times."

131

"It's all right," he said. On the phone, his voice sounded as warm as his eyes had looked on New Year's Eve. "You're here now."

"Yes," I said. "I'm here."

I sat there with the phone pressed to my ear, staring at the orange metal locker, thinking of him, until Lindsay, whom I'd nearly forgotten was standing above me, cleared her throat.

"My new friend Lindsay from work wants me to invite you to a dinner party on Saturday night," I said.

"You got a job," he said.

"Yes."

"Where?"

Lindsay began drumming her fingers against her creamy thigh.

"I'll tell you on Saturday," I said. "If you want. If you're free. Which you're probably not."

"I'm not," he said.

"Oh, good," I said, though I found to my surprise that I was disappointed.

"Good? So you don't really want me to come?"

"I do," I said. "I thought it might not be your thing."

Lindsay nudged me in the shin with a pedicured toe, and I turned all the way away

132

from her.

Did people still call something they liked their "thing"? In exactly how many ways was I making an idiot of myself?

"Seeing you is my thing," he said. "If we could leave the dinner party a little early, I could get to this other place a little late. Do you like rock music?"

I knew the right answer was yes. But I gave him the true answer: "No."

He laughed. "A friend of mine is in a band that's playing at a club downtown, and I told him I'd go see him. So how about if I go to the dinner party with you, and then you come to the club with me."

"All right," I said.

Then I hung up and sat there, so lost in thought I really did lose sight of Lindsay and everything else around me. I had my first date in nearly a quarter of a century.

CHAPTER 8

It was when I was getting dressed for Lindsay's dinner party that Diana called. Maggie was reclining on the chaise — trying to "baby," as she put it, the embryo she hoped had taken hold inside her — flipping through a Japanese style magazine and passing judgment on everything I tried on. Negative judgment. She thought I should wear the old jeans of Diana's I'd grabbed when I left home, but I was afraid Thad would consider them too casual. I couldn't stand Thad, but I still wanted him to think well of me.

"Whatever you wear on bottom," Maggie said, "the top's got to be really feminine. Lacy."

"I don't want to look like I'm wearing my underwear."

Her eyes lit up. "That's a good idea. Why don't you go over and check out what's in my top drawer. I have a couple of amazing lace camisoles."

I was about to protest when, from my red tent, I heard my cell phone ring. Please let it be Lindsay or Thad canceling the dinner, I thought. Please let it not be Josh, telling me that the longer he's thought about it, the more certain he is that I'm an old lady in disguise.

So sure was I that it would be one of these people that I was stumped when I first heard the trademark crackling line from Africa, as if Diana was calling from several decades as well as several thousand miles away, and my own daughter's voice.

"Mom?" she said. "You sound different."

"No," I said. "I'm just . . ."

Trying to act your age? Getting ready to go out with a man who might have gone to high school with you?

I'd left a message with her field office telling her I'd gone back to work at Gentility and was staying in Manhattan with Maggie, that she should call me on my cell phone in case she needed to reach me. That was all she needed to know.

"You sound different too," I said, attempting to reclaim my Mom voice.

Then I realized part of the reason I was so surprised that it was Diana on the phone. I was accustomed, whenever my cell phone rang, to calculating the time in Africa to anticipate whether it might be her. And right now, in her time zone, it was the middle of the night.

"Where are you?" I asked, holding my breath, half expecting her, despite the static on the line, to tell me she'd just landed right here in New York. I'd be thrilled, blown away. But I'd also be, I had to admit to myself, a tiny bit disappointed at having to cancel my own party when it was just getting under way.

Diana laughed uneasily. "I'm taking the weekend off, and I spent the night in town," she said. "With a friend."

"Oh," I said. "That's good. That's very good."

I liked thinking of her in a place with electricity and a toilet and no lions prowling nearby.

"Mom," she said. "I have to tell you something."

I held my breath. She sounded nervous, as if I wasn't going to like what she had to say. But she'd already dropped out of school and gone halfway around the world. What could she possibly have to say that was going to make me feel worse?

"I've decided to stay here," she said in a rush. "At least until the spring."

"Oh," I said, relief flooding out of me. "That's great."

"That's great?" she said. "I thought you'd be mad."

"Why would I be mad?"

"The whole time I've been here, you've been pressuring me about when I was going to come back. At New Year's, when I told you I was staying longer, you sounded so crushed."

And so I had. But now, intoxicated with my own experience of adventure and novelty, I felt only ashamed that I'd leaned on her like that. She was at a time in her life where she *should* be going out in the world and doing what she wanted, for as long as she wanted, without any sense of obligation to come home and keep me company. I didn't want her to wait twenty years, as I had, to get a taste of this kind of freedom.

Plus, now that I'd claimed it for myself, renting out the family nest and making myself a new young secret — at least from my daughter — life, I wasn't ready to hand it back.

"Listen," I said, "I'm sorry for that. I see now how unfair that was. You're doing this really amazing, adventurous thing, and I think you should make the most of it."

There was a silence so long I finally said,

"Diana?" worried that we'd lost our connection.

"I'm here," she said. "I just can't believe you mean that."

"I do," I said firmly. "In fact, I think it makes sense, since you've gone through all the hard work of getting acclimated over there, to stay as long as you're able."

Another long pause, and then she said, "Really?"

"Absolutely," I said.

I looked out the open door of the tent to see Maggie, still reclining on the chaise, but pointing at her Dale Evans watch and mouthing something frantic-looking to me.

"Listen, sweetheart," I said, "I have to run now, but you have a wonderful weekend, okay?"

"Where are you going?" Diana asked.

"To a dinner party here in the city," I said.

"How's everything going there?"

"Great," I said, with what I instantly feared might be too much fervor. "I'll e-mail you. And really, don't worry about rushing back. The house is rented out for at least a couple of months. Stay as long as you want."

And then felt guilty, as soon as I hung up, that it sounded like I didn't want her to come home. Of course I want her to come home, I reassured myself, just not quite yet. Not quite yet.

When I finally arrived, huffing and puffing and shiny with sweat from running down the five flights of stairs from Maggie's apartment, through the streets of the Lower East Side to the Second Avenue subway stop, and then eleven blocks up Madison Avenue to Thad's apartment building, Josh was already waiting for me, leaning against its imposing limestone facade. Looking adorable. Wearing torn jeans.

"Oh," I panted, looking at the skin of his knee poking through the denim.

"Oh," he said, taking in the black satin pants and black lace blouse and black velvet peacoat I wore, along with a long emerald velvet scarf wound around my neck. On my feet, in anticipation of the long run ahead, I'd worn boots, but I held red satin high-heeled mules in my right hand, a bottle of champagne, now extra-extra-bubbly, in my left.

"You look amazing," he said. "Maybe I should go home. Put on a suit."

"Hmmmm," I said.

"Except I gave all my suits and ties to this group that helps inner-city kids get corporate internships."

"Oh."

"I've still got the navy blazer my mom bought me in high school," he said. "I could wear that."

"Oh?"

"But I guess it would take me a while to get out to Brooklyn and back."

"How long?"

"Maybe" — he cast his eyes toward the dark winter sky, calculating — "an hour and a half."

"It doesn't matter," I told him, taking his arm and suddenly wishing I'd taken Maggie's advice and worn jeans myself. "I don't think this is going to be your kind of thing anyway. I'm just happy you said you'd come."

"I'm happy," he said, "because I'm here with you."

He was taller than I remembered. As we stood in the lobby of Thad's building, waiting for the elevator, he pulled off his stocking cap, and I felt like running my fingers through his hair. He smiled down at me, and I found myself tongue-tied. Small talk seemed impossible; if I opened my mouth, I felt, I'd start pouring out my heart.

I was relieved to see, when the door opened, that we were the first guests to arrive and that Lindsay was dressed up in

140

something shiny in her usual black, and Thad wasn't — though for Thad that meant he was wearing crested velvet lounging slippers instead of shoes, and a cashmere cardigan instead of a jacket. But at least he was well mannered enough not to comment on Josh's jeans and T-shirt, instead taking his worn leather jacket and offering him a martini. I was relieved when Josh accepted, and then further relieved when Thad's face broke into a smile as Josh specified straight up, with olives, and gin rather than vodka.

"I never did understand this vodka nonsense myself," Thad said to Josh, ignoring me after issuing his standard hello peck on the cheek. "I thought Lindsay would have everything ready in time for the girls to sit down and have a drink with us, but apparently there's some high-level brouhaha in the kitchen, so you'll have to make do with just me for company until the others arrive."

I figured that since, in Thad's view, I didn't exist, I was free to leave Josh with a little wave and follow Lindsay into the kitchen. Actually, I didn't quite have a chance to follow her in there: as soon as the guys were out of sight, she grabbed my arm and yanked me into the tiny stainless steel space.

"He's so hot!" she whispered, presumably

referring to Josh, not Thad. "Is he, like, some kind of rock star?"

Why would Lindsay think Josh was a rock star? But more urgently, why was every surface of the kitchen covered in debris? There were grocery bags strewn across the counters with food spilling out of them. A dozen tiny plates held a dozen tiny mountains of chopped somethings — onions, mushrooms, parsley. And why did nothing seem to be actually cooking?

"How's it going in here?" I asked.

"Awesome!" Lindsay chirped. "I guess. I mean, I thought everything was under control." She looked around the kitchen, seeming to notice the jumble of uncooked food for the first time. "But now, I'm not sure —"

And then she burst into tears. I was stunned to see Lindsay, who'd always presented herself as being in utmost control of everything from her job and her relationship to her pubic hair, lose it so instantly and completely.

"Sssssh," I soothed, moving in, awkwardly at first, but then enfolding the girl in my arms, as I had done countless times with Diana. "It'll be okay."

"I can't do it," Lindsay sobbed. "It's a disaster. Thad is going to leave me."

142

If only it were that easy, I thought, but what I said was, "Don't be silly, sweetie. I'll help you. What do we have to do?"

Lindsay looked wildly around the room, like a racehorse panicking at finding herself in the starting gate. "I don't know," she wailed. "Everything!"

"Don't worry," I said. "Dinner will be on the table in no time. But first things first."

I ducked out of the tiny kitchen and snagged the bottle of Bombay Sapphire that Thad had left open on the antique sideboard in his dining room, pausing for a moment to marvel that he had a dining room. He probably considered that more essential than a kitchen. Pouring a healthy measure in each of two crystal glasses, I moved back into the kitchen and handed one to Lindsay.

"What's this?" Lindsay said.

"This is courage," I said, raising her glass as if in a toast. "This is nerve. Now drink up."

I heard Lindsay sputter as the gin hit her tongue, but I had no problem swallowing my own mouthful. The taste of it was so redolent of a thousand suburban dinner parties that it seemed almost like the magic potion that would transform me back into Super Housewife.

143

"Okay," I said, noting with satisfaction that Lindsay had managed to drain her glass as well. "What are we having?"

"Caesar salad," Lindsay said. "Oh, fuck, I forgot to make the croutons. And pasta. Pasta something or other, with lots of chopped vegetables. The recipe is on the counter there, somewhere under the bags."

Looking at all the ingredients in such disarray made even me feel overwhelmed.

"Did you consider just making a roast?" I asked.

Lindsay looked horrified. "Oh, no," she said. "Thad might have liked it, but I'm vegan. And there's at least one other vegetarian, a nondairy, and a raw foodist coming tonight, though he's eating at home before."

The doorbell rang, sending Lindsay back into panic mode.

"You should be out there with what's-his-name, your rock star," said Lindsay. "I'm supposed to be taking care of this."

"Nonsense," I told her. "You're the hostess. Your job isn't to be a maid or a chef, it's to make your guests feel comfortable."

Lindsay looked intrigued, if still doubtful.

"Seriously," I reassured her. "Here. Let's pull some hors d'oeuvres together. Do you have any cheese? Good — your nondairy

144

person can just eat around it. Here, throw some nuts in this bowl. Okay, now take that out and say hello to everyone, and whatever you do, act like everything's all right."

"What will I say if Thad asks me when dinner's going to be ready?"

"Pretend you didn't hear him and suggest he pour everybody another drink."

"But an article I read in *Bon Appétit* said —," Lindsay began.

"Just do it."

As soon as Lindsay wafted out of the kitchen, I set to work unpacking the bags, lining up the ingredients, tearing up lettuce, and putting a big pot of water on to boil. This shouldn't take long, as soon as I got everything organized. Back in Homewood, I threw parties for a hundred three or four times a year, and got so practiced I could pull the whole thing together in less than twenty-four hours.

By the time Lindsay returned, the ingredients were lined up along the backsplash in order of when they needed to be cooked, the countertops were cleared and wiped clean, the lettuce was washed and nestled, wrapped in paper towels, in a salad bowl, and three enormous cloves of garlic were soaking, smashed and covered in kosher salt, in a bath of olive oil for the Caesar dressing.

"How did you do this?" Lindsay asked, her mouth open.

"It just took a little tidying up. The only thing I couldn't find was the dessert."

"Oh, no," said Lindsay. "I knew I forgot something."

"Don't worry. We'll call down to that deli on the corner and get them to send up eight packages of Hostess cupcakes. Everybody will love it. How's it going out there?"

"Great." Lindsay grinned. "Thad is already on his third martini, and Josh said everything smelled great."

I laughed. "The power of suggestion. Okay, let's get busy."

I hadn't realized how much I'd been missing this kind of thing in the time since Gary had been gone. I'd tried once or twice to throw dinner parties in Homewood on my own, but all our old regular guests had seemed uncomfortable coming to a party with no Gary, even though when Gary was there, all he did was sit at the head of the table looking as if he'd rather be watching TV.

But I loved cooking, I remembered as I sliced and sautéed and stirred, especially cooking for a crowd, on a deadline, with the sound of laughter rising from the next room.

146

"Where did you learn to cook like this?" Lindsay asked, as she darted around, acting as my sous-chef.

"I know it might seem hard to believe," I said, not letting her see my smile, "but I learned to cook in New Jersey."

As the work neared its crescendo, I sent Lindsay out to set the table and reveled in spending the final moments in the kitchen alone, tossing the salad and running the bread under the broiler for just long enough to make me faint with the aroma of hot buttered garlic.

"Now it really does smell awesome."

Josh was standing in the kitchen doorway.

I shot him a smile. "The secret ingredient is always garlic."

"I'll eat it if you will," he said.

"You have to eat it because I already have."

"Let me taste," he said, moving toward me.

And then before I had a chance to actually respond, his lips were on mine, the tip of his tongue flicking out to taste me.

"Mmmmm," he said. "Definitely delicious."

My whole body flamed. Oh, God, perfect time to have my first hot flash.

"Go tell your buddy Thad," I said, "it's time to sit down."

If Lindsay was worried about Thad questioning her role in preparing the dinner, she needn't have been: he accepted the appearance of the food as nonchalantly as if it sprang fully prepared, all by itself, from his stove every night. The other guests gushed about how delicious the food was, and I insisted that Lindsay take all the credit.

Thad held forth at the table, ignoring not only me but all the other women there, addressing his comments to the men, especially Josh. Yet Josh made a point of redirecting every one of Thad's questions and remarks toward one of the women at the table. "I don't know," he'd say. "What do *you* think of the Supreme Court decision, Lindsay?" Or Alice or Liz or Sarah, the other two women who were there. "Interesting, Thad — I'd love to hear Alice's take on that."

He even tried to help Lindsay and me clear the table when we were done eating, but Thad stopped him — I actually thought Thad might throw himself bodily across the path of Josh's hand as he reached for a dirty teaspoon. For what I hoped was the last time in my life, I found myself supporting Thad.

"Go ahead," I told Josh. "I'm just going

to give Lindsay a hand, and then we can leave."

But after one pass over the table, I realized I was working alone. As I moved around the table clearing the last of the wineglasses, I heard Thad droning on in the living room and caught sight of Lindsay perched on his lap.

Screw it. I'd been intending to tie on an apron and begin loading the dishwasher, but then I told myself, Stop being such a mommy. Anybody can do dishes. Even Thad.

I went into the living room and laid a hand on Josh's shoulder.

"It's time to go," I said.

Thad looked up in surprise. "I'm just finishing up a story about when I was publisher of the *Crimson,*" he said, opening his mouth to resume his speech.

"Sorry," Josh said, standing up and putting one arm around me, at the same time extending his right hand. "Great night. Thank you."

God, he was smooth. If he ever wanted to get rid of me, I'd be cut loose before I even saw the glint of the knife.

Out on the street, Josh slipped his hands inside my coat and pulled me close. At first

I was nervous, thinking of what I'd thought when he so adroitly extricated us from the clutches of Thad. Then I was nervous, thinking about what might lie ahead tonight. And then finally I let myself relax against him, resting my head against his chest, unsure if what I heard was the beating of his heart or my own.

When at last I looked up at him, he said, "Thank you for introducing me to your friends."

"Thad is not my friend."

Josh laughed. "That's who I was afraid of becoming."

"You're nothing like him."

"It can happen so easily," said Josh. "You don't even realize it, and suddenly you're this stodgy prick."

He was right. That had happened to Gary. Gary hadn't always been an endodontist with a thirty-eight-inch waistline. He had been a poet, slender and romantic. But it was so much easier to pull off being a slender, romantic poet at twenty-two than it was at forty-four.

Sitting on the subway beside Josh, hurrying down the dark streets with him, my hand tucked in his pocket, I could sense his energy but his insecurity, too. It was the insecurity more than the self-confidence, I felt, that had driven him to go to business school and get engaged when he claimed never to have wanted those traditional trappings. His conventional side, under wraps now but still in there somewhere, was more frightening to me than the sneaker-wearing gamer. Just as I was more afraid of my own inner housewife than of the young woman I was pretending to be.

It was the inner housewife who threatened to betray me when I squeezed into the hot and crowded club behind Josh. It was so loud in there, louder than anything I had ever heard in my life. And the music sounded unbearably horrible, all squawks and squeals and arrhythmic pounding. I wanted to — my inner housewife wanted to — clap my hands over my ears and scream, "Stop that racket!"

But Josh, whose left arm was stretched out behind him so he could keep hanging on to my hand even as he continued pushing forward toward the stage, was nodding his head to the music, as, it seemed, was everyone else in the room. Most of the people there looked to be about the same age as Lindsay and Thad and the other dinner party guests, but it was as if this crowd was being young in a different era. They had shaggy hair or shaved heads, pierced noses and tattooed necks. The girls were wearing huge trousers or tiny skirts — or sometimes both — and tops that barely existed, cropped and shredded across their breasts. The guys looked as if they had stepped off a fashion runway or rolled out from under a car.

I felt something bump me on the left and was startled to find a couple dancing there — or rather grinding without touching, the girl in front facing away from the guy and rotating her butt. The guy in back thrusted toward her and looked as if, any second, he was going to come. I moved closer to Josh.

"Are you okay?" he called back to me.

I nodded, thinking of how primed this man seemed to be considerate. He'd been so generous when he'd complimented Lindsay on her food, when he hadn't smirked, not once, at Thad.

"Wanna dance?" he shouted into my ear.

Quickly, I shook my head no. He didn't seem like the kind of guy who would mimic intercourse with me in a public place, but this was one chance I wasn't willing to take.

Josh turned to watch the band, and a little while later I felt someone tap my shoulder from the other side.

"Eeeee?" a girl said into my ear.

"What?"

She looked momentarily confused, but then obviously decided to change tactics. "Exxxxxxxxxxx?" she asked.

I scrunched up my face and shook my head in the universal language for, "I don't know what the fuck you're talking about." The girl opened her palm and thrust what looked like a handful of miniature smiley-face buttons under my nose.

"Ecstasy!" the girl said.

I let out a yelp.

"Oh, no!" I cried. "No, thank you!"

I felt so straight, so out of it, so *old.* But at the same time, I realized I would never have fit in here, no matter what my age. I had always been the girl curled up on the window seat, reading about nineteenth-century England, while all around me people got high and blasted music and danced wildly.

"I have to go," I said suddenly.

If this had really been college, if he had been a boy I'd been out with back then, I would have suffered on through the concert, would have even pretended to enjoy it. But despite Josh's good behavior at the dinner, despite my genuine fondness for him and a powerful desire to press my cheek against one of his very broad shoulders, I simply could not go on.

He looked down at me, surprised, starting to protest.

"I'm sorry," I shouted, already pulling away. "I've got to go."

Where was I going, exactly? And why? I felt confused about everything except my need to escape that place. It was as if I'd dived into an ocean that had looked fun and exciting from the shore, but had found myself getting knocked down by waves that up close proved far too wild for me. All I could think about was making my way back to the sand.

It wasn't until I was out on the street, gulping the clean air and beginning to look around for a taxi, that I realized Josh had followed me, that he was even now smiling and opening his mouth to speak as he reached for my arm.

His grip was so perfect, not too grasping, which would have only made me tear away from him, but not too flimsy either. Maybe if we were on a desert island, I wanted to say, and we didn't have to deal with the world around us, we could be together. Maybe if I weren't so determined, after all these years, to remake my life exactly the way I wanted, we could find some middle ground. Maybe if I wasn't so scared of revealing my real self, I might be able to get close.

"I really like you, Josh," I said, letting myself touch his arm, which in itself nearly did me in.

His smile faded. "Why do I sense a 'but' at the end of that sentence?"

Of course there was a but. So many buts.

But you're way too young for me. But I'm way too old for you. But there's no way we can ever find a middle ground.

"But this isn't right for me," I said, gesturing toward the building, the people huddling on the sidewalk around us, all of it.

"This place isn't me, Alice," he said, attempting to pull me toward him again.

Part of me, a bigger part than I wanted to admit, longed to melt into his embrace, to let go of the control I was struggling so hard to maintain.

But I couldn't let myself melt. I couldn't lose control. I had to be true to my new self, to my determination to do things differently than I'd always done them before.

I swung around and, without another word, darted off into the dark streets of downtown Manhattan, alone and — it didn't even hit me until I was nearly at Maggie's — entirely unafraid.

CHAPTER 9

"Why did you run away?" Maggie asked me.

We were in the big ABC Home store, where Maggie was shopping for a mirror. Not too big: her Snow White's Wicked Stepmother mirror covered that base. And not too small: she needed enough reflective surface to fulfill her purpose.

What Maggie was looking for was a pretty mirror to hang on the wall opposite the main door of the loft. The reason: Maggie, the skeptic, the nonbeliever, had consulted a feng shui expert on reconfiguring her loft to maximize her baby luck. I half expected the feng shui guy to decree that my red tent had to go, but *au contraire,* he thought its location and color most auspicious. His most insistent recommendation was placing a mirror across from the door, to send any bad chi flying right back out to the hallway.

For Maggie, though, such a purchase could involve hours, days, even months of searching for the perfect item. It stood to reason that a person who'd lived in one place for twenty years and had managed to collect only two pieces of furniture was fairly picky.

"I don't know," I said, picking up a square mirror in a hammered silver frame and showing it to Maggie, who made a face as if she'd tasted cleaning fluid. "He's just not right for me."

"I thought you really liked him," Maggie said. Her eyes were not on me but on the huge jumble of brightly colored wares as we drifted through the store. "I thought the only issue was that he was young."

"But that's so big," I said. "I mean, his age kind of determines everything else about him: his tastes, his values, how he likes to spend his time —"

Maggie stopped and looked straight at me then. "Don't you think that's a little hypocritical?" she said, putting her hands on her hips.

She was wearing her black sleeping-bag coat again, and standing like that, with her elbows out and her legs planted apart, she completely filled the aisle, intimidating as Ursula the Sea Witch in *The Little Mermaid*. Afraid that at any moment she might sic her electric eels on me, all I could do was stammer that I wasn't sure what she meant.

"You're rejecting him because of his age!" she thundered, waving her padded arms, threatening to send iron candlesticks and silk shantung pillows and Venetian chandeliers rocketing to the ground. "It's the very thing you hated when people were doing it to you!"

My shoulders sagged as all the air left my body. "You're right," I said.

Maggie let her arms drop and smoothed the front of her coat. "Damn right I'm right. I thought what was important here was who somebody was inside. I thought the whole point was that age blinded people to each other's real and essential qualities. I thought we were trying to transcend all that and triumph over age prejudice."

What could I say? It was all true.

"I guess I'm a prime offender," I finally admitted.

"I guess you are," said Maggie. "Maybe that's why age was so important to you in the first place."

My shoulders sank even farther, so that now my head was hanging toward the floor. I was staring at the toes of my new red sneakers.

"You're right," I repeated. "I'm a terrible

person. I should just give this whole thing up."

"Oh, don't be ridiculous," Maggie said, resuming her mirror search so precipitously I nearly fell over trying to collect myself to scurry after her.

"You've done splendidly!" she was saying when I finally caught up. "It's only been a month, and you've gotten yourself a job, a friend, even a guy! Now you just have to stop being afraid of embracing it."

"I'm not afraid," I said.

She stopped short. If we had been cars, I would have rear-ended her.

"Then tell me this," she said. "Why didn't you sleep with that cute boy last night?"

I laughed nervously. "I already told you," I said. "The age thing aside, he's not my type. He's kind of scruffy, he likes horrible music, he has this totally impractical dream of being a video game designer, of all things. I just can't take him seriously."

"Hmmmph," said Maggie. "You want the BLT?"

As if she hadn't given it to me already. As if she was even going to wait for my answer.

"He sounds like exactly your type," she told me. "In fact, he sounds exactly like Gary. The young Gary. The Gary you fell in love with."

That insight hit me with the force of a Pakistani armoire — we were now surrounded by them, red and green and crying out to shelter a TV — toppling onto my back. Once again, whether I liked it or not, Maggie was right. Josh was quite a bit like the Gary I'd gone crazy for on the streets of London, the Gary who'd made my soul soar along with my body.

"Furthermore," said Maggie, using the word for perhaps the first time in her life, "I think that's exactly why you ran away from Josh last night. I think you take him *too* seriously, and that totally freaks you out. You're afraid you're going to fall in love with this guy."

"That's ridiculous," I said. But I could feel my heart pounding. "The first time I met him, he told me he wasn't interested in a commitment."

She paused again and peered at me here, as if she were trying to diagnose a disease of the skin. But I was afraid she was looking deeper than that. I put up my hands and covered my cheeks, as if that might keep her from seeing right through me.

"So maybe that's what's worrying you," Maggie pointed out. "You're wildly attracted to him, you really like him, and you're worried that he's going to reject you.

You're afraid to risk going forward, no matter how much you want to."

Suddenly her focus shifted and she looked up, beyond me to a spot somewhere to the right and above my head, as if harking the voice of an angel who'd appeared on high.

"Wait a minute," she said, nudging me out of the way and standing on her toes to reach way up.

"Be careful," I said, thinking of the bean-sized baby that might be hatching inside her.

At my words she cradled her stomach with one hand, and then returned to earth grasping a round mirror, the size of a dinner plate, rimmed in a red frame embedded with a hundred smaller mirrors, glistening like stars.

"This is it," Maggie said, her face breaking into a smile as she stared at herself in the glass. "I feel luckier already."

"So do you think you'll marry him?" Lindsay asked.

We were sitting in her cubicle, where I'd come to thank her for dinner, though what I really wanted to talk about was work. I wanted to get Lindsay's thoughts on an idea I had for marketing the classics line, see whether she'd back me up on the editorial side and how she thought I should present it to Teri. As I'd discovered in the short time I'd worked with her, Lindsay was brilliant on everything to do with the publishing business. The trick was getting her to talk about it.

"I don't see that happening," I said.

I hadn't told Lindsay about fleeing from Josh outside the club. I'd already chewed over the incident with Maggie, and I couldn't tell Lindsay the real reason behind my misgivings anyway. Besides, I was afraid if Lindsay thought I wasn't going out with Josh, she'd renew her efforts to fix me up with Porter Swift.

"Why not?" she pressed.

"I'm not really interested in getting married right now," I said. "Listen, Lindsay, what do you think of the idea of getting modern women novelists to write new introductions for the classics line?"

"You can't distract me that easily," Lindsay said, grinning. "Come on, I want to know the story. He's one of those guys who's terrified of commitment, right? Thad's like that. You're probably doing the same thing I'm doing: playing it cool because you're afraid that if he knows you want to get married, he'll run the other way."

"But I don't want to get married!" I told her. "I want to work! I want to do well at this job!"

"Oh, you'll do well," Lindsay said, waving her delicate pale hand, as if success was something you could conjure at will from the air. "You have so many great ideas. Like that one you just said."

"So would you help me with that?" I asked her. "I mean, ask some of your writers if they'd consider doing that?"

"Of course, of course," she said, making a note to herself on her calendar to call two well-regarded writers I already had on my unspoken wish list. Then she dropped her pen and looked me straight in the eye. "Now tell me why you don't want to marry Josh."

"I don't want to marry *anybody*," I said.

That momentarily stumped her, sending her swiveling to and fro in her big black-upholstered chair, which completely swamped her little black-clad body.

"Okay, maybe not *today*," she said finally, "but soon this is something you're going to have to get serious about, if you want to have children. I figure it's nearly too late for me already."

I could tell Lindsay had spoken without a drop of irony, but I couldn't help letting out a chuckle. "Oh, come on, Lindsay," I said. "You have *tons* of time."

"No, we don't," Lindsay said, not so much as cracking a smile. "I figure I've got ten years, tops, to get married, spend a little alone time with my husband, and have all my children. And that's if I have the whole plan in play right now."

Lindsay launched into a rundown on the math of her reproductive future as if it were a bonus question on the SAT for life. Even if by some miracle Thad were to propose tomorrow, she said, she would need a minimum of a year to plan the wedding, then another year to spend on their own before they got pregnant, then *another* year if everything went perfectly to conceive and give birth to the first child, then a two- or three-year gap before the second . . .

"But what about your career?" I interrupted her. "What about just being young?"

"We don't have time to be young," she said.

"Speak for yourself," I told her. "What makes you so sure Thad's the one?"

Especially when it seemed so clear to me that he wasn't.

"He has a good job," she said, looking away from me for the first time, opening her top drawer and taking out a pen, which

164

she proceeded to chew. "He makes a lot of money. He'd take good care of me."

"It looks to me like you're doing a good job taking care of yourself," I said gently.

"Yeah, but that's because I *have* to do it," she said. "That doesn't mean I'll always *want* to do it. Definitely when I have kids, I'll want to take some time off."

Suddenly, the air in Lindsay's cubicle seemed to drop ten degrees. I felt her before I saw her, the hairs on the back of my neck standing on end.

"What's this little coffee klatch?" Teri Jordan said from behind me.

Feeling my face flame as if I'd done something wrong, I turned around and said, as casually and convincingly as I could, "Oh, hi, Teri. I was just asking Lindsay her opinion of an idea I had for the classics line."

"The classics line, hmmmm?" Teri said. "I heard something about taking time off after having kids."

"That was me," Lindsay said. "That's something I want to do."

"Big mistake," snapped Teri. "All these young girls think they can take a few years off and then step right back onto the merry-go-round, but it doesn't work like that. By the time you try to start up your career again, it's often too late."

I had to admit, Teri had a point. But before I could agree with her, Lindsay started talking again.

"Nothing personal, Teri, but I don't want to be in some office when I could be home with my baby," said Lindsay. "Once she's in school, fine, then maybe I'd look for something part-time, something flexible."

"But if you stop working, you won't have the seniority to command flexibility," Teri said. "And when your kids are older — I mean middle school and high school older, when they've outgrown their nannies but are ripe for getting into trouble with drugs and sex — that's when you really want to be able to work at home sometimes."

"Things have changed," Lindsay said. "Women have more options now."

Teri raised her severely plucked eyebrows. "Yes and no," she said. "In theory they've changed, but in practice I've had a lot of experience with this and seen a lot of other women face the realities of trying to balance family and career, and I know it's still really difficult."

It was really disturbing me to be having this conversation with these two women, and find myself so thoroughly on Teri's side.

Lindsay opened her mouth to speak,

closed it, and then opened it again. "I appreciate it that older women like you opened doors for us," she said finally. "I think it's going to be different for me."

Teri Jordan may have been a bitch, but she was no fool. She clamped her mouth shut and turned stonily to me. "There's work waiting on your desk," she said.

I stood up, but waited until she left. It wasn't that I felt I had to defend my boss's honor, but I couldn't let that last remark of Lindsay's go unaddressed.

"I don't think it's really so different," I said. "Even after all this time, I don't know whether I could handle kids and a career."

"Well, I think I could," she said. "If that's what I wanted."

"Maybe that's the real issue," I said. "What do *you* want out of life?"

"I want everything," Lindsay said simply, gazing back at me with those unclouded eyes.

And so she should, I thought. When I was Lindsay's age, I mean really her age, I would have outlined my future very much as she just had, entertained the same gauzy vision of my possibilities. In fact, talking to Lindsay was disturbing not so much because she saw things differently from me, but because she saw them so much like I once had.

"Then I'm sure you'll get it," I said, patting her hand even as I began to back away. "I'm just going to try and manage one thing at a time."

CHAPTER 10

He called me. Then I called him. Then he called me again. Each time, what started out to be a brief conversation turned into an extended talk. I took the phone under the covers in my red tent. I whispered to him from the supply room at work. It was like I was in middle school again, when I first discovered the telephone, and I never wanted to hang up.

It seemed easier to open up to him when it was only his voice I was dealing with, when the physical reality of him and his age weren't in the picture. And when I was a mere voice myself, which seemed somehow like a truer, more timeless version of me.

I might have been satisfied to play out our entire relationship on the telephone, but then, inevitably, he wanted to meet. He suggested a place, but I was afraid our embryonic romance wouldn't survive another night of grinding dancers or their equivalent. I offered to cook him dinner. That night at Lindsay's had reawakened my cooking instincts, and I knew, if nothing else, the process would relax me.

He assured me that the place he was subletting in Brooklyn had a decent kitchen and what looked to him like a full complement of pots and pans — though he'd never actually attempted to prepare anything more elaborate than frozen ravioli.

I set out to shop on Saturday at noon, a full six hours before I was due at Josh's. The city seemed quiet and the ice had all melted and the temperature had thawed a bit. My internal sense of time no longer moved to the rhythm of the school calendar, but I realized it must be the start of Presidents' Week, a time when we always took a family vacation. But inevitably, if we went skiing it was so warm that the snow had turned to mud, and if we went south the weather was as cold as it was back home.

Not my home anymore, I told myself firmly, at least not for now. In fact, Maggie's Lower East Side neighborhood was beginning to feel more like home than I ever imagined it could. I'd developed my own little routine in the mornings and the evenings and had assembled a cozy village of shopkeepers and restaurant people I chatted with — the tall Albanian guy who started preparing my cappuccino with skim milk, no cinnamon, two minutes before I customarily walked in the door of his café every morning, the counterman at Katz's deli who knew just how to trim the pastrami sandwich I sometimes treated myself to, the tiny eternally busy woman at the vegetable stand, and the waitress at the restaurant where we'd gone on New Year's Eve, who'd just landed a part in a tampon commercial.

Today was a chance to expand my range. I stopped at the old-fashioned butcher shop that was always closed by the time I got home from the office, as if it didn't want to trade with working women. But today, the courtly man behind the counter discussed at length with me my various roast options — Josh assured me he'd happily eat whatever I wanted to cook — and then meticulously trimmed the fat from the leg of lamb he helped me select. At the Chinese bakery I bought two pork buns, and then a block later, at the Italian bakery, I couldn't resist a beautiful loaf of semolina, so warm and crusty and fragrant I ripped off a hunk and munched on it as I strolled down the street.

The sidewalks were wet, and the sun shone warm on my face. When Maggie first moved to the Lower East Side, all the stores were Hasidic, shut down on Saturdays. And then for a while, when crack first made its debut, the neighborhood became so dangerous it was terrifying to simply walk through the streets, even in daytime. Now there was a whole new generation of street life: groovy bars and restaurants, a café owned by a rock star that served a hundred varieties of tea, a sneaker shop that drew entire suburban families and kept its priciest wares locked inside thick Plexiglas boxes, like the Hope diamond. I strolled along, putting everything I bought in a backpack so my hands were free to examine the apples at the fruit stand, to carry a cappuccino and shop for a shirt I ended up changing into and wearing out of the store.

When I reached the entrance to the subway, I decided on impulse to ride up to Fourteenth Street to see what I could find at the Union Square Greenmarket. It was amazing to me that this outdoor farmers' market operated year-round. If I closed my eyes, blocking out the bare trees and the stall operators and shoppers in their turtlenecks and heavy coats, I could almost imagine it was spring. I bought parsnips and carrots for a puree, apples and peaches to make a pie.

My pack was full and I carried a bag in

each hand by the time I headed out to Josh's house in Brooklyn. I'd gotten so involved in my shopping that I'd almost lost sight of why I was doing it, what this night might hold, so it wasn't until I was walking toward his building, peering at street signs and addresses, that I remembered to get nervous.

"You're still in control," Maggie told me. "This is the age of AIDS. People don't sleep together on their first date."

"It's our second date," I pointed out. "Or maybe, if you count New Year's Eve as well as the night I stood him up at the bar, it's Date Two and a Half. Plus it's also the age of *Sex and the City*."

"Oh," said Maggie. "You're right. It's obviously time to fuck his brains out."

Had I been making a pro-fucking-his-brains-out argument? I hadn't been aware of that. In fact, if I let myself even think about fucking his brains out, I wanted to hurl the groceries into the street and hightail it (note to self: don't say "hightail it" if you want people to think you're under forty) back to New Jersey.

It's just dinner, I told myself, in rhythm to my feet. A mere leg of lamb.

Josh had told me he was subletting his apartment from a musician, so I wasn't expecting the sweep of elegant space behind him when he opened the door. It was more a loft than an apartment, nearly as big as Maggie's, and nearly as unfurnished, but in a different way. Everything was sleek and modern: a steel-armed charcoal sofa facing an enormous flat-screen TV, a rectangular black dining table with wheels on its legs, and in the far corner a bed as flat and vast as a field, blanketed in bedding as soft and white as snow.

Quickly, I turned my eyes from the bed to the long wall crowded with recording equipment along with what I guessed were Josh's own computers and video screens, speakers mounted in all four corners of the ceiling, and shelves filled with thousands of records and CDs.

"What kind of music do you like?" Josh said. "We've got it all here."

"Oh, I don't know," I said. "I need to put down these groceries."

I definitely wanted to avoid the music question. I didn't really know any music that had been made since the seventies, early eighties at the very latest. After that I'd gotten too busy being a mom, and when Diana had gotten old enough to be interested in music, I bought her a Walkman so I wouldn't have to listen to it. Sting was my idea of a new musician. Elvis Costello,

174

someone extremely modern. Even better, I liked the music we'd listened to at dance parties in high school and college, Motown, mostly.

Josh led me into the tiny stainless steel kitchen, which looked like the kind of place where you might invent a cure for cancer. It looked as if it had rarely been sullied by anything so plebeian as raw meat or mud-crusted parsnips. I set down the bags and began unpacking my backpack, looking around and thinking about where the cutting board might be, trying to distract myself from the fear of melting into a pool of my own nervous perspiration.

"Come on," he said, running a hand along my hip. "Let's dance."

I giggled, perhaps girlishly.

"There's no music," I said.

"We don't need music."

He pulled me close, one arm around my back, the other holding my hand close to his heart. It was the way people danced at weddings, which at least was something I knew how to do.

"Come on," he murmured in my ear. "Tell me what kind of music you like."

"Martha Vandella," I said finally. "Marvin Gaye."

It was nice, dancing in the silence. I liked

175

swaying with his arms around me, resting my cheek on the soft cotton covering his substantial shoulder.

"Oh," he said. "Oldies."

I stopped moving.

He laughed. "Don't worry," he said. "The guy I'm renting this place from has everything. It's all arranged chronologically."

He went over to the shelves that held the CDs and reached toward the top, which I figured was somewhere near the beginning of time — but not, I was relieved to see, the *very* beginning. I guessed there might be a few Billie Holiday and Elvis Presley recordings up there before it.

"Here's something I think you'll like," Josh said, pulling one down. "It's a favorite of mine."

It was Sam Cooke, "You Send Me."

He held me more tightly now as we began dancing again. I felt something nudge my hip and realized it was him, growing hard. I wasn't thinking about groceries anymore.

Unfortunately, what I was thinking about was even less romantic. I was remembering the visiting professor I'd slept with at Mount Holyoke, the poet who was in his late forties when I was barely twenty, of how slack his skin felt compared with that of the handful of boys I'd had sex with. He'd felt somehow *worn,* like an old shirt.

I was horrified by the idea that Josh would feel that way about me, would divine, once I was naked and in bed with him, by the look of my skin or my feel or my scent, that I was older — much older — than he'd thought I was.

He took off his T-shirt.

"Uh, I don't think so," I said.

He stared at me.

"I'm sorry," I said. "It's not you."

Like the boys always said: It's not you, it's me. Except in this case, it was true.

The music was still playing, but we had stopped dancing. I reached out and touched his shoulder, so hard, so tight. I couldn't resist running my hand along it, over its curved edge like the lip of a waterfall and down the smoothness of his biceps. I trailed my hand across his chest to his nipple, hard as a pebble. I moved closer and kissed him there, flicking out my tongue to feel its ridge.

He groaned. "Alice," he said. "This is too hard."

I ran my hand down his flat stomach, unsnapped his jeans, and touched his penis.

"It's too hard for me, too," I said.

He grabbed my hand.

"Please," he said.

I pulled my hand away and used it to push his pants down around his knees. He stepped out of them. He wasn't wearing any underwear. The Sam Cooke song had ended, and something unfamiliar had come on. I knelt down before him and took his penis in my mouth. This was something I couldn't remember ever wanting to do before, but I wanted to do it now. Maybe because this was a way to have him without taking off my clothes.

"Oh, God," he said, digging his fingers into my scalp and arching his back so that he thrust deep into my throat. "I want to see you, Alice."

I stopped and looked up at him.

"Let's just do this," I said.

"Come on," he said, nudging me upward. "Please."

I stood up, and he began unbuttoning my new shirt, its buttons difficult to work through the still-stiff buttonholes, finally pulling it off my shoulders and reaching into my bra, cupping my breasts in his hands. Then he unsnapped my pants and pulled them down in the exact way I'd tugged at his. I was wearing black cotton underwear, bikinis, not new. He seemed to smile when he saw these, but then reached inside and put his finger into me, not seeming to mind at all the thicket of pubic hair he encountered there.

"Oh," I said.

"Yes," he murmured, pressing it in more insistently. "Oh."

"Oh."

I thought I might have my first person-to-person orgasm before we even started on the actual sex.

"Let me take my clothes off," I said.

"I'll do it for you."

I stood there like a child, holding my arms out from my side while he eased my shirt and my pants all the way off, while he unhooked my bra and pulled down my panties. From the recesses of my mind came the memory that I was nervous about him seeing me without my clothes, but my desire for him immediately overrode my anxiety.

It was immediately evident that he was too excited, too, to notice anything other than that I was standing before him naked, and that we were about to make love. He took my hand and led me over to the CD player, which he switched off, and then to the big white bed.

At the bed, he pulled me down, pressed his mouth to each of my breasts and then between my legs. I could have danced to the beat of my heart. I had never felt like this before, truly. All the years in recent memory, my sex life with Gary had been routine and unenthusiastic, an occasional lunch with a boring colleague. The months in bed with my pregnancies and then the months recovering from those losses, the years at home with a small child and then a curious adolescent — these had all taken their toll. And before that, with Gary and with the few lovers I'd had in college, the problem had been mine alone. I remembered the excitement of kissing, the thrill of getting undressed, and then losing interest when it didn't progress beyond a certain point. Waiting for him to come, and feeling as if I never ever would.

Now I felt overcome by my excitement, so that I lost all sense of myself and of what we were doing. Did he feel so different because he was not Gary or because he was young and so strong, so eager? Who cared? It was thrilling that as strong and eager as he was, I felt every bit as strong, and a lot more eager. All that exercise — I'd taken more Krav Maga classes with Lindsay, and was back at the gym running on the treadmill and lifting weights — fueled my energy now, and I felt as if I could keep going all night. At one point it seemed as if he came, but that barely slowed him down. He lay on his back with his eyes closed while I moved slowly above him, and then he joined back in.

I wanted to talk to somebody, afterward. Is it like this, I wanted to ask, for you? I thought of all the women I'd known, my old Homewood friends Elaine and Lori, my neighbors and the moms of Diana's friends, even Maggie, even Lindsay, and I couldn't imagine they felt this way about sex. If they did, they'd be having it every second. They'd be grabbing men — or women, in Maggie's case — in the street and doing it every chance they got.

But maybe I just felt this way because it had been so long. Because it had been, I thought with a laugh, forever. I was a forty-four-year-old virgin, I thought. A forty-four-year-old virgin who had all the mechanics down pat.

"That was amazing," Josh said.

I looked at him in surprise. I'd nearly forgotten he was there.

"Really?" I said. "It was for you, too?"

"Of course," he smiled, turning onto his side and running his fingertips lightly over my torso. "You're incredible."

"I am?" I said.

He nodded solemnly. "You seem like you

really like sex."

"Doesn't everybody?" I asked, really meaning, Don't all young women like sex? Because I was thinking it was probably just my generation that had so much trouble getting started. Girls today, with the magazines, the how-to books, with *Sex and the City,* seemed to have such an easier time.

"Not that much," he said. "You're different."

"You're different, too," I said.

He was different from Gary, of course, and from Thad, from all those men who lived within their own egos. And he was different from the dreamier young men I'd dated in college, too: less gallant and more interested in my life, not as macho and more willing to let me take the lead. He's a lot, I realized now, like I always wished men would be, back when I was dreaming of Prince Charming. A lot like I assumed Gary was, back when I was blinded by love.

Or maybe Gary was really more like this back then, when he was studying in England and writing poetry. His poems had been beautiful, and he had been so serious about them, about his search for beauty and truth. I would come home to our tiny apartment in the early days of our marriage, during my first tour of duty at Gentility, to find Gary staring unseeing and openmouthed at the wall, or a few times with tears streaming down his face, immersed in the feelings and the words.

"Can I ask you a question?" Josh said.

He was not quite looking at me, I noticed.

"All right."

"How old are you?"

I stopped breathing. He knew. He had guessed. He could tell by my crepey skin, my stomach, my thighs.

I hesitated for a moment, trying to decide which I wanted more: to tell the truth or to keep him wanting me. "I'm older than you," I finally said.

"That's what I thought," he said.

I was relieved, now that it was out. I was glad that he had brought it up, because I was obviously too much of a coward to do it myself. When he learned the full truth, I wondered, would he run away? But better to have it all clear now.

"Really?" I said. "What are you, twenty-five?"

"Bingo," he grinned. "How did you know that?"

"Lucky guess," I said. "That's how old Lindsay is, too."

"I figured she and I were about the same age," Josh said. Then he laughed, his eyes dancing. "Though I figured Thad for at least fifty-eight."

And then I had to ask: "How old do you think I am?"

Please, I thought. Don't let him say over forty. Though I fully intended to tell him the truth.

He grimaced, and I held my breath.

Finally he spoke. "I'd guess you're . . . twenty-nine."

CHAPTER 11

Teri arrived a few minutes early at the office, clutching a Starbucks cup as big as a vase in her black-gloved hand. I'd already been there for an hour, working, as had become my habit, on my classics project, sketching rough ideas for a new cover direction. As soon as I saw Teri I curled my arm over my notebook, just like I used to do when Bobby Mahoney tried to copy off me at St. Valentine's.

"What's that you're doing?" Teri said, stopping dead in her tracks and sliding her enormous dark glasses — on her sharp little face, they made her look like an alien — down her chiseled nose.

"Oh," I said. "It's just something I'm working on."

"What is it?" Teri said, a smile flickering on and off her lips like a lamp with faulty wiring.

"It's not quite ready," I said. "I want to

185

get it completely pulled together before I present it to you."

Lindsay had advised me to outline my idea in writing and give it to Teri in a memo. That way, Lindsay said, she'd at least have to give me credit for what was documented as mine.

"Let's have a preview," Teri said, dropping her briefcase and already reaching across my desk.

What could I do? Tell the teacher? I showed her the notebook — I wanted to be able to carry my notes back and forth from Maggie's with me, and besides, I was paranoid about entrusting the plan to the computer before I was ready to show it to Teri — and explained my idea in broad terms. Teri listened, looking not at me but at the paper, nodding as I talked. I felt vaguely guilty, thanks to my Catholic girlhood, for working on this project without telling her, or maybe I was just afraid that she was pissed off. Which she looked. Though she looked like that almost all the time.

"This has possibilities," she said when she'd finished reading. "I'd like to see this more fleshed out."

My heart soared with relief and pleasure. I was finally on the right track. My boss liked my idea and had given me the green

186

light to develop it. I imagined myself presenting the idea to Mrs. Whitney, with Lindsay providing backup, Thad lending his support, Teri looking on with the pride of a mentor.

Which she certainly could be, now that I was open to giving her a chance. Maybe the problems between us had been more my fault than I'd acknowledged. I'd been holding back from her, not bouncing my thoughts off her or asking her to tell me about marketing. Maybe, as Maggie pointed out about my attitude toward Josh, I was just a big old age bigot, and I'd discounted Teri's expertise because I knew she was a lot younger than me. If Lindsay saw Teri as being from a different generation, so did I, but in my case it was a younger, more callow, less creative and less sensitive generation — the kids who came of professional age during the dot-com boom and congratulated themselves, rather than history, for it.

But she had more than a decade in the workplace on me, I reminded myself. She had a degree in marketing, a field I barely knew existed a month ago, and she successfully balanced a high-powered career with a houseful of kids, something I hadn't managed to do. Sure, she was tough, but you had to be tough to accomplish as much as she had. Teri Jordan deserved my respect, and I vowed to improve not only my job performance but my attitude.

Most of the day I spent energetically working my way through the in-box on my desk, which Teri always managed to keep piled with projects. That day I tripled my efforts, actually managing to deposit the last completed item on Teri's desk just as she was leaving for a meeting with Mrs. Whitney.

"Is there anything else you have for me right now?" I asked her. "Because if not, I thought I'd spend some time on the classics project."

"Good idea," Teri said, disappearing in an efficient hustle out of her office.

This was great. Now I could work on my project during regular hours rather than having to do it before Teri got in in the morning or at Maggie's at night. I could be open about what I was doing rather than having to sneak and hide. The new openness fueled my energy for the project itself, so that I managed to finish my list of titles and possible authors for the introductions while Teri was still in the meeting. Printing it out, I brought it into her office to set on her desk with the pile she always took home with her to read in the evening.

That's when I saw it: the memo Teri had written to bring into her meeting this afternoon. She usually asked me to spell-check and copy her meeting memos, and it briefly crossed my mind as odd that she hadn't today, but I'd dismissed my misgivings. Maybe she'd decided not to do a memo, and maybe she simply saw how hard I was working and decided not to bother me with what was essentially a mop-up job.

But now I saw the real reason Teri hadn't asked me to prepare the memo. There it was, in the heading for the very first paragraph: NEW DIRECTION FOR CLASSICS LINE. And there was an outline of my idea, presented as Teri's exclusive work, even including the cover ideas I'd been working on when she'd arrived this morning.

"What are you doing in my office?"

It was Teri, back from her meeting. I was standing there, holding the memo. Despite myself, I felt my cheeks color.

"I was just putting something on your desk," I said, feeling my face begin to burn even hotter, "but then I saw this."

"You have no business rifling through my papers." Teri wasn't looking at me. Instead, she hurried to position herself behind her desk, gathering everything into a pile.

"I can't believe you presented my idea when I told you it wasn't ready," I said. "And you didn't give me any credit at all."

"I've made it very clear," she said, "that I'm the only idea person in this department."

"But you're not!" I cried, forgetting about what I should or shouldn't say. "I mean, this was completely my idea, and I think I deserve at least some of the credit."

"That's not how it works," Teri said.

"But that's how it should work," I told her.

"Listen," she said, finally looking at me. "This was all outlined during the interview. I've already had one problem with you around this issue on your very first day of work. I'm starting to think that maybe there's no way you're going to be happy in this job."

I opened my mouth to speak, and then I just stood there, the words choked in my throat. How had we gotten to this point with such dizzying speed? Was she about to fire me? I was afraid that if I asked that question, she'd say yes. And then it would be over. And I was not going to let her get rid of me so easily. I was not going to do that to myself.

"I can be happy in this job," I said finally.

"Good," she said, beginning to pack up again. "As long as we understand each other."

"We understand each other."

I understand, I thought, that you're a self-aggrandizing control freak. But I'm not going to let you get the better of me.

"Good," Teri said again. "Then it should be clear to you that it's a compliment that I take these ideas into a meeting with Mrs. Whitney."

Teri took her coat off the hook and shrugged it on, then slipped on her sunglasses, even though it was already nearly dark outside. "Now that I know you're capable of so many excellent ideas," she said, "I'll expect nothing less of you."

"Right."

"I already set up a meeting with Mrs. Whitney for Thursday to present the full concept, so you'll have a memo ready by then."

"Thursday?" I croaked.

She patted my arm so enthusiastically I was afraid she was going to raise a bruise. "I have complete confidence in you," she said. "Remember, we're a team."

"Of course, Teri," I said to her retreating back, wondering whether it was possible to sue for spiritual harassment. Was there any way for me to hang on to my job and at the same time keep her from sucking my soul?

"Just don't tell her your ideas," Maggie said.

She was working on a new sculpture, only now she had moved on from encasing a cow's heart in a cement cube to embedding a duck's heart in a papier-mâché sphere. She'd dropped the duck heart into a condom — more symbolically powerful than a balloon, she claimed, even though, like the heart itself, no one would ever know it was there — blown up the condom, and then layered the papier-mâché over that until she'd created an enormous globe.

"I have to tell her my ideas," I said miserably. "She's already set up a meeting with Mrs. Whitney for Thursday to do the full presentation." I shook my head. "I never thought I'd long for the day when all she expected from me was a good cup of coffee."

"Insist you be included in that meeting," said Maggie.

"And then announce in front of everyone that the concept is really mine?" I shook my head. "Teri would flip."

"What if you held out some ideas from the main proposal?" Maggie said. "I mean some of your best ideas. And then at the

192

meeting you could pipe up with them as if they'd just occurred to you."

She stepped back and cocked her head, surveying the ball. "Does it bother you knowing there's a lot of air around the duck heart?"

I gave her the look that remark deserved. "It bothers me knowing about the heart, period," I said. "Everything else seems beside the point."

"I'm afraid it's going to rattle around in there," she said.

I didn't think a real live — or in this case, real dead — heart could actually rattle, but rather than debate that hypothesis, I pointed out that it was unlikely that anyone would be able to shake a sphere as big as a Volkswagen around to find out.

I wished my mind were clear enough to focus on such problems as the sounds emitted by dried duck hearts, but I was too distracted by my concerns about handling Teri and the upcoming meeting. I worried I wouldn't have the nerve to publicly present an independent slate of ideas, having already experienced Teri's wrath.

"She's not going to attack you in front of everybody," Maggie pointed out, "and the important thing is that you get credit for your great ideas. Make sure your little friend, the editor, is in the meeting, and her boyfriend the honcho too. That way you'll have more ammunition on your side in case Teri tries to fight back later."

I knew Maggie was right. If I was going to succeed, I was going to have to swallow my anxieties and take on Teri at her own game. I was going to have to be brave enough, finally, to act like a grown-up.

Maggie moved back a few paces and then stepped forward to smooth a bubble from her papier-mâché.

"Did I tell you?" she said. "The Vietnamese adoption people are coming to check me out."

"They're coming here?" I cried. Maggie was still hoping she was pregnant, but she was also going ahead with the adoption application, to keep all her bases covered. "When?"

"Sometime this week," she said, applying a fresh sheet of wet newspaper. "They deliberately leave it vague."

"What?" I said, looking wildly around the room. I wasn't sure how a place with so little furniture in it managed to look so messy. "We've got to clean this place up!"

Maggie shook her head with an elaborate show of unconcern.

"It's fine," she said. "They just want to

see how I live. I don't have anything to hide."

"But they want to be sure this would be a good place to raise a baby," I told her. "We should at least pick up a little, clean up all this glue, maybe put a rug down."

Maggie stopped working, holding her sticky hands in the air like a surgeon's.

"I have no intention of putting on a big show," said Maggie. "I'm an artist, and any child of mine is going to be raised in a creative environment."

"Of course," I said. "It's just —"

"I don't want to get a baby under false pretenses," she said.

"Right," I said, feeling as if a big faker like me didn't have a right to argue with Maggie's purity. "Of course."

She was still holding up her hands. "Shit," she said. "I have to go to the bathroom. I guess I should start wearing rubber gloves, but I just love the feel of that cold glue on my hands."

I heard the water blasting in the bathroom as she hurried to wash her hands before she used the toilet, and I experimentally reached out to touch the glue, which did feel weirdly cold, as if it had come from somewhere deep in the earth. I wished then with a pang sharper than I ever could have anticipated that I had a creative career of my own, something I alone was in control of, something no one had to give me and that no one could take away. I thought of the aborted novel I'd never looked at after I'd packed it away in the attic. It seemed now that, as with so many other things in my life, I'd given up too easily because I was so terrified of failing. That was something I couldn't let happen again.

"Shit," I heard from the bathroom. "Shit shit fuck fuck."

The bathroom door burst open, and there stood Maggie, looking as if she was about to cry, something I hadn't seen her do since third grade.

"I got my period," she said.

"Oh, God," I said, feeling devastated for her. She had been sure that the insemination had taken. "I'm so sorry."

"I guess now it's especially good those adoption people are coming so soon, huh?" She wiped an incipient tear from the corner of her eye.

"Yes," I said. "It's great you have the other option under way."

And then I thought of the thing I'd wanted to say before, the thing I'd bitten back because Maggie had been so adamant about not wanting to change anything about the loft to impress the adoption agency. I'd never be able to live with myself if I thought my living there was the reason Maggie didn't become a mother.

"You know, it might be better if I wasn't here when the adoption people came," I said gently. "I could pack my stuff up in the tent, find somewhere else to stay for a few days. I mean, it looking like someone else lives here might complicate things for you."

Maggie stared at me. "But that would be lying," she said finally.

"Not lying," I reminded her. "Don't ask, don't tell."

She gazed at me another minute. "I'm not going to do that," she said finally. "In fact, I'm going to make a point of telling them you live here. You're my best friend. You're a mom. What could be bad about that?"

I could think of a hundred possibilities, but before I got the chance to begin enumerating them, Maggie stepped back into the bathroom and slammed the door.

CHAPTER 12

I offered to stay home that night with Maggie, but she shooed me away, saying she could certainly weather getting her period by herself, and besides, she wanted to be alone with her duck heart. While I would have been happy to spend the evening comforting Maggie, I was also dying to see Josh again.

We'd been out a few times during the week, but tonight, he was cooking me dinner. I expected maybe bratwurst and frozen fries, or a hearty pot of chili — the kind of thing Gary used to make on the rare occasions when he cooked. And since, after all my shopping, I hadn't gotten around to actually making anything too elaborate for Josh last time, he didn't have a very high standard to live up to.

So I was surprised and impressed to find a gourmet meal in progress when I arrived at Josh's place. Vegetables and exotic herbs were spread across the kitchen's stainless steel countertops, and something that smelled wonderful was bubbling on the stove.

"I didn't know you knew how to cook," I said, kissing the corner of his mouth. He'd obviously been tasting his efforts; the preview was delicious.

"I don't," he said. "I called my mom, like, ten times today."

His mom. I forgot about people having moms — I mean, people I was having sex with. I could only hope that she was older than me.

"So what are we having?" I asked.

"Some salad thing. Let's see, shrimp with garlic and vegetables. And this kind of mushroom risotto — that's my mom's specialty."

That was one of my specialties, too.

"How about a cocktail?" I said.

"I got something better," he said, holding his fingers to his lips and making a sucking sound. "A little . . ."

I had no idea what he was talking about, and my confusion must have showed on my face.

"I got us a couple of blunts," he said. "You know, spliffs."

And when I still looked baffled: "Pot."

"Ooooh," I said, the light dawning. "I don't think so."

I had smoked pot, of course. Round about the last time I'd gone on a date — twenty-five years ago.

"Oh, come on," he said. "If nothing else, it'll make my food taste better."

This really made me nervous. I had pleasant memories of my few experiences with marijuana, but I'd spent so many years warning Diana of its dangers that I'd begun to believe them myself. It can damage your lungs. It can muddle your thinking. And it can lead to harder drugs. By the end of the evening, I might find myself down under the Williamsburg Bridge, selling my body for a hit of crack.

But what really scared me was what I might say to Josh under the influence. My dim memories of smoking include lots of outrageous statements and wild laughter. Who knew what I might confess, with all my inhibitions dismantled?

I was about to suggest that I mix us a nice martini instead, when Josh lit up the joint. He took a really deep drag and held it out to me.

Maybe more than I was afraid of becoming a crack ho, I was afraid of Josh seeing me as uncool. I accepted the joint and took a light puff, trying not to inhale. Josh, in turn, poured me a glass of white wine, and I sat on a stool near the kitchen counter sipping the wine while he stirred his risotto and we passed the joint back and forth, companionably quiet.

Then Josh suggested we put on some music and said there were some things he wanted to play for me to update my taste from Marvin Gaye.

I looked skeptical. "Not like the rock they were playing in that club that night," I said. "Because if it's that —"

"It's not that," he said. "Do you like rap?"

"Uhhhh, I don't think so." An Everest of pot was not going to make me that cool.

"But if you like Marvin," he said, "and Aretha, I really think you'll like this."

He put on something then that was a little bit rap and a lot more soul. "I'm going down . . . ," a woman sang, and I thought, Sister, I know just what you mean.

We made love. Maybe, I thought, if Gary and I had smoked pot, our sex life might have been better. But then I thought, naaaaaah.

Josh's playfulness was what enchanted me more than anything, so that I felt like a child, not merely a young woman. In the middle of kissing, of touching, of the most

201

intense passion, he'd say something that made me laugh so hard we'd have to stop whatever we were doing so I could lie back and chortle, a more intense release than any orgasm. The only thing we seemed to do more than touch each other was to laugh.

The risotto burned, so we decided to ditch the plans for an elaborate sit-down dinner and eat in bed. Josh set down the pot holding the shrimp and the salad bowl directly on the sheets, handed me a fork, and suggested we dig in. It was delicious, the best dinner I'd ever eaten, it seemed. For dessert, instead of making the sundaes he'd planned, we fed each other ice cream and caramel sauce directly from the containers, and then squirted whipped cream into each other's mouths.

"Let's play a game," he said, after we were finished eating.

"All right." I stretched. "How about Scrabble?"

He looked at me as if I'd suggested we play a little croquet, right there on the bed.

"I had something electronic in mind," he said. "Do you know Doom?"

Oh, I knew Doom all right.

"Not really."

"Final Fantasy?"

"Nope."

"I know. I'll just teach you the game I've been working on. My own design."

"I'd like that," I said. "But I've never really played video games."

I don't think he really understood what I meant by never, because he handed me the controls, gave me a brief tutorial, then seemed to think I'd know what to do. But my pathetic little guy kept getting instantly annihilated by the alien space guns, incapable of making even the feeblest attempt to get out of the way.

"I know you don't have any brothers," Josh said, "but didn't you have guys as friends? Boyfriends, maybe, who tried to teach you to play?"

"No," I said, attempting and failing yet again to get the little man to jump over the rock. "I never even tried to play one of these."

Josh shook his head and took the controller back. "You press X with your left hand and Right Arrow with your right, like this," he said. The little man leaped handily into the air, only to encounter another rock.

"Okay," I said, taking the controller back. "I get it now."

The little guy slammed head-on into the rock, and the game evaporated him completely.

"That's it!" Josh cried, snatching the controller from me. "You're banned!"

Laughing, I grabbed for it.

"Oh, no," he said, holding it beyond my reach. When I lunged for it, he slid it across the floor and then clamped his hands over my wrists, wrestling me back onto the floor. I jerked my knee upward — a Krav Maga move — and managed to startle him onto his side, but he quickly recovered and rolled me over again onto my back, straddling me, breathing hard.

"What have you been doing all these years?" he said.

It sounded like teasing, but I could feel my guard go up. I wanted to tell Josh the truth. And I'd decided that when I couldn't, I'd try not to say anything at all.

"You know," I said, my voice light and teasing.

"No, I don't," he said seriously. "I know you went to Mount Holyoke. I know you spent some time traveling. But I don't know how much time, or where you went, or what you did. And if you're twenty-nine now, that leaves a lot of years unaccounted for."

"What do you want to know?"

"Well, how did you get your name, anyway? Alice sounds so . . . old."

"I was named after my grandmother," I

said, relieved that he'd asked a question that allowed me to both reveal something about myself and answer honestly. "She was Italian — Alicea."

"Alicea. That's pretty. Maybe I'll call you that. Or Ali. You seem more like an Ali."

I made a face, remembering the horrible restaurant guy. "I really prefer Alice."

"What did you do for work before you got this publishing job?" Josh asked. He put down his game controller, his face suddenly serious.

"I didn't really work," I told him. "I tried to write a bit, but it didn't go anywhere."

"So what did you do?" he asked. "How did you support yourself?"

"I didn't support myself. I got money from my . . . family."

"From your mother."

"My mother paid for college," I said truthfully. "But then I had other family money." Namely, Gary's money.

"I'd like to meet your family," he said.

I laughed, until I realized he meant it.

"But I told you. My father died when I was a child, and my mother died last summer. I'm pretty much on my own now."

"What about Maggie?" he said. "You always say that Maggie is like your family. Why can't I meet her?"

Maggie had actually expressed curiosity about meeting Josh, too, but I was afraid such a get-together would raise more issues than it would settle, with Josh wondering how I had gotten to be friends with someone "so old," and Maggie getting way too much material for the boy-toy jokes she already teased me with.

"I just don't think it's a good idea," I said.

"Are you ashamed of me?" Josh asked.

Ashamed? How could he imagine such a thing? I wanted to show him off to everyone I'd ever met in my entire life. In theory, of course.

"Of course not," I assured him.

I stood up and walked across the room to the refrigerator, suddenly in need of a beer. Maybe, too, the sight of my naked body would serve to distract him.

"Why all these questions?"

"My parents were asking me," he said. I could hear him pull in a shaky breath. "They want to meet you."

"No!" I squealed, clutching the cold beer to my heart.

"Jesus, what's the problem? They're coming into the city, and they want to take me out to dinner, and they wondered whether you might like to come along. No big deal."

"Good," I said. "I'm glad it's no big deal.

Because I don't want to go."

"Why not? My parents are very nice people."

I was sure they were. He'd already told me they lived in Fairfield, Connecticut, that his father worked as a lawyer for the state and his mom had become a nursery school teacher once Josh and his sister were in high school. They had an old house — a lot like my house in Homewood, I'd bet — and his mother loved to garden. I'm certain she and I would have a lot in common, much more than Josh had ever bargained on.

"Listen," I told him. "I really like you. I want to be with you. But I thought the deal here was neither of us was interested in a commitment. You're moving to Tokyo, Josh. From the very beginning, we knew this was a temporary thing."

"But why do you have to put all these limits on it? Even sometimes when we're just talking, it's like you have a limit on how much you'll tell me — like you're afraid you might give away too much."

There he was, the person I had been afraid of all along, the Harvard MBA lurking inside the gamer. "When I met you, you talked about how you didn't want to get married," I reminded him. "How you didn't want to get serious about anything or anybody. That's the only reason I wanted to go out with you in the first place."

Josh looked at me as if he were seeing me for the very first time. "That was the only reason?"

I took his hand, softening. "No, of course not. Of course that wasn't the only reason. I like you a lot, Josh."

If last week I felt twenty-eight or twenty-nine, tonight I felt fourteen.

He breathed out through his nose and seemed vulnerable as a little boy — not, I must note, a real turn-on for me. But I had reduced him to this state.

"But it's *because* I like you so much that I want to be sure we're in agreement about how far this relationship is going to go," I tried to explain. "I don't want a big committed relationship right now. I need to be free to put my energy into my job, to put myself first. I haven't done that for a long time."

Josh looked at me curiously. "Why not?"

I shook my head as if to clear that statement from our collective memory. "This is about you too, Josh," I reminded him. "You made this huge change in your life, went through all this pain to break commitments you'd made, so you would be free to go to Tokyo and study gaming. That's got to be your priority."

"But I feel like I'm falling in lo—"

"Stop!" I screamed. "Don't say that."

"Why not? Why can't I say it? It's what I feel."

"Because it scares me," I told him. The truth.

"Because it makes me want to run away." The truth.

And because it was only if he didn't say it that I could let myself enjoy him feeling it, and that I was able to feel it myself.

CHAPTER 13

On Thursday morning, I sat at my desk, peering around the edge of my cubicle every few moments to check whether Teri might have somehow sneaked into her office without my spotting her. Maggie's reassurances notwithstanding, I'd been trying to leave her place even earlier every morning than usual, so as not to collide with the adoption people. I used the time to work on my proposal, which was literally under my fingertips, awaiting Teri's approval. I'd counted on having time for revisions before the meeting — not that Teri ever had anything to change or add. She simply okayed my work and put her name on it. But now, on the day of our big proposal, she was a full twenty minutes late.

The phone on my desk trilled, making me leap off my chair. I was relieved, and then alarmed, to hear Teri's voice.

"My kids have the flu," Teri said. "All

three of them."

"But can't the babysitter watch them?" I said. "I mean, at least long enough for you to get to the meeting."

"The babysitter has it too."

"The backup babysitter?" I gasped.

In one of her lectures on working mother-hood, Teri had told me that the key was having not merely reliable child-care help, but a rock-solid backup, "like hospitals have emergency generators in case of a blackout or an earthquake."

"She moved to Montana with the pizza guy," said Teri. "But that's not the point. The point is, I'm not coming in."

"But the meeting —," I said.

"We're going to have to reschedule. Or postpone."

"All right," I said, flustered. "What should I tell Mrs. Whitney?"

"Tell her . . . shit," Teri said. "This is a problem, not a solution. She's not going to like this."

"No, she's not," I agreed.

I felt my brain slipping into the high problem-solving gear that I'd perfected over my years of caring for a house and child. Furnace broken down/dinner burned/book report due by tomorrow morning? No matter how daunting the combination of problems, I could always come up with a dozen solutions.

The trouble, right now, was that I wasn't sure what the problem was. How to put off the meeting without ruffling Mrs. Whitney's feathers? How to arrange child care so Teri could get to the meeting? Or how to conduct the meeting without Teri? Which, it was beginning to dawn on me, might mean I didn't have a problem at all.

"I could talk privately to Mrs. Whitney's assistant — maybe this meeting isn't even on Mrs. Whitney's radar, and she won't notice if we reschedule," I said.

"Mrs. Whitney told me yesterday how anxious she was to hear my plan," Teri said.

My plan, she'd said, not our plan, never mind *your* plan. Screw her, I thought. Her not being there was the best thing that could have happened to me. I'd go in there, do the presentation giving myself full credit, without having to suffer her angry looks.

But as soon as those thoughts occurred to me, an arrow of guilt pierced my heart. It wasn't Teri's fault that her kids had gotten sick, that her babysitter was out of commission. In fact, for the first time she seemed fallible, sympathetic — downright human.

"I know," I said.

Did I really want to say what I was thinking of saying? She didn't deserve it. On the other hand, it was the right thing to do, the thing that, should I ever claw my way to a position like Teri's, I'd want my assistant to do for me.

"I could take the train out there," I said. "I could babysit for you. I'll bring the memo along so you can review it on the train back in, and then you can run the meeting yourself."

"Impossible," Teri said, without even pausing to consider the offer. "There is absolutely no way you could handle three sick children."

"Really, I wouldn't mind," I said. "I've babysat before, lots and lots. I took care of this one little girl through the stomach flu, pneumonia, through the chicken pox, mono —"

A procession of Diana's sick faces, weak and pathetic, paraded across my mind.

"I don't know what kind of mother would leave a child that sick with a young babysitter," Teri said. "It's totally out of the question; you'd have no idea what to do. I'd feel more confident leaving you in charge of the meeting."

"Honestly," I tried again. "I assure you —"

"I've made my decision," Teri said. "You

will conduct the meeting, and just ignore my absence. In fact, tell Mrs. Whitney that I've delegated this project to you. That way, if it fails, it won't be my fault."

"But I better tell you . . . ," I said. "You haven't even seen . . ."

There was a distant sound of retching, and then a blood-curdling scream, followed by a hurried, "Oh, God," from Teri.

"E-mail me the proposal," Teri snapped. "If I have any changes, I'll send them to you. Just make sure it's my name on the top of that report."

And with that she hung up.

My hands were slick with sweat. My stomach was cramping. I had to force myself to pull in a long slow breath, and then consciously direct myself to let it out. I was so nervous, waiting my turn to present my report to Mrs. Whitney, that I thought I might collapse over the arm of my chair and throw up.

Steady, I told myself. You've been waiting for this moment for more than twenty years. The only one who knows more than you about Gentility Press, the only one who *believes* more in Gentility Press, is Mrs. Whitney herself, and she's right here, waiting to listen to you. She is a smart woman, she is a fair woman. Plus, as I knew from dissecting the historical sales figures, she was a desperate woman, her company on the edge of bankruptcy if somebody didn't come up with a fresh marketing solution, fast.

My idea was Gentility's best hope, I was convinced of that. Yet I wished, perversely and fleetingly, that Teri was there to back up the ideas with her marketing expertise. But her name was on the proposal, I reminded myself — it just wasn't on the portion of the presentation that was mine alone. Only Lindsay knew that I had prepared ideas with only my name on them, and from across the room she shot me an encouraging smile. She'd given Thad a sneak preview of my thinking, and even he had been impressed.

"Alice Green?"

Mrs. Whitney was looking around the room. I fumbled to my feet.

"Here I am, Mrs. Whitney."

Florence Whitney looked hard at me.

"We had another Alice Green who was here very briefly, years ago," she said.

I was stunned that the head of the company would have any recollection of my name. I felt the heat rise to my face.

"Smart girl, bright career ahead of her,"

Mrs. Whitney was saying, continuing to study me. "As I seem to recall, she left to have children. Utter shame." She seemed to meditate for a moment on the tragedy of childbearing. Then she looked up at me sharply and said, "You look enough like her to be her daughter."

I burst into relieved laughter. "Well, I'm not."

Mrs. Whitney's memory of my long-ago self made me somehow feel less anxious, more substantial. I was not someone totally inexperienced, I reminded myself, someone just starting out. I'd been doing things, difficult and interesting things — including raising a child, which hadn't been a shame at all — for over two decades.

Drawing in one more deep breath, feeling at last like the oxygen was crossing into my cells and animating my brain, I moved around the room, passing out copies of the report to Lindsay, Thad, the sales director, the art director, the publicity person, a handful of other editorial staff, and Mrs. Whitney herself.

"This is the report that Teri talked to you about, outlining our new ideas for marketing the classics line," I said. "The last major change Gentility made in the line was ten years ago, when Teri came on board and did away with the introductions by the big women's-lib writers from the sixties and seventies."

"Like me!" Mrs. Whitney laughed. "Yes, I'm afraid we'd become old hat. Teri argued that the women she was at college with didn't think of themselves as feminists anymore. And your generation has never even heard of us, have they, Alice?"

"I have," I said. Though when I'd mentioned *Why Men Must Die* and similar titles to Lindsay and Josh, I'd been met with completely blank looks.

I propped a chart that Josh had helped me devise on the computer against one wall.

"Gentility's strength in the women's market has always been its female-centered viewpoint," I said. "But we haven't taken advantage of —"

I stopped myself. I was putting it in terms of a problem. I began again.

"It's time we took advantage of the most recent phenomenon in books written for and marketed specifically to young women, with their bright sexy covers and lively writing. These books are selling millions of copies."

"I like those numbers," said the sales manager. "But I don't see how we can hope to do anything like that with Jane Austen."

217

"Yes, yes," said Mrs. Whitney impatiently. "Where is the solution in this?"

"I'm . . . we're . . . proposing that we enlist the stars of the new generation of female writers to help sell our classics, just as we did with Mrs. Whitney and other famous writers of the feminist era," I said. "A lot of those writers are fans of Austen's and Wharton's and the Brontës' and would be honored to write an introduction to a book like *Pride and Prejudice* or *The Age of Innocence.*"

"We don't have the money to pay these big modern writers," said one of the editors.

"But we can offer them status," said Lindsay, standing up and brandishing a sheaf of papers. "I have here preliminary commitments here from ten of the top women writers to write introductions to our classics. For free."

Mrs. Whitney frowned. But I knew her well enough to recognize it as the frown that meant: This is intriguing, but I'm not convinced it's going to work.

"We've been working on a new cover look, too," I chimed in. "This is a new and surprising direction."

I'd picked out covers I remembered my reading group friends finding especially attractive, and Lindsay had helped me back up the success of those books by researching sales figures. I had even asked Maggie to do a few drawings for me — a red lace bra peeking out of the bodice of a nineteenth-century gown, a stilettoed foot arching beneath the hem of a long dress — though I'd been uncertain, when I expected Teri to be in the meeting, whether I'd actually show them.

Now, though, I lifted the first rolled-up drawing above my head and let it unfurl.

The room was silent, but I was stuck behind the drawing, my arms beginning to ache, so I couldn't see anyone's reaction.

"Wow," the art director said finally, getting up from her chair and, I could hear, walking over to where I stood. "Is this a Maggie O'Donnell?"

I peered around the edge of the heavy paper at her.

"Yes," I said. "How did you know?"

"I love her work," the art director said. "I've been trying to get her to do a cover for me ever since I started working here. How did you persuade her?"

"She's an old friend."

"Well, I'm very impressed," said the art director.

"So am I," said Mrs. Whitney. "Bravo, Alice."

Then she did the most amazing thing. She began applauding. At first, the rest of the room was silent, but then Lindsay began clapping, followed by Thad and the art director, and then the sales manager, until everyone had joined in.

"I want you all to look into implementing Alice's idea as soon as possible," Mrs. Whitney said, standing up to signal that the meeting was over. "I want these writers contacted about doing the introductions, I want new covers commissioned for all the books as soon as possible, and I want press releases on this new direction to go out once we have everything in place."

I cleared my throat. "Lindsay did a lot too," I said. "And Teri, of course. I'm part of Teri's team."

Then Mrs. Whitney paused and looked directly at me.

"Where is Teri, anyway?" she asked.

"She, uh, she had a scheduling conflict," I answered.

"Well, tell her how pleased we all are with the new direction. This kind of fresh young thinking is exactly what our marketing department needs."

I was thrilled. Until I imagined Teri's re-

action when she heard about the meeting.
Then I was terrified.

CHAPTER 14

Directly after work, Lindsay and I headed downstairs to Gilberto's to celebrate our success. We sprang for two champagne cocktails, toasting our brilliant futures, and then Lindsay suggested we order another round.

"I can't," I said. "I'm meeting Josh."

He had been the first person I'd called after the meeting, and he wanted to take me someplace special tonight in honor of my triumph.

"Blow him off," Lindsay said. "Go out with me."

"What about Thad?"

"He left for a weeklong business trip to California right after the meeting," she said. "Come on, this is our chance for a big girls' night out."

I hesitated. I certainly wanted to encourage Lindsay to make a move independent from Thad. But I also felt terrible about canceling on Josh.

"I can't just pull the plug on Josh," I told her. "He was so supportive about this project, doing all those charts for me, really getting into helping me figure out how to handle it."

"I thought you weren't serious about this guy."

"I'm not. But I really like him. I mean, I really really like him."

"But you don't want to marry him."

I shook my head firmly. "No."

"Never."

"No."

"So do you see yourself, like, living with him forever, like Goldie Hawn and Kurt Russell or something?"

"He's going to Japan in a couple of months, and I have no intention of letting our relationship drag on after that."

"So what do you feel bad about?!" Lindsay cried. She drained her second champagne cocktail and waved to the bartender. "I think I'm going to switch to apple martinis," she said. "What about you?"

"I definitely can't handle apple martinis."

"Well, you need something to loosen you up. I don't understand you, Alice. If you have no intention of making a commitment to this guy, why are you wasting time being all monogamous with him? You should be going out! Having fun!"

I had to admit, she had a point.

"I'm the one who's practically married," Lindsay said, "at least in my dreams. But until that ring is on my finger, I'm reserving my rights as a free agent."

"A free agent?" I'd never heard Lindsay refer to herself this way, or even admit she found any appeal in the concept.

"At least in theory," she said. "I'm sick of Thad taking me for granted. Maybe if he didn't assume I was sitting at home every time he went away on a business trip, he'd be motivated to propose."

"There's no reason you shouldn't go out," I told her.

"You either," she said, reaching over to undo my blouse two more buttons. "You're not in the Third World anymore."

She insisted on sitting there watching me as I dialed Josh's number and told him that I couldn't meet him after all tonight, I was going out with Lindsay. He was so under-standing, so sweet, I felt even worse about not seeing him, wished all over again that it was him I was going out with. As I began apologizing again, for probably the tenth time, Lindsay grabbed the phone out of my hand.

"Don't wait up, Joshie baby," she said, giggling into the phone and then snapping it closed.

"Come on," she said to me. "I'm going to show you how to have a good time."

Instead of ordering her apple martini at Gilberto's, Lindsay hopped off her stool and marched out the door, leaving me to scurry behind, calling back over her shoulder that we were heading to Martini, a bar that specialized in all varieties of the drink. I was surprised at how warm it was outside, and how light. There was an almost festive feeling to the evening, a celebration of nothing more or less profound than having made it through another winter, that fueled Lindsay's and my high spirits.

We walked for nearly an hour, laughing and reveling in the success of our presentation. This *was* fun, and I felt glad I'd let Lindsay talk me into going out with her. I was always claiming that Josh and I weren't serious, that ours was a short-term relationship, yet I was letting my feelings for him run away with me. As I had with Gary, as I had with everything else I'd ever cared about in my life. It was good I was forcing myself to be more independent, bolder, *wilder,* the way I swore I would be when I first wished I could be younger.

225

Finally we reached Martini, a dark, gleaming bar with blue lights and curved steel walls. From the menu listing 128 different kinds of martinis, Lindsay ordered us both Speeding Tickets: vodka and cold-drip espresso served straight up in a glass with a sugared rim.

"For energy!" Lindsay said, lifting her glass.

We were standing near the bar, surrounded by a crush of people. Every single woman, it seemed, was beautiful. And every single man was gay.

"What's with the guys here?" I said in Lindsay's ear.

"What?"

"They're all gay."

Lindsay surveyed the room.

"No, they're not."

I looked again. I saw guys in tight black T-shirts and black leather pants, guys wearing bracelets and boots with heels and bright striped shirts fluttering open over bare skin. One guy had on a T-shirt that read "Vixen."

"They look gay to me."

"Metrosexual!" cried Lindsay.

I knew about metrosexuals, guys who liked clothes and food and art and shopping, but were straight. Josh had the interests and the temperament but not the wardrobe of a metrosexual; Thad was the anti-metrosexual. But these guys in the bar, I was convinced, had crossed over to the other side.

"I don't believe you."

"Okay," said Lindsay. "I'll prove it."

I laughed. "How are you going to do that?"

"You'll see. Who do you think is the most gay-looking guy in the room?"

There were so many choices, but I finally zeroed in on a delicate-looking man with blond hair and a lavender shirt.

"Good choice," Lindsay smirked. "This won't take long at all."

"What are you going to do?"

"Follow me."

I waded through the crowd behind Lindsay, and then hung back as she approached the lavender-shirted man.

"Fuck," I heard Lindsay say, in a southern drawl that was pure theater. "I'm hotter than butter sizzling on a griddle."

I couldn't help rolling my eyes at the ceiling, but I heard Lavender Shirt laugh in response.

Lindsay went on to flirt outrageously, so that every time I stole a glance in her direction, Lavender Shirt had moved in closer. First he was just laughing, but soon he was leaning in and touching Lindsay's elbow, then her waist, and then he had his hand resting on Lindsay's hip, and finally I saw him move in and begin grinding against Lindsay to the rhythm of the background Beyoncé in what I supposed was a dance move.

Before I could so much as stick out my tongue in disgust, Lindsay kissed Lavender Shirt lightly on the cheek and darted back in my direction, taking me by the wrist and leading me toward the door.

"Convinced?" Lindsay said, when we had made our way outside.

"I am. But maybe one of those other guys would have turned out to be gay."

Lindsay shook her head. We were walking fast down the street, past knots of people standing outside bars smoking.

"You can't tell by how somebody looks," she said. "Or even necessarily by what they do. Didn't they have metrosexuals in the Third World?"

I laughed. "Shouldn't we stop and get something to eat?"

Walking through the crowded streets, I realized I felt lightheaded not only from the liquor but from the lack of food.

"We're drinking our calories tonight," Lindsay said.

"I think I need something to eat."

"Then order your martini with an olive."

We turned onto a narrow street lined with stately town houses, their facades painted white and gray and pink, and then onto another residential lane. We were heading farther and farther west into the Village, where the streets were darker and less populated. Finally, Lindsay grabbed my hand and led me across a busy avenue and pointed to a knot of people on the sidewalk ahead, on a block that dead-ended at the whizzing lights of the West Side Highway, with the river and the hulking cliffs and high-rises of New Jersey beyond.

"That's our place," Lindsay said.

The only thing that distinguished the red brick building from the blank facades of what might have been warehouses or industrial offices that surrounded it was the crowd of people lingering outside, and the velvet ropes that cordoned off the shiny silver steel door. Lindsay pushed her way confidently through the crowd, kissed the enormous Asian doorman on the cheek, and pulled me through the battered steel door behind her. We wound down a black-lit stairway into a cavernous basement space, which was packed with people dancing to what sounded like disco music.

Maggie and I had gone to see *Saturday Night Fever* a dozen times, dancing to the sound track in my bedroom with all the lights off except the disco globe that had cost me nearly twenty hours' worth of babysitting money. At Mount Holyoke, liking disco was considered highly uncool — the girls there were more into Joni Mitchell and the Roches — and so I had kept my curiosity about Studio 54 and my love for the BeeGees under wraps. And now, I thought as the music hit me and I began to move my shoulders in time to the beat, I could let it all out.

"Night Fever!" I called over the noise to Lindsay.

Lindsay looked at me strangely.

"My friend Maggie and I used to listen to this back in —"

And then I stopped. Realized what I was about to say, and also that I couldn't say it. And at the same time, began to suspect that this song wasn't "Night Fever" after all.

Lindsay ordered us another pair of martinis, and I knew as I began to sip that I was about to slip over the border from being pleasantly tipsy to being truly drunk. I hadn't been drunk in — how long? Since the night after Gary left me, and before that, since my honeymoon, drinking margaritas

230

all day with Gary while lounging in the sun. And before that, it had been college.

"Is this disco music?" I said into Lindsay's ear.

We were dancing now, drinks in hand.

"Trance," Lindsay said.

"It's just called dance?"

"No, *trance*. You know. Trip-hop."

I shrugged and took a long pull on my drink. Lindsay danced away from me and toward someone else, so I danced for a minute with a tall man wearing a red sweater and then closed my eyes so I could dance happily alone. I'd always loved to dance, but it had never been one of Gary's specialties, and then, as Diana had gotten older, she'd teased me about my dancing so relentlessly that I had stopped being able to let go and enjoy it at all, even when I was alone.

But I was enjoying it now, in the dark with the lights pulsing, the crush of bodies all around me. Everyone in the room, I felt, was younger and more beautiful than me, but rather than making me feel self-conscious, that made me feel free. It had been liberating, before Maggie made me over, to be a frankly middle-aged woman, whom no one ever noticed. I'd come to fully appreciate the liberating quality of being invisible only now that I was once again prey to so much attention based on my looks. But in this place, I was nothing special, invisible once more — which might have been a bad thing if I'd been looking for sex, but was a good thing for dancing.

"Martini time!" Lindsay sang into my ear. We elbowed our way back to the bar and ordered more drinks. The room was definitely starting to spin now. And then I noticed something else I hadn't seen before.

"All right," I said to Lindsay, pointing at all the pairs of women arrayed around the bar, making out. "Is this some kind of joke?"

"What do you mean?" said Lindsay.

"Now, *this* is a gay bar!" I said.

"No, it's not," said Lindsay, looking utterly serious.

"Come on." I gestured toward the kissing women. "We're not just talking about clothes here. This is genuine action!"

"Oh, that?" said Lindsay. "They're not gay."

"What are you talking about?"

"Where have you been? It's a thing. Even the pledged virgins do it."

Now I was totally lost. "Pledged virgins?"

"The girls I went to college with back in Nashville who wore the rings pledging they would stay virgins till marriage. Even they go to bars and make out with their girlfriends."

I asked the only question that made any sense to me. "Why?"

"Oh, you know, it's 'wild,' " said Lindsay, making little quote marks with her hands. "And it's safe."

"I don't get it," I said, looking with wonder at the gorgeous women going at it. This was definitely a fresh twist on the LUGs — Lesbians Until Graduation — at Mount Holyoke. I wondered whether Maggie knew about this, and if so, why she wasn't out here getting in on the action herself. Or maybe you weren't allowed to participate if you actually *were* gay?

"It's fun," Lindsay said. "Watch."

But instead of doing something, as she'd done before, that I could observe, she leaned over and kissed me. On the lips. With tongue.

I was so stunned, my first impulse was to pull away. But I was also undeniably turned on.

"Never kissed a girl before?" asked Lindsay, when she finally took a breath.

All I could do was shake my head no. I'd seen Maggie do it, of course. And the girls at college. But I'd always been too much of a straight arrow — straight in every sense of the word — for that.

"It's nice, right?" said Lindsay. "Soft."

And then Lindsay moved in again. Yes, soft was the word, her lips more tender than Josh's, her tongue so small and quick. I could feel her breasts beneath my own, her long sweet-smelling hair against my cheek, her small hand against my hip. I liked it, I definitely liked it, but I had to make myself forget it was Lindsay I was kissing — not so much because Lindsay was a girl, but because she was my friend. It was like playing Spin the Bottle in eighth grade, squeezing your eyes shut so you could concentrate on the kiss and block out the fact that it was Tommy DiMatteo who lived down the block and sat in front of you in math who you were kissing.

When we finally looked up, there were two men standing beside us, watching. I turned away, hating the idea that I'd inadvertently provided these guys with a show. I was about to motion to Lindsay that we should move to the other side of the bar when Lindsay, to my horror, began talking to the guys.

They were dancing as they talked, these men, the better-looking of the two beaming in on Lindsay and the other one checking me out as if trying to decide whether he could make do with me, since we were obviously the two leftovers. A fresh martini appeared at my fingertips, and the men raised their glasses in a toast. Lindsay laughed loudly, and then leaned forward as the better-looking guy said something in her ear. She nodded, and the two of them started walking away, but then she turned around and motioned for me to follow.

There was a circular booth in the back of the club near the bathrooms, and we crowded in there. The better-looking man slipped a folded square of paper from the front pocket of his jeans, opened it, and took out a tiny plastic envelope. Inside the envelope I could make out chunks of something white, like sugar left out during a rainy spell. He shook one of the chunks onto the back of a credit card and began chopping it with a blade he unfolded from the tiny Swiss Army knife that dangled from his keychain.

"Is that cocaine?" I gasped.

"Sssssh," the three others said in unison.

"We have to get out of here," I said to Lindsay.

"I wanna do this," Lindsay said.

The better-looking man rolled up a dollar bill and handed it to Lindsay, who handily snorted a line of the cocaine.

"That's enough," I said, pulling on Lindsay's arm. "We've got to go."

I'd actually done cocaine, in the early eighties, at a club in London a few nights before I met Gary. It had been fun, I remembered; it had made me feel wonderful, until I woke up in bed with someone who smelled so bad I thought I might throw up. Then I met Gary, and in short order fell in love, and found to my enormous relief that a safe and happy future was mapped out before me, and the memory of the cocaine was connected for me with all the danger in the world from which I had been lucky enough to escape.

Now the better-looking man was snorting his own line, and then handing the rolled-up bill to his friend. And then he leaned over and kissed Lindsay, bringing his hand as he did so directly to her breast.

"Lindsay," I repeated, more insistently.

Lindsay kept kissing the guy, and his friend was eyeing me. If he tried anything like that with me, I'd tear his windpipe out with my fingernails. I even thought I'd enjoy doing it.

Josh, I thought. All I wanted was Josh.

"Lindsay," I said, pulling on her arm this time, standing up so I had the traction to drag her out of the booth. The better-looking man tried to hold on to Lindsay's other arm, but I leveled a look at him, holding the windpipe-ripping image in my mind as I'd learned in Krav Maga class.

"Let her go right this instant," I said, in the firm voice I'd used to let my child know when I was really serious about something, "or I will crush your balls."

He let go instantly, and Lindsay, giggling wildly, fell away from him and spilled onto the lap of his friend, who put his arm around her.

"It's time to go home," I said.

"I don't want to go home," said Lindsay.

She turned deliberately away from me then and to my astonishment began kissing the second-best guy. The good-looking friend smirked at me and slid over to press himself against Lindsay's back, reaching around to cup her breast as she kissed his friend.

"Lindsay," I said loudly. "We have to leave right now."

Lindsay looked up at me with drunken eyes. "Leave me alone," she said. "You're not my fucking mother."

I wanted to leave right then, but I couldn't let myself abandon her. I stood by myself at the bar, drinking club soda and watching. At least she stopped letting herself be used as sandwich material by the two creeps, though she stayed with the better-looking guy. She knew I was there, too. As she left the club with him, she glanced at me, but then quickly looked away.

By the time I worked my way outside after them, they had vanished. I stood there for a moment breathing in the cigarette smoke, trying to decide what to do. Finally, I hailed a cab myself and gave the driver Maggie's address. But then, as we were heading across town on Houston Street, I changed my mind and asked the driver to go to Williamsburg. To Josh's. Josh was a night owl, often up watching TV or even working long after I'd dropped off to sleep, and I suddenly felt like I had to see him, the way you crave a shower after spending time in a room filled with smoke and grease.

The taxi driver, angry at feeling he'd been duped into going all the way out to Brooklyn in the middle of the night, dumped me off on the dark street and sped away. This was the difference between Brooklyn and Manhattan: whereas Maggie's street was populated at any hour of the day or night, Josh's shut down by midnight, no open bars or restaurants, no pedestrians in sight. The only movement came from somewhere near a parked car in front of Josh's building, a flash that I first thought was a cat and then realized, with a little scream, was a rat.

Rushing to the door, I pressed his buzzer frantically and then, when he didn't answer, hurriedly punched his numbers into my cell phone. The rat was still pawing around near the car, probably trying to eat the tires, and I was afraid it was going to lunge for me next. When Josh didn't answer his phone either, I began to think that maybe he'd gone out for the night. Met someone. Hadn't come home.

Gingerly, I stepped back on the sidewalk, craning my neck to get a look at Josh's windows. Shit. They were dark. That meant either he really had gone out, or this was the first night he'd fallen asleep before midnight since I'd known him.

If there were other cabs around or if it were early enough to safely take the subway back to Manhattan, I would have left right then. If he'd really gone out, I couldn't stand there waiting until who knows when, and if he was sleeping, I hated to wake him up, especially after ditching him for my misguided night out with Lindsay.

But I was stuck. I tried buzzing and calling again unsuccessfully, and then finally edged over toward the curb, scooped up some gravel, and tossed it at his window, calling, "Josh! Josh!"

Finally I saw a light go on in his apartment, heard the rumble of the window sliding open. And then I saw blessed Josh's head appear.

"Josh!" I pleaded. "Let me in."

It took him a moment, through his half-open eyes, to tell what was going on. Then he let out a low chuckle. "I don't believe it," he said. "Come on, get in here."

I took the steps two at a time, not pausing for breath until I was safely inside his apartment, not a rat in sight.

Then I hurled myself into his arms, and stood there hanging on to him, feeling like a ship that had finally sailed into port. He held me for a long time, until finally he pulled away and said, "What happened? Girls' night out gone wrong?"

I shook my head no, reluctant to somehow be disloyal to Lindsay, and then I nodded a woeful yes. "I should have been with you."

"Should have been?" he asked.

"Wanted to have been. Wished I had been."

He kissed me then, a soft kiss using only his lips, again and again, like the kisses I remembered from junior high, before sex made everything so complicated. I felt, with him, that I was home, and that home was the only place I wanted to be. So much for my wild young self. The first man I'd been with since the husband I'd married at twenty-one, and all I wanted to do was be at home with him every night.

For the first time, taking off my clothes, climbing into bed with Josh, twisting myself around him as if it were possible for us to become one, I began to consider that maybe our relationship didn't have to end just because he was going to Tokyo. Maybe I didn't have to put so many limits on it, could allow our feelings to determine how involved we got. I began to wonder whether, since I'd successfully defied time, I might be able to think about forever.

Chapter 15

My tenants were moving out, back to their own newly renovated house, leaving me to decide once again what to do about my house. One option, of course, was moving back in, but the only reason I could see to do that was if Diana came back home. Did Diana have any intention of coming back home? Her e-mails and phone calls, spotty as usual, made no mention of what she was doing, and I, absorbed in my own new life, had stopped hounding her.

But now I had to know. I left a message for her at her field office in Africa, and then waited three days for her to call me back. No, she said, she had no plans to come home.

"That's good," I said.

"That's *good*?"

"I mean, that leaves me free to rent out the house again and stay with Maggie in New York."

"It sounds like maybe you want to move there permanently."

"No, no," I told her, though to my surprise I wasn't totally appalled by the notion. "It's just more convenient right now. Don't worry about rushing home."

"All right, I won't," Diana said. "In fact, I'm thinking about signing on for another year."

Another year. I felt my heart sink at the prospect of not seeing my daughter for another whole year. But maybe I could persuade her to come home for the holidays this December. Or maybe, now that I was earning money, I could even go over there to visit her.

"I'm glad things are going well for you," I told her, really meaning it. "Maybe staying would be a good idea."

Over the next few days I found the idea of renting out the house for a longer term or maybe even putting it on the market growing on me more and more. I'd started this whole younger thing as a lark, a one-night experiment. And then I'd pushed it a bit further to see whether it would help me get a job, jump-start my life.

Now everything was going so well, I found that I didn't want to give it up. Any of it. Maggie said that while the adoption board had seemed curious about her "unusual living arrangements" — she'd made quotes in the air around these words — she thought the visit had gone well, and so I felt more at ease about being in the loft. And at the office, with Teri still at home — once all her kids were finally better, she came down with the flu herself — I was sailing forward with my project.

The only weird thing was Lindsay. Since we parted outside the club, she'd seemed cool to me, though she claimed everything was all right and she was merely swamped with work. Well, I was swamped too. Figuring Lindsay was embarrassed about what had happened or annoyed with me for trying to tell her what to do, I decided to take the opportunity to lay low, holing up in Teri's office to work on the project from early in the morning until late at night.

When I wasn't working, I spent all the time I could with Josh. His departure for Japan was still far enough away that we could relax and have fun without worrying that our time together was about to end.

And why did it have to end at all? I was beginning to wonder. I mean, eventually, of course, I'd have to own up, maybe, but why should it have to be in two months or two years or any set amount of time?

How long, I tried to calculate, could I pull off pretending to be roughly fifteen years younger than my true age? When I was fifty, could I fake being in my mid-thirties? Closing in on sixty, could I pass myself off as fortyish?

Sure, I had the advantage of looking naturally young, but that wasn't going to last forever. I could exercise every waking hour and things were still eventually going to sag. Lines would form, skin would grow crepey, gums would recede, and hair would thin. It was happening already to women my age or a little older; certainly, it would happen to me too.

And then there was that guilty feeling I got, way beneath the skin. At work, even with Lindsay, I could tell myself I wasn't hurting anyone, that my performance as an employee, even as a friend, had nothing to do with my age, real or fake.

But with Josh, the guilt was more persistent. Our relationship may have started out as a fling, but without either of us willing it, it had turned into much more. Our feelings for each other were serious and genuine; shouldn't I be just as real with him about my age?

Yet suppose we decided to stay together for the longer term, and I confessed my real age, and Josh accepted that. Suppose I came out as forty-four to the entire world. Wouldn't it still make sense for me to try to look as youthful as I possibly could? The business world definitely was more welcoming to someone who looked young, and even if Josh knew the truth, I'd want to look like his girlfriend, not his mother. That didn't mean resorting to plastic surgery, necessarily, but less radical methods. Creams and peels. Botox. Restylane. Gloves that sent little shocks to your skin.

When I mentioned to Maggie, as casually as possible, that I was thinking of trying one of these age-defying techniques, she squealed and spilled her espresso. "What?"

"It's not a big deal. It's completely natural."

"You're completely out of your fucking mind! Why in hell do you want to give your face shock treatments?"

"To look younger," I told her.

"You look young enough already!" said Maggie. "I'm tired of this! I want my friend back!"

"I'm right here," I said.

"Oh, no, you're not," said Maggie. "Not completely."

That stunned me into silence. I had no idea what she was talking about.

"How am I not there for you?"

"In little ways," said Maggie. "I miss hearing you talk about your garden. I'd rather hear about your tulips coming up than some stupid club you went to with your baby buddy."

I nodded, though I remained unconvinced. I suspected Maggie found both topics equally deadly.

"And I miss you inviting me out to your house for a nice ham dinner," Maggie said.

That, at least, made me laugh. "You know you would never come, not once, when I invited you to New Jersey for a nice ham dinner."

"I'd come now."

"You would not. You're just saying that because I don't live there anymore."

From the street far below Maggie's loft, salsa music drifted up to where we sat, side by side on the chaise, sipping our espresso.

"I was thinking," I ventured.

"Uh-oh."

"My tenants moved out," I told her, "and I was thinking about what I wanted to do. And I think I might want to move in here. For, you know, for good."

We were both silent for a long time then, until finally Maggie said, "I don't think that's a great idea."

"Oh," I said, feeling my heart smash onto the hard wooden floor. "Of course not. I'm crowding you, you have your work —"

"That's not it," Maggie said quickly. "But while you've been working sixteen hours a day and then spending your nights out in Brooklyn, I got some bad news."

"Oh, Maggie," I said, feeling myself flush with the realization that, in fact, I *had* been so caught up in my own life that I had completely lost touch with what was going on with her.

"The Vietnamese adoption people turned me down," she said. "I completely flunked the home study."

"Oh," I said. "I'm so sorry, Mags."

"It's not your fault — you tried to warn me. I'm applying to another agency now, and I'm going to take your advice."

"Really?" Frantically, I tried to search the dusty archives of my mind for what advice that might be.

"You said I should fix this place up," Maggie reminded me. "I'd love it if you would help me with that."

"Oh," I said, brightening at the thought of moving more comfortable furniture, some soft pillows and cozy afghans, into Maggie's spare loft. "Of course."

"And I think you should move out," Maggie said.

I felt like I might fall onto the floor. My whole self, along with my heart.

"Not forever," Maggie rushed to say, "but it turns out you were right. It was a problem with the first agency that you were living here."

"Oh," I said, feeling my flush deepen.

"If domestic partners are living together, they both need to be checked out," Maggie said.

"But I'm not —"

"Duh. But given my sexual orientation, they didn't necessarily believe me. And it turns out that even lesbians who are adopting together usually establish separate residences and have just one person apply and then the other parent adopt once the child is part of the family, because it goes much more smoothly that way."

"I had no idea," I said.

"I didn't either, until now. But I can't afford to make the same mistakes again. I'm realizing I really need to be smart about this," Maggie said. "Do you mind terribly?"

"No," I hurried to assure her. "Of course not."

"You can always move back in," Maggie said. "Later. Though I'm not sure when."

"Sure," I said, my mind spinning in search

of alternatives. "Of course."

"Hey," said Maggie. "Maybe we could go out to New Jersey this weekend, get some stuff to fix up this place. Do you have anything that might make it look more, you know, normal?"

Well, I thought, what *wouldn't*? If anything, Maggie's loft had become more quirky over the past few months, with many of the wire women now suspended from the ceiling to make room for the cement blocks that crowded the floor. But the wire figures were so large that you couldn't simply walk beneath them. Instead, they dangled down to three or four feet above the floor so that you had to crouch and dodge your way through the space, or risk getting bashed in the head with an iron thigh.

"I have a couple of dark blue velvet armchairs that might look good with this chaise," I said, working to keep the doubt out of my voice. "And a nice Persian rug that would look great on this pine floor, maybe a coffee table —"

"That's why I need the old you back so badly," said Maggie, clapping her hands in excitement. "I need your straight eye. Straight eye for the queer guy. Girl."

"Thanks," I said. "I guess."

"Can we go to a mall when we're in New

Jersey?" Maggie asked.

A mall? I guess she really wanted to do the full Jersey experience. "Sure."

"Will you bake me a ham? And a pie?"

"If I remember how."

Thinking of spending the weekend in New Jersey, back in my old house, my old life, filled me with an unexpected shiver of fear. I felt as insecure about trying to be the person I'd been before as I'd felt, not that long ago, about launching my new life in New York. I was certain I wasn't ready to go back. But it was Maggie who'd asked me. And for Maggie, I'd do anything.

I measured the flour, two cups, into my favorite green-and-blue spatterware bowl.

"Do you want a crumb top, or a crust?" I asked Maggie.

Maggie, who was sitting at the scrubbed pine table, drinking a glass of wine, gazed at the ceiling, as if asking the advice of the goddess of pies.

"I love them both," she said finally. "Whichever is easier for you."

"Either is easy. Remember that saying — easy as pie?"

"I have the feeling there's a good reason people don't say that anymore." Maggie grinned.

"Ah, come on," I said. "It's really not hard. Want me to teach you?"

Maggie looked, in equal measure, intrigued and terrified.

"Really," I said. "We'll make crumb. It's virtually foolproof."

"Okay," Maggie said, standing up and tying on one of my old aprons. "What do I do?"

"All right, get out a bowl," I told her. "It has to be a beautiful bowl."

"Why?"

"Because then the whole experience will be more pleasurable. Pick one you like."

While I continued working on the bottom crust, Maggie rummaged around in a lower cabinet, surveying and rejecting bowls, until she came up with an old apple green pouring bowl my mother used to use for pancake batter when I was a kid.

"Perfect," I said. "Now dump in some flour."

"How much?"

"Doesn't matter. You can scoop some out with a coffee cup if you want."

I suddenly had a memory of doing exactly this with Diana when she was five or six, her kneeling on a chair beside the place where Maggie now stood. The image of Diana was so vivid, I felt that I could blink and she would be there as her little-girl self, pouring the flour as slowly as if it had been ketchup into the bowl. She'd been so nervous, just like Maggie, about making something without a recipe, but had loosened up as she went along, nibbling her crumb topping-in-progress and eventually mixing it to perfection.

"This is something you can do with your child one day," I said, smiling as I pictured a little Asian girl with straight black bangs kneeling on a chair as Diana had, helping Maggie scoop out the flour.

Maggie looked up at me and grinned. "I never pictured myself as the baking kind of mom. I kind of figured I'd take her out for sushi every night."

I could tell she was only half kidding, and who knew, maybe Maggie would be lucky enough to get the kind of kid who'd sit quietly in a restaurant, chowing down on raw fish. My child had been more the Cheerios-in-front-of-the-TV type, but maybe that was because I hadn't demanded anything more sophisticated.

"What if you have a boy?" I said, teasing her.

Maggie looked taken aback, as if this had never occurred to her. Then she said, "Well, I'll take him out for sushi too."

253

"Maybe you have the right idea," I said. "I think I made everything so comfortable for Diana, smoothed the way for her so thoroughly, that it came as a great shock when she started school and discovered the world really didn't revolve around her."

"Diana's a great girl," Maggie said. "Really, you should be proud of the job you did raising her. Seeing how well she turned out, watching how gratifying motherhood was for you — that was a big part of what finally made me want to have a child of my own."

I was so touched, I felt tears spring to my eyes. "Wow," I said. "And here I always worried you thought I was wasting my life, compared to doing something important like being an artist."

"Diana is your work of art," Maggie said. "And now you're starting this whole new phase of your life. Come on now, what's next?"

"Well," I said, "it's time for the sugar."

We'd bought white and brown on our grocery run, and now Maggie held a cupful up for my inspection.

"However much you think is right," I smiled. "You decide."

"So you really think I can do this on my own?" she said, dumping in the sugar with

254

a wobbly grin, not quite meeting my eye.

I knew she was asking about more than the pie crust. We hadn't had a straight-out discussion about the baby issue since New Year's Eve, when I told Maggie I thought she might be too old to take on the demands of motherhood. I'd done my best to be supportive since then, but now I realized I'd come to truly believe in Maggie's quest for a baby. She'd extended herself so far for me, opened up herself and her world in a way I knew she couldn't have even a few years before, that it was clear she was more than ready to let a child into her life.

I still couldn't, for myself, imagine having the energy to take care of an infant, to keep up with a toddler, but neither could I imagine my life feeling complete if I'd never had a child at all. Thinking about this, my heart filled with joy for Maggie, that she'd realized what she wanted before it was too late, that she was doing everything in her power — and more — to make her dream of motherhood come true.

I reached out and squeezed her arm. "The BLT?" I asked.

"Of course," she said. But she looked apprehensive about hearing what I had to say.

"I do," I assured her.

She looked up at me then. "You honestly

think I have what it takes to be a good mother?"

"I know you do," I said. "You're already doing things for this child I never knew you were capable of."

Maggie looked at me questioningly.

"Wearing khakis, for instance," I said, letting a smile steal across my face. Maggie had always been militantly anti-beige in all areas of life, but today in J. C. Penney — J. C. Penney of all stores! — she'd picked out a pair of part-polyester khakis for herself, positing that the adoption people would feel reassured if she were dressed in "momwear."

I gestured to the green bowl, where she was using her fingers to mingle the sugar and the flour.

"And baking," I pointed out.

She frowned at her mixture, white and powdery. "This doesn't look much like crumb topping."

"It needs brown sugar," I said. "And butter. And a couple of spices — cinnamon, nutmeg — whatever you want."

"Oh, I definitely want spices," Maggie said, grinning. "As many and as much as possible. That's okay, isn't it?"

"It's completely up to you."

"Is it really?" Maggie asked, suddenly

turning serious again. "What I mean is, do you think I can still be myself and be a good mother, too? Because I'm uncomfortable with this, all this changing."

I was about to answer quickly that yes, of course, she could still be herself and be a good mother, that the changes were just temporary, only superficial, nothing that would undercut the essence of Maggie's most essential self.

But then I thought, Are they really? I'd thought, on New Year's Eve, that I was just coloring my hair, only changing my shoes. And now I felt as if not only my life but my very self had changed at least as radically as the surface me.

Yet weren't those changes positive? And wouldn't the changes in Maggie that would inevitably come with motherhood be equally positive, even if less predictable? Sure, it was frightening to find your life turning inside out. But I remembered Maggie herself, way back in high school, telling me that fear and excitement were two different aspects of the same emotion.

"One of the smartest things anyone told me," I said to Maggie now, "was that before you have children, you try to figure out how you're going to fit your kids into your life. And then once the baby comes along, you

257

try to figure out how you're going to fit your life into your kids."

Maggie blinked. "I'm not sure I totally get that," she said.

I was about to explain how the notion had played out for me, how it had played out for every mother — and a good portion of the fathers — I knew. But then I thought that, like age, like love, it might be one of those things you had to live through to fully comprehend.

"You will," I told Maggie. "You will."

Late that night, as I lay in my old bed on my own crisp white sheets, wide awake with the strange familiarity of it all, with the unaccustomed quiet of the night outside, I heard my phone ring. Not the phone on my bedside table, but my cell phone, all the way downstairs in my purse. I had no problem, in the moonlight, finding my way through the hall and down the stairs and to the purse I'd left as had long been my habit on the bench in the front hall.

I expected it to be Josh. I'd told him I was going away for a girls' weekend with Maggie — "Can I come?" he'd joked — and I figured he was calling to tell me he missed me.

So I was startled to hear Diana's voice on

the line.

"Honey," I said quickly, feeling my pulse pick up. "Are you okay?"

"Yeah," she said. "Are you?"

"Of course." I looked around me. Even in the dark, I could almost imagine her small self, skipping through the rooms. "Do you know where I am now? I'm home. In New Jersey. In our house."

I waited, expecting to hear Diana's cry of surprise, or even a grunt of indifference before she launched into a story of her latest adventure. I was shocked when, instead, she started crying.

"Sweetheart!" I said, alarmed. "What is it? What's wrong?"

"I miss it," Diana said. "I don't feel like I have a home anymore."

"Oh, darling! Of course you have a home! Even if I sell the house, you'll always have a home with me."

"So that's it," Diana said, her voice growing stony. "You're going to sell the house."

"No, no, that's not what I'm saying. I mean, maybe someday, but —" I realized I was confused. "I thought you weren't ready to come back."

"I thought you didn't want me to come back."

"Oh, no. Of course I want you to come

back," I said, trying to telegraph the conviction I felt through the phone wires, "if that's what you want for yourself. I'd love it if you were here, but more than anything I want you to feel happy and satisfied with what you're doing."

There was a silence so long I thought we had lost our connection, until finally I ventured, "Diana?"

"Well, I don't know if I want to come back right now," she said, sounding as if I had roused her from a reverie. "I still have a lot of work I need to do here."

This felt more like mother-daughter business as usual.

"Whatever you decide," I told her. "I just want you to know that if you want to come home, I want to have you here."

CHAPTER 16

I was sure when I went into the office Monday morning, I would find Teri there. But she was still at home, although well enough to begin looking at work that I would messenger to her.

Getting the first package ready to send to her, I felt my mouth go dry and my heart begin to thump, much as if I were coming down with the flu. But my problem was emotional, not physical. I was suddenly worried, for the first time, what Teri was going to make of all the work I'd done on the classics project. As long as she'd been completely out of the picture, I'd been secure in Mrs. Whitney's support and the power of the ideas themselves. But now I began to consider that Teri might feel seriously threatened by how far I'd run with this project.

Should I send her everything I'd done? I wondered. Or maybe I should hold some memos and e-mails back, break the whole thing to her gradually. Gee, Teri, Mrs. Whitney was pleased with our presentation. She asked me to take it a step further. My expanded plans for the line were a big success. And now, ooops, it looks like I'm gonna be *your* boss!

That last part was still in my fantasies, but I couldn't help imagining how Teri would react if *she* saw that as the logical progression of things. Which, from what I knew of how her mind worked, she very well might.

I needed Lindsay's advice, but when I went to her office, she was sitting there ashen-faced — which, considering how pale Lindsay was normally, was saying a lot — moving piles of paper from one side of her desk to the other. She didn't even look up when I said hello.

"What's wrong?" I asked.

She picked up a stack of manuscripts, then thumped them down on the other side of her desk.

"Thad broke up with me," she said, still not looking at me.

"Oh, God!" I said. "I'm sorry."

Then, finally, Lindsay met my eye. "Are you?" she said. "I thought you might be glad."

I felt my cheeks flush with guilt: Although I *was* sorry that Lindsay seemed so miserable, I was also glad on some level that she was finally out of what I saw as a not-great relationship. Thad seemed so controlling, so ready to quash Lindsay's free spirit, which she seemed blindly willing to trade for the security of marriage — a kind of security, I knew, that didn't necessarily last.

But I didn't feel as if I could say anything that straightforward to her. I was her friend, not her mother, as she'd made abundantly clear to me that night at the club. As a theoretical contemporary, how did I have any more perspective on this than she did? And she'd long deemed my disinterest in marriage as completely wacky, rendering any romantic advice I might offer null and void.

"Did you?" I asked. "Why would you think that?"

"Oh, please," Lindsay said. "You've never liked Thad."

I guessed I hadn't been hiding it as well as I hoped.

"This isn't about whether I like Thad," I said. "It's about whether he's really the best guy for you. What happened, anyway?"

"When Thad found out about that guy from the club," she said, "he was furious

263

and broke it off."

This wasn't computing. "But this all happened a week and a half ago," I said. "He's been out of town. How did he find out about it now?"

"I told him," she said miserably. "When he got home."

"Why on earth did you tell him?" I said. "What happened to being a free agent until that ring was on your finger?"

"But that's exactly why I told him," she said. "When he came back from California, he seemed to assume I'd been sitting around knitting the whole time he'd been gone. I wanted to make him see that if he wanted that kind of commitment from me, then we were going to need to get engaged."

Or maybe, it occurred to me, she told Thad about the other guy because she wanted to provoke a breakup. Maybe she knew in her heart that Thad wasn't the right man for her, that she needed to have more experiences before she settled down.

"It might be for the best," I said gently. "Now is the time you should be going out, having fun —"

"I knew you'd say something like that," Lindsay snapped.

"Listen," I told her. "It's you I care about. Your happiness. And I believe you might find more happiness somewhere beyond Thad."

"My life is ruined," she said, covering her face with her hands and beginning to sob.

"Lindsay, come on . . . ," I said, laying my hand on her shoulder.

"Just because you're determined to screw up your own life," she told me, shaking off my touch, "doesn't mean I'm going to let you screw up mine."

Was I determined to screw up my own life? That wasn't the way I saw it, though Lindsay's words kept echoing in my ears. Certainly, I felt less secure at work, more worried about what was going to happen when Teri returned, without her and Thad in my corner. And I plain missed her friendship, the fun she brought into my life. Taking the long bus ride home to New Jersey every night, traveling, it seemed, into my own past and future at the same time, had reopened a lot of questions I'd been working hard to set aside.

The question of Josh, for instance.

At the same time I wanted to start telling him only the truth, I found myself lying more and more. My burgeoning number of little lies all stemmed from one major lie: I was hiding the fact that I had moved home to New Jersey, given that he'd had no idea in the first place there *was* any home in New Jersey. Via the miracle of cell phones and meaningless area codes, I could be anywhere, as far as he was concerned — so I pretended I was either working late or recovering from working late at Maggie's loft.

It wasn't that I didn't want to see him. It was more that seeing him confused me even more than I was already confused. Going back to New Jersey, reclaiming my home, rediscovering every minute of every day who I'd been all these years — as well as being reminded how many years I'd been that person — made me feel as if I could not go and see Josh and play a role any longer. But how could I confess to him the enormity of my charade? I wanted to come clean, but each time I imagined it, I ended with the certainty that it would mean losing him. And one of the few things I felt sure about was that I didn't want that to happen.

"I miss you," Josh said.

I was talking on my cell phone, sitting in the living room of the house in Homewood. I had thrown the windows open to the warm spring evening and had also built a fire, just because I could. The little Chinese lamp was turned on; the only other light came from the candles I'd lit around the room. Everything was back in place now, all the photos of Diana in their sterling frames on the mantel, all my favorite pillows and books, dishes and knickknacks, placed just the way I liked them. I still hadn't decided what I was going to do about the house, beyond making the most of it in whatever time I had here.

"I really miss you," he said, apparently thinking I hadn't heard him the first time.

I sighed deeply and involuntarily with the force of all the feelings and thoughts I was holding inside.

"I miss you, too," I said at last. "I'll see you soon."

But I found myself wanting to gobble up every minute I had in my house. With Teri still out, I was free to fudge my hours, coming in a bit later in the morning, rushing out the door in the afternoon, savoring all the things about home I'd forgotten I loved so much. I made myself drink my coffee in the sunniest place in the kitchen each morning, angling my chair so that I could see the cherry tree budding in the yard. When I read, I curled up in the big window seat rather than sitting lazily on my bed. I took baths in the huge Deco tub off the master bedroom, the tub that had been one of the main reasons I'd wanted the house but that I'd rarely let myself luxuriate in before.

And I used all my favorite things, everything I'd collected for so many years. The white cotton sheets with the hand-crocheted edging. The chunky blue spatterware mugs, and the cream dishes. The sterling napkin rings with the *A* engraved on them, and the dented coin-silver spoons that were so perfectly contoured for grapefruit.

I arranged my favorite kilim and hooked rugs so that my feet could glide from one to the next, never touching wood, as I wound my customary path through the house. When I ate, I used the etched crystal wineglasses — Gary's grandmother's, though he seemed to have forgotten about them — and lit every one of the golden beeswax candles in the hand-forged iron chandelier.

I washed the red cross-stitched bedspread by hand, and suspended it from the branches of the lilac tree to dry. Then I ironed it stiff, along with the linen napkins and hand towels. I polished the silver candlesticks and the copper pots, and buffed the pine floors on my hands and knees. I used Gary's abandoned toothbrush to clean the grout between the old subway tiles in the bathroom.

For every meal, I leafed through my bulging recipe file, indulging myself by cooking all of my favorites, not minding somehow doing all that work just for myself. I made Grandma Giovane's spaghetti sauce from scratch, simmering it on top of the stove until the house was drenched in the sugary scent of tomatoes. I baked myself a chocolate cake and an onion tart; I constructed a Cobb salad and even fried myself the homemade precursor to chicken nuggets, the treat that, as a girl, I'd always requested for my birthday dinner.

The place I spent most of my time, though, was my garden. This had always been my favorite time of year here, with everything popping from the ground so fast it seemed you could stand there and watch it grow. I cleared out all the old leaves and dead stalks from last year, and rooted out the yellow columbine that would take over if I didn't get it now. I pruned the roses and laid brick for a new path and planted white geraniums in all the window boxes.

I couldn't afford to let my time at the house drag on without making a decision about renting it again, or at least beginning to investigate its sale. But before I did that, I wanted one uninterrupted weekend there alone. Besides, I rationalized, this was my chance to tackle the larger organizational tasks that I'd always put off in the past, and now would have to do if the house were sold.

I went through all the bookshelves, carting boxes full of books to the library for donation, to the university club for sale.

I sorted through all the unworn clothes in the attic, getting rid finally of all the ordinary gear from Diana's childhood, all of my own clothes bigger than size 10, and every single item that had belonged to Gary.

I threw out Gary's notes from dental school, my notes from Russian lit, and Diana's seventh-grade social studies project. I finally gathered Diana's childhood drawings into pretty portfolios, and went through boxes of papers from my mother's house, ditching old gas bills but framing an award my mother had won for penmanship in 1933.

And then, at the dusty bottom of one of the attic's dustiest boxes, I found it: the manuscript of the novel I'd started writing when Diana was a toddler, the chapters I'd labored over for months, only to lose heart. I thought I'd thrown this away long ago, but now I sat down right on the splintery boards of the attic floor and started reading. And kept reading.

I imagined coming across this manuscript

at Gentility Press. I'd be excited, I thought. The story felt familiar yet not stale, a domestic comedy about the suburban mother of a young child, feeling that she wants more out of life but not knowing how to get it. It was the not-knowing-how-to-get-it part of the story that tripped me up, I saw now. I didn't know how to keep writing the novel because I didn't know how to get more out of my life. Couldn't imagine how, for my heroine or myself. I thought I'd run out of ideas and energy writing the book. But what I'd really been clueless about was how to go forward with my own life.

Now, though, it seemed so obvious what the woman in the story should do, how she should fail, what she should try next. If I had had a pen, I would have started writing right there on the attic floor, but instead I moved downstairs to the chair near the fireplace, my laptop balanced on my knees, forgetting that I was covered with dust, stopping only when I realized it had gotten too dark to see.

Then I roused myself to build a fire, make some tea and smear some peanut butter on a hunk of Italian bread, and rush back to my chair to start writing again.

I was still sitting there when I heard a car door slam outside and then, alarmingly, footsteps on the porch stairs and a key in the lock.

I stood up, heart hammering, scribbling pages falling from my lap, just in time to see my daughter Diana burst through the front door.

"Hi, Mommy," she said. "I'm home."

CHAPTER 17

No matter how much I wanted to stay home and be with Diana — and after her long absence, that's all I wanted to do — I couldn't call in sick. Teri was finally coming back to work. But I also couldn't let Diana see me duded up in my usual young-assistant working gear. The night before, when I'd been wearing old sweat clothes and covered in dust, when her eyes had been bleary from her long trip, I'd just looked like the same old mom to her. We'd curled up together on the couch just as we had when she was tiny, her head on my shoulder while she talked softly and I smoothed her hair and scratched her back. Although it tore me apart to leave the house without at least a glimpse of my sleeping daughter, I got dressed on tiptoes and saved my elaborate makeup application for the bus, where the only redemption for having to leave Diana was using the long trip to work on my novel.

By the time I made it to the office, I was exhausted — from the late night, the excitement of Diana's arrival, my tense leave-taking. And then there was the buzzer sounding from my phone the moment I stepped off the elevator.

"Alice," came Teri's voice as I breathlessly lifted the receiver. "Come into my office immediately."

Her door was shut, and when I let myself in, she was sitting grim-faced at her desk, several sheets of paper arrayed before her.

"Someone's been using this office," she said, the second I stepped through the door.

I'd worked sprawled out on the floor, careful to replace the stapler and paper clip holders in the exact position I found them, not even using her phone for fear of leaving a telltale fingerprint behind.

But now, I had no choice but to 'fess up. As the guardian of the office, my only other option — claiming ignorance — would have been worse than the truth.

"I did some work in here, when I needed quiet," I told her. "But I really didn't think I wrecked anything —"

"That's not the point," Teri cut in. "The point is that it doesn't belong to you."

"Right," I said, feeling my cheeks begin to

274

burn. "Of course."

"Or did you forget that?" Teri said. The flu had left her face looking even sharper and more pinched than it had before. "Maybe you started to think that as long as you were stealing my ideas, you could grab my office and even my job."

For the first time in my life, I understood what people meant when they said they couldn't believe their ears. I'd been bracing myself for Teri's return, anticipating that she would confront me about claiming what I saw as my rightful credit for the ideas for the classics project. But for her to say that I'd taken the ideas from her . . .

"You know that I didn't steal any ideas from you," I said, keeping my voice even.

"I know nothing of the kind," Teri said. "Not only did you take my ideas, but you perverted them in a way I don't even recognize, much less condone."

All I could do was shake my head, words choking in my throat. "I don't know what you're talking about," I finally managed to say.

"This is a travesty," said Teri, thumping the top page of what I recognized as my most recent memo. "Abominable. It's beyond me how you could take it upon yourself to suggest that we use . . . trash! . . . to market the greatest books ever written by women."

"What?" I gasped. "I assure you, Teri, no. I thought that you were as excited about this concept as I was."

"My idea was to improve sales of the classics line," Teri said, "not to get Jane Austen onto the shelves next to the feminine hygiene products. That's what's so offensive about this, Alice. It's . . . morally reprehensible to tart up Jane Austen or Charlotte Brontë like some stupid girls' book."

"But don't you think that whatever makes people read Jane Austen and Charlotte Brontë is good?" I asked, feeling more conscious than ever of the blond dye in my hair, of the pink color on my lips. "Isn't anything that makes the novels look younger and more exciting for the better? They're still the same great books."

Teri shook her head and set her mouth in a hard line. "I'd fire you right now, except somehow you've fooled Mrs. Whitney into believing this is a good idea. I don't know what kind of a stunt you're trying to pull, but I intend to get to the bottom of it."

"What do you mean?" I asked weakly, but Teri was done talking. She simply pointed to the door with a finger bonier than the

Grim Reaper's, and when the silence became unbearable, I slunk away.

Later that morning, I tried to talk with Lindsay about what had happened, but the door to her office was closed, and her assistant claimed she was in a meeting. It seemed that as far as I was concerned, Lindsay intended to remain in a meeting for the rest of her life.

At about three, Diana called me, wondering when I was coming home. I explained to her that I'd try to leave at five and should be home by six or six-thirty.

That was the one bright spot so far in my day: telling my daughter when I'd be home, and knowing she was there waiting for me.

Teri stayed closeted in her office the entire day, not emerging even to yell at me, and so a few minutes before five I began gathering my things. I could hardly wait for the clock to strike the hour so I could dash out of there; if I timed it just right, I'd meet Mrs. Whitney on her way to her train home — she always took the 5:14 — and then even if I encountered Teri, she wouldn't be able to give me a hard time.

I was one breath away from making my break when my phone rang. When I heard Josh's voice on the other end of the line, all the air went out of me. All weekend I'd been looking forward to tonight, when Josh and I were finally supposed to get together again. But then, in the thrill of Diana's homecoming, our plan had completely flown out of my mind.

"I was just wondering where we were going to meet," he said, determinedly perky.

"Oh," I said. "Josh. I'm sorry. I can't do it tonight."

There was a long silence, and then he said, "You promised."

"I know," I said. "I'm so sorry. Something completely unexpected came up."

That was when he exploded. "What's going on, Alice? I haven't seen you for a week now, I don't have that much time left, and you've completely vanished."

"I know, I know, I just feel so stuck."

"Stuck," he said. "Is there something you're not telling me?"

Now it was my turn to hesitate. I hated to lie to him. It felt like an insult to all the closeness we'd felt, all the revelations we'd shared. I owed it to him — to Diana, to *myself* — to tell him the truth.

And I would. Just not right this minute.

"I promise," I said. "In the next few days, we'll get together. But tonight I have to go home."

"Home?"

"To Maggie's," I said, smarting at telling a big fat lie.

And then, even as I was telling him good-bye, I started worrying about how I was going to pull off seeing him, and when, and what I was going to tell him when I did. The truth? Or something that, in the moment, seemed even sweeter?

When I finally turned the lock in the door at home, again writing for the duration of my bus ride home, I nearly didn't recognize my little house. It looked as if the place had been ransacked, with dirty clothes strewn all over the front hallway, laundry baskets of clean but unfolded clothes upended on the furniture, magazines and books scattered on every surface. Rap music was blasting from the kitchen, along with the smell of something burning.

"Hi, Mom," Diana said.

She was perched on a kitchen stool, eating ice cream direct from a carton. She had apparently been shopping: chips spilled out of a bag onto a counter, next to an open tub of guacamole. The other grocery bags stood, still full, in front of the pantry.

"I went shopping for you," Diana said proudly.

"Oh, thank you."

I moved to hug my daughter, to drink her in in a way I hadn't been able to in the shock of her arrival last night. She looked both older and thinner to me, her skin brown, her arms muscled, her sandy hair streaked with blond.

"I've been starving ever since I landed," Diana said, reaching back to her ice cream.

"Why don't you let me cook you dinner?" I said, brushing her hair back from her face. "I could make vegetable lasagna."

Always her favorite.

"Thanks, Mom," Diana said. "That would be great."

She went back then to eating the ice cream, reading the magazine, and moving her head in time to the music, largely ignoring me. At first I was hurt that, after all these months of not seeing me, Diana hadn't said a word about how much weight I'd lost, or my new blond hair and groovy haircut.

But then I thought, Phew. I can relax now, and just be Mom again. In fact, the more I thought about it, the better I felt about the fact that Diana had been able to slide so instantly back into her old way of being here with me. It had been so cataclysmic when Gary announced his departure, and then

Diana had taken off for Africa before our tears were even dry, making it feel as if we'd never again enjoy a normal evening like this.

I hummed as I set about constructing the lasagna, then moved through the house, stacking papers, folding laundry, sorting the contents of Diana's spilled suitcases, putting everything back in order. I found myself thinking about my novel, getting an idea for something my character might do, wondering whether I'd get a chance to write tonight, but then chiding myself: It's Diana's first night home. You want to be with her. And then tomorrow night, of course, I had to go to Josh's. Imagining what kind of excuse I was going to have to make to Diana about that sent me hurtling back toward panic, so I forced myself to concentrate on setting the table, lighting the candles, sliding the bubbling lasagna out of the oven and cutting it into nine tidy squares.

When Diana came to the table, I already had the spatula poised under her favorite piece.

"Center square?" I asked, smiling.

Diana sat there contemplating the lasagna, and suddenly pushed her chair away from the table.

"I can't eat that," she said.

I was shaken. "Why not?"

"It's disgusting, Mother, all that dairy. You could feed my whole village on that."

"I wish I could feed your village," I said evenly, thinking that she must have spoiled her appetite with that ice cream. "I know this is an awful lot just for the two of us. We can freeze whatever we don't eat."

"It's just . . . ," Diana said, looking around the house, her lip curling, "all this *excess*. I'm serious. I wish we could sell all this junk and donate the money to people who really need it."

"Well," I sighed, reluctant to bring up anything too precipitous when Diana was still in this weakened state, "we may end up having to sell this place. But I'm afraid the person who really needs the money is going to be me."

"Ach," Diana said, standing up. "That's ridiculous. I'm sorry, Mom. Maybe I'll have some cereal later."

I ate the lasagna at the dining room table alone, blinking back tears as I gazed out at the daffodils on the lawns and the green fuzz on all the trees. I was so excited about Diana being here, had been delighted to devote my entire evening — would have loved to have spent the whole *day* — trying to make things special for her. And not only did she take it for granted, she seemed to assume I had no feelings of my own.

It was my own fault, I thought. I'd always been so selfless, so willing to serve, asking for nothing in return. I'd *raised* her to treat me like a doormat.

Don't be so hard on yourself, I thought, or on Diana. She'd be better as soon as she got some serious rest and readjusted to being back in America. Even coming home after my summer in London, I'd remembered feeling seriously disoriented. Until then, I'd have to be patient.

Late that night, as I sat in bed writing, I heard Diana rummaging around in the kitchen. I thought about getting up to see if she wanted anything, but then I told myself no, better let her take care of herself. It was time for things between us to start shifting, for her sake and for my own. In the morning I found the lasagna pan in the refrigerator, uncovered, empty except for one tiny dried-out square in the corner. Not wanting to wake her, I crept back upstairs and looked in on Diana in her old room, snoring in her little girl's white bed.

For years, when I looked at her as she slept, I could see the baby Diana in her more grown-up face. But now there was no trace of the infant or toddler or even the child she had once been. Instead, I realized with a shock as I watched her, what I saw there was myself — the young self I'd been trying to resemble, the young self I'd once been.

CHAPTER 18

"Where are you going?" Diana asked.

I leaped into the air and let out a little scream. I'd been tiptoeing through our darkening backyard, a garbage bag in my hand. Trying to think fast, I raised the bag and waved it around.

"Just putting out the trash."

"You're all dressed up," Diana pointed out.

She was standing in the open kitchen doorway, wearing her pajamas. When she'd gone to bed right after I got home from work — the jet lag had turned her schedule upside down — I waited a few hours and then figured I was safe to slip away to meet Josh. I'd already called and told him. In the morning when Diana noticed I was gone, she would assume I'd left for the office. I hadn't counted on her seeing me like this.

Narrowing her eyes, she leaned toward me. "Are you wearing *makeup*?"

285

"Oh," I said, my hand fluttering to my face as if I'd forgotten it was there. "Am I wearing makeup?"

I hated lying to my daughter. But I was even more loath to tell Diana the truth: "Oh, honey, I'm just running off to see my young lover. The sex is fantastic, and he's just a few years older than you!"

"Yes, Mother, you're wearing makeup. And high heels. And tight pants. What are you trying to do?"

"I'm trying to look good," I said, standing taller, feeling as if the person I was really trying to convince was myself. "Don't you think I look good? You haven't said anything about all the weight I've lost."

"I didn't want to say anything," said Diana, making a face as if she were trying to keep from throwing up. "I thought you might have, like, an eating disorder."

That kind of nasty adolescent comment at least made it easier for me to leave.

"Listen, I'm going," I said.

"When will you be back?"

I hesitated. Josh would naturally expect me to stay the night. I *wanted* to stay the night.

"I'll see you tomorrow after work," I told her. "I'm just getting together with Maggie."

286

"I want to see Maggie," Diana said. "I'll get dressed and come with you."

"No!" I cried.

And then, at Diana's shocked look, I hurried to explain, "Today was her final insemination attempt. She's going to be flat on her back. She doesn't even want me to be there."

That part, at least, was true. Maggie's apartment had passed muster with the adoption people, and her doctor had greenlighted one more round with the sperm bank. This time, she'd vowed to spend the entire weekend with her hips in the air, staying as still and quiet as possible to maximize the sperm's chances of survival.

"But you are going to be there."

"But I'm just going to help her," I pointed out, deciding I needed to make the prospect even less appealing. "Emptying bedpans, cleaning toilets, that kind of thing."

"Oh," said Diana, looking as if she was about to cry. "Maybe another time."

I was immediately overwhelmed with guilt. I'd never been able to say no to my daughter. And I hated lying to her.

"I don't have to go," I said. "I could stay here with you."

"No, no, go ahead," Diana said, retreating back into the house. "I don't really want to

hang out with a bunch of old people anyway."

I hadn't let myself remember how hand-
some Josh was. How sexy. How sweet. I had
blocked out how crazy he was about me.
And vice versa. Completely blocked the vice
versa.

I hadn't banked on Josh's huge grin when
he opened his door, on the pressure of his
lips at the corner of my mouth, the feel of
his hand against my hip, instantly inspiring
my nipples to stand at attention. I hadn't
counted on how my entire body would melt
under his gaze, how I would hear myself
laughing and working to make him laugh,
working to make him keep wanting me.

He was telling me about his preparations
for Tokyo, something about his sublease, a
mix-up over the apartment he thought he
was getting in Japan, and all the while I was
thinking: How am I ever going to tell him
the truth?

There was simply no graceful moment, no
easy transition. I couldn't imagine how to
get from his:

You wouldn't believe the price of a tiny
room in Tokyo.

To my:

God, that's worse than New York. And

guess what, I'm a forty-four-year-old house-wife!

Not just a housewife, I reminded myself. Or even just a mother, or assistant to the marketing director from hell. A writer now too. At least that was something important about my life I could share with him.

"I've been working on a novel," I told him.

His face lit up, and he threw his arms around me. "That's so fantastic!" he said. "Tell me all about it."

"Oh, there's not much to tell," I said. "I started it a long time ago, and just recently I found it again, and I've been working on it."

"Where was it?" he asked, still grinning.

I looked at him, confused. "What do you mean?"

"Where did you find your novel? Was it in, like, a suitcase, or had you stored it somewhere in Maggie's loft?"

"It was in a trunk," I said, trying to avoid an out-and-out falsehood. "Stored."

"Oh," he said, looking as if he were going to ask me more but then shaking his head a little and, to my relief, deciding to pursue a different line of questioning.

"Can I read it?" he asked, with as much excitement as if I'd told him I'd resurrected a long-lost play of Shakespeare's. "I'd love to read it."

"No," I said quickly.

"Okay, okay," Josh said, laughing. "I understand. Just tell me what it's about. What's the title? Tell me everything."

I hadn't planned on telling him any of this. But as he pried one detail after another out of me, I found myself growing more and more animated. And with every detail I told him, he asked for more. What was the first sentence? How many chapters had I finished? What was the main character like? How had I written so much so quickly? Was he in it?

I felt myself blossom under Josh's attention. This was the thing that made him so different from Gary, so much more appealing than all the older men I knew. It wasn't his looks or his staying power in bed — though that was pretty remarkable, too. It was his willingness — no, his *desire* — to focus at least as much attention on me as on himself.

I wished I could pour my heart out to him about Diana. I didn't want to burden Maggie with the perils of parenthood, not now when she needed to feel only optimistic. But Josh, I felt, would understand anything I told him. I'm so hurt that my daughter treats me like my greatest pleasure in life should be doing her laundry, I wanted to tell him. But the worse thing is, I see now that I made her like that! I made her like that by letting washing her socks *be* my greatest pleasure for far too many years!

I'm trying to be patient, I wanted to tell Josh. I'm still the mother; I've got to give her the time to adjust to a new way of being with me. I've got to show her the way.

And meanwhile, all I want to do is be here with you, jumping your bones.

As if reading my thoughts, he leaned over and kissed me softly on the lips.

"I've missed you," he said.

"I've missed you too."

Truth. Truth with cherries on top.

"I have something I have to tell you," I said, feeling as if I were peering down from the top of a very high dive.

"Can't you tell me in bed?" he asked. "If I don't tear your clothes off and lie naked on top of you right this very minute, I will die."

One last time, I told myself. I'll sleep with him one last time. And then I'll definitely tell him.

I lay naked and spread-eagled across the bed, breathing deeply, sweat coating my body. At the other end of the loft, I could hear Josh moving around, filling two glasses with ice, running the water so it could get cold, ice tinkling as he walked back across the room toward me. I could feel him standing beside the bed, imagined him holding the water out to me, but I felt incapable of so much as opening my eyes, never mind reaching up for the water.

"That was the best sex of my entire life."

He laughed lightly. "Me, too."

"Yes," I said. "But I've lived longer than you."

He laughed again. "But that doesn't mean you've had more sex."

I was about to contradict him, but then I thought, he's probably right. There had been only a handful of men before Gary, and I'd gotten pregnant so soon after our marriage, and then the threat of the miscarriage had ruled out intercourse for several months, so that we'd gone almost instantly from our brief honeymoon period to weekly sexual routine. Once a week for, say, twenty years. How many times was that? A thousand. That didn't seem like very many, though throughout my marriage I'd always been maneuvering to do it less. Yet with Josh, I felt that if we made love a thousand times this year, I'd still crave more.

Now, my entire body was still vibrating, my lips swollen and tingling. I felt the bed dip under his weight as he sat down, and I rolled toward him, lazily opening my eyes. He was so beautiful, his skin so smooth and tight, his muscles so perfectly formed, as if he'd been created just this morning. I couldn't resist reaching out and touching him, running my hand down his back to his waist and his hip. I wanted to commit this to memory, to make the memory powerful enough to last forever.

And then I surprised myself again by bursting into tears. I was curled on my side like a child, sobbing, yet every time I tried to gather myself together and apologize, I found myself crying all the harder. Josh finally set down the glasses of water he'd still been holding and lay down beside me, folding me in his arms. The smell of him enveloping me, the pressure of his fingers against my back, the weight of his leg draped over mine, only made me feel worse.

There was something I knew now that I didn't know when I was in my twenties: relationships like ours were near-impossible to find. I might, with a great deal of luck, a long time from now, meet another man who was more appropriate for the real me. But I knew I was never going to find someone else as wonderful in exactly the same ways as Josh.

And what about him? Would he have the same trouble connecting with someone new the same way he did with me?

My first automatic response was, No, it would be easier for him, he was so much younger, his life was less complicated, and besides, he was a man, with a larger universe of women at his fingertips. When he was forty-four, his age would even be an advantage in attracting twenty-five-year-olds.

But for me, there would be no twenty-five-year-olds after Josh. Even Josh, so warm against me, his breath made manifest with the rise and fall of his chest against mine, seemed ephemeral. Any minute now, he would disappear. I could try to hold on: keep putting off telling him the damning truth, even follow him to Tokyo. But no matter what I did, time would keep passing, making it only more certain that he would no longer be mine.

CHAPTER 19

My heart lurched when I arrived at work early Monday morning to find Teri already there, standing by my desk.

"You're in early," I said, working to keep my tone unworried. "Is there a meeting this morning?"

"Come into my office," Teri said, turning her back on me. Her hair had been freshly cut, coming to a sharp point at the nape of her neck. "I need to speak with you."

I followed her into her office, feeling my breath catch in my throat. I had barely sat down when Teri said, "I've come across something very disturbing."

She pushed a piece of paper across the desk at me: a copy of my application for the job at Gentility Press.

"What's the problem?" I asked.

"You tell me," Teri said coolly. "It seems that all is not accurate on this application."

"What do you mean?" I was now barely

able to speak.

"It seems you didn't really graduate from Mount Holyoke with a degree in English literature, as you claimed."

I let out my breath.

"Yes, I did," I said.

I'd actually come across my diploma this weekend, while checking on the important documents I'd stored in the safe Gary had installed at home.

"I called Mount Holyoke myself," Teri said. "I asked them to look through all their student records, not only for literature graduates but for all graduates, and you weren't there." She gave a triumphant little smile. "Not at all."

"What years?" I managed to whisper.

"What?"

"What years?" I said more loudly, suddenly clear about what I was going to do. "What years did you check?"

"Yes, I noticed that you very cleverly left your graduation date off your résumé, which made my job a little harder," said Teri. "But I had them look at their records for every year dating back to 1990. When you would have been, at my best estimation, roughly ten years old."

"Thirty," I said.

"What was that?"

296

"In 1990, I turned thirty," I said, feeling, along with the fear, the release of telling the truth.

Teri opened her mouth, and then sat there staring. "I don't believe you," she said finally.

"It's true. I graduated from Mount Holyoke in 1981." I lifted the phone on Teri's desk. "Go ahead, call them," I said. "They'll confirm it right now."

Teri shut her mouth. "You still lied."

"How did I lie?"

"You represented yourself as a recent graduate."

"How so? There's nothing on this résumé or application that says when I graduated or claims I've done anything I haven't."

"Exactly!" Teri said, slamming her hand on her desk. "It's what you don't say that's inaccurate. If you graduated from Mount Holyoke in 1981, what have you been doing for the past twenty-something years? Surely you haven't been 'touring Europe,' as you note here, for all that time."

"I've been home raising a daughter. I've been home mopping floors and being the class mom and, I don't know, baking hams. Or, as more than one personnel director called it when I went to job interviews with all the dates on my résumé, 'doing nothing.' "

Teri stared at me. "You lied," she said finally.

"I didn't lie. I'm a mom, Teri, just like you. But when I tried to return to my career after staying home with my child, I found the door barred to me. So I simply omitted a piece of my history — a piece that wasn't even relevant to my profession."

I should have known Teri wouldn't have any sympathy for the difficulty of reentering the workforce after being a stay-at-home mom.

"Other mothers keep working despite the sacrifices involved," she said. "If you choose to sit at home, you have to be willing to pay the price."

"But why should the price be eternal marginalization?" I began. "I'm ready to give my job my all now —"

"You're dishonest," she interrupted me. "You're sneaky. This isn't the only problem."

I caught my breath. "You're talking about the classics project."

"Yes. You went behind my back on that. Tried to steal all my ideas."

I opened my mouth. Closed it. And then opened it again — very wide.

"How dare you," I said. "You're the one who's been stealing my ideas from day one.

And not only did you steal my ideas, you stole my exact words to express them with."

"That's ridiculous," she said. "I have no idea what you're talking about."

"You know very well what I'm talking about. You even acknowledged it to my face — you remember, the whole 'your ideas are my ideas' thing. You just didn't call it stealing."

"It doesn't matter what you say," Teri said. "You're a liar, and once what you've done comes out, no one will believe anything you say."

"Lindsay already knows all about your taking my ideas," I said. "Even Thad knows some of it. And Mrs. Whitney is undoubtedly putting two and two together, which is probably the real reason you need to get rid of me."

I stood up then. I'd been so afraid, just a moment ago, that Teri was going to fire me. But now I knew what I wanted to do — *had* to do.

"I love this company, I really do," I told her. "I even love my job. But I can't work for you anymore. I quit."

"But," Teri stammered, "I'm firing you."

"There you go again," I said, even managing a smile. "Trying to steal my ideas."

■ ■ ■ ■

I wished I could talk to Mrs. Whitney before I left, to make sure she knew my version of the truth, but that was going to have to wait for a calmer time. For now, the only person I had to see was Lindsay. The entire company would be buzzing with gossip about my real age within minutes, I knew, but I wanted Lindsay to hear the truth from me.

Lindsay's assistant was away from her desk — probably in the ladies' room, already getting the story on me — so instead of knocking, I opened Lindsay's door and stepped inside her tiny office. She looked up and scowled: she was still unofficially not speaking to me. Before she could protest at my intrusion, I held up my hand.

"I'm just here to say good-bye," I said. "I quit."

Immediately a look of concern crossed over her face, which at least gave me hope that my friend was still in there somewhere.

"What happened?" she asked. "Did she try to take credit for your work again?"

"No. I mean, yes, that was part of the problem. But we had a confrontation because Teri found out that I — I guess you would call it, *misrepresented* myself on my résumé. That I wasn't entirely truthful about my background."

"Did you inflate your experience?" Lindsay asked. "Or expand the dates when you worked someplace? Because if it's something bogus like that, I don't care, I'll talk to Thad myself —"

"It's not that," I interrupted. I drew in a deep breath. "I didn't tell the truth about my age, Lindsay. To Gentility, to Teri, even to you."

"To me? I don't think you ever said exactly how old you were. I just assumed —"

"That's the problem. I let everybody assume I was a few years out of school, somewhere in my twenties. But I'm not, Lindsay. I'm forty-four."

Lindsay's mouth dropped open, and she sat there staring at me, shaking her head. "How can that be?"

"I've always looked young for my age. And my friend Maggie, the artist who sketched those covers for the classics meeting, helped me do my hair, do my makeup, put together a younger-looking wardrobe." I laughed a little. "Don't you remember how appalled you were by my failure to get a bikini wax?"

"So that was just because you were old and out of it," she said. "The whole Third

301

World traveling through Europe thing was a lie, too."

I didn't know which stung worse, being called old or having what I'd said to Lindsay characterized as a lie.

"I never meant to lie to you or hurt you in any way, Lindsay," I said. "That's why I had to see you before I left — not only to tell you who I really was, but to try and explain why that made me feel the way I did about your relationship with Thad."

"What are you talking about?"

"I was married for more than twenty years, Lindsay. I was a full-time mom; I have a daughter who's nearly as old as you. And when my husband left me last year, I was totally lost."

"And so you decided to go out and perpetrate this major fraud on the world?"

"It wasn't like that," I said. "It started as a lark, and then it just snowballed. I feel terrible now about all the people I lied to, even Teri. It was so wrong."

"Yes, it was," said Lindsay, crossing her arms over her chest.

"But don't you see," I said, "that's why I have to tell you the truth now. I think one reason I wanted to be friends with you was because you remind me of myself when I was your age. I was like you, so anxious to get on with the grown-up part of life. But now I realize that I missed out on so many pleasures of being young. No, more than that — I used my marriage and my child as an escape from the hardest part of becoming an adult myself."

"Just because you screwed up," Lindsay said, "doesn't give you the right to assume that I would."

"No," I said. "Of course not. But I did have this perspective that made me feel you shouldn't be in such a hurry to get married, shouldn't be so quick to say you'd throw away your career when you had children —"

Lindsay leaped to her feet as if I had burst into flames. As if she had.

"You don't know anything about me," she said. "My generation, we're not like you. We love men. We want to enjoy our children."

"I loved my husband," I said, stunned. "I wanted to enjoy my daughter, too. I *did* enjoy her. But that doesn't mean I feel un-ambivalently happy about having spent my twenties and thirties sitting in a house with a child. I wish I had worked longer back then, had seen more of the world —"

"And I wish you would get out of my office," said Lindsay.

I stopped talking.

"I mean it," said Lindsay. "I want you to go."

"I thought you'd want to hear the truth," I said.

Lindsay pointed to the door.

So for the second time that morning, I left.

I called both Maggie and Josh from the street to tell them, in varying amounts of detail, what had happened, and though they both wanted to see me right away, I felt that all I had the strength for was dragging myself to the bus and going home. I promised Josh I'd see him tomorrow, when I vowed to myself that I was definitely going to tell him the truth, the whole truth — despite the disastrous consequences of today's revelations. And I made a plan to get together with Maggie later in the week, when she said she'd feel more mobile following the insemination and I suspected I'd even more seriously need her moral support.

Diana was still sleeping when I got home, which was a relief. I curled into a corner of the sofa, pulled the one afghan Maggie hadn't taken up around my neck, and promptly passed out.

I wasn't aware of anything until I felt a

hand shaking my shoulder and opened my eyes to see Diana staring down at me, a concerned look on her face.

"Are you sick?" she asked.

"No," I said. "I came home early."

I expected then that Diana would ask me why I'd come home early, and I would tell her that I'd quit my job, if not the whole reason behind my departure, and she'd commiserate, maybe brew me a cup of tea, and we'd sit in the sun of the living room, and I'd feel happy to be home with my daughter.

But instead she said, "Oh, great. You know what I'm dying for? Some of your pancakes."

Never mind that I'd offered to make them for her this weekend, and she'd snubbed me, claiming they were too fattening. Never mind that all I did, in any case, was pour the mix into a bowl and slosh in some water and stir it all around, something she could have done handily herself.

Although I knew it was ridiculous, some part of me felt gratified that my big girl still needed me to be her mommy — more precisely, still *wanted* me to be. I heaved myself off the couch, swallowing any resentment I might have felt about her seeming lack of interest in me, and went into the kitchen, Diana trailing behind me. She sat at the pine table leafing through the morning paper as I put a fresh pot of coffee on to brew, mixed the pancake batter in my mother's green bowl, heated the griddle I'd had since her childhood, with its four perfect silver circles worn into the surface where the pancakes had always been cooked.

I'd made Diana pancakes for breakfast nearly every day of her entire growing up, progressing from homemade batter to the ready-made stuff, adding in chocolate chips or blueberries, putting whipped cream on top or pouring the pancakes in the shape of the letters of her name, according to her whimsy. How many pancakes was that? Four a day for an average of six days a week for, say, fifteen years — close to 20,000 pancakes. Twenty thousand and four, counting today.

"Remember all those mornings," I said to her now, sitting in the same chair she'd always occupied, "I made pancakes for you growing up? If I put chocolate chips or berries in them, you always insisted I use exactly five pieces in each pancake. You'd even count."

Diana smiled, but she didn't look up. I felt a jolt of annoyance go through me, but pushed it back down.

"What do you have up today?" I asked her.

"I'm going to Dad's," she said, yawning widely. "Can I take the car?"

"Sure," I said. "When are you planning to be home?"

"I don't know," she said. "I'm spending the night, and I may be back by dinner tomorrow, or stay a couple of extra days. I want to play it by ear, all right?"

"Of course," I said, flipping the pancakes. "It's just, if you're going to take the car —"

Diana snapped the paper and looked up at me. "Mother, you have to stop treating me like a child, okay? If I'm going to live here with you and we're going to get along, you need to treat me like the fellow adult I am."

I drew in my breath, watching the steam rise around the edges of the pancakes, waiting until I'd lifted them onto the plate and set them on the table in front of Diana to speak.

"You're right," I said then, surprised at how measured my voice sounded. "And you need to treat me like a fellow adult too. Not like the mommy whose only function is to cook you pancakes in the morning."

Diana blinked, syrup draining out of the bottle she held tipped over her plate. "Well, you didn't have to make the pancakes if you didn't want to."

"I did want to," I assured her. "I'm not saying I don't want to be your mother or I don't want to do things for you. I'm saying I want you to have some consciousness that I'm a human being, and that if I'm home in the middle of the morning from work without being sick, there must be a reason."

Diana set down the syrup bottle with a thud, but it was too late, the pancakes were drowned in a swamp of goo.

"What's the reason?" she said.

I started crying then, not just from the confrontation right then, but from the force of what had happened all morning.

"I lost my job, all right?" I managed to say.

"What do you mean, lost?"

"I quit. But if I hadn't quit, I would have been fired."

Diana didn't say anything, but suddenly I heard her chair scrape back and then she was at my side, her hand on my shoulder, gingerly at first, but then pulling me closer.

"Don't worry," she said. "You'll find another job."

"No, I won't," I sobbed. "It was so hard to find this one, and now no one else will ever hire me."

"Come on, Mom," Diana said, patting my back as if I was the baby. "You said it was going so well. You had all those great ideas, and everybody loved them. It was just that your boss was a jerk."

I shook my head against her shoulder. "You don't really know the whole story," I said.

"Well, tell me!" she burst out, rearing back and holding me at arm's length. "Maybe I don't ask you things sometimes, but you don't tell me, either! I'd love to know the whole story."

I looked her in the eye, trying to gauge her readiness to hear what she called the whole story, as well as my own readiness to tell it. Maybe she was right, that I had to be willing to tell her more, along with her being willing to ask. Maybe I would even do that, some day soon.

But not today, I thought, remembering Lindsay's reaction this morning, anticipating Josh's tomorrow. Losing a job, a friend, even a lover — those blows were awful, but ultimately ones I knew I could bear. But if I lost my daughter, I might as well curl back up in the corner of my sofa and die.

CHAPTER 20

When I rounded the corner from the subway onto Josh's block, I literally could not believe my eyes. There stood Josh — or at least someone who looked exactly like Josh — outside his building, leaning against a very shiny red Mustang convertible, with the top down. His face lit up when he saw me, and he waved the keys in the air in triumph.

"What's this?" I said.

"A surprise. I thought you needed some fun in your life."

"God," I said, "that's so *sweet*. But where did you get this car?"

"I borrowed it," he said. "From my buddy Russ, the guy who has the band we went to see that first night. But don't hold that against him."

I laughed. "I don't understand," I said, surveying the car, its black upholstery polished to a high gloss, its chrome details shining as if they'd been minted yesterday. "Where are we going?"

"Jersey," he grinned.

"New Jersey?" I said, trying to contain my horror. "Why would you want to go there?"

"Not me," he said. "*We*. Come on, doesn't it look like a car that some guy in a Springsteen song would have driven? This car is longing to be in Jersey."

"Well, maybe I'm not," I said stiffly.

Josh shot me an odd look. "Come on, babe," he said, opening the passenger door. "I never took you for a snob."

"No, it's just . . . ," I said, horrified that he would take me for the kind of New Yorker who sneered at New Jersey, the kind of person I'd always hated. "I really have to talk to you."

"About your job," he said, nudging me toward the seat of the car. "I know. I have a plan."

"And other things, too," I called out as he walked around to the driver's side.

"I have other things I want to talk to you about, too." He had slipped behind the wheel now, was fastening his seat belt and reaching for the ignition. "We can discuss everything once we get there."

"Once we get *where*?" I said, serious panic now beginning to set in.

For the first time, he hesitated. "Well, I just figured we'd get to New Jersey and then look around for something good. Have you ever been to New Jersey?"

"Yes," I admitted. "I grew up in New Jersey."

"Cool," he said, a wide smile breaking over his face. "Then you can direct us."

He turned the key, and the Mustang roared to life. Roared was the right word: the engine was so loud, and once we started driving, the wind whipped around my head so fiercely that conversation was impossible. I directed Josh with my hands, pointing him toward the Williamsburg Bridge, crossing to Manhattan and then winding our way through the crowded streets of Chinatown and Soho toward the Holland Tunnel.

"Isn't this awesome?" Josh caroled as we sped across the bridge.

"Awesome," I called back, hoping not too much grit had lodged in my teeth.

In Manhattan, in the odd moment when he wasn't shifting gears, Josh grabbed my hand, smiling and nodding at me above the blare of the horns and the smell of truck fumes. It was getting harder and harder to smile back, imagining the conversation we were going to have once we crossed into my native state.

"Maybe we should stop here," I said to him, during a momentary lull in noise and traffic on West Broadway, gesturing toward the sidewalk cafés. "This would be a perfect place to talk."

He shook his head firmly. "I want to get this baby on the open road. Go somewhere completely new with you."

"I've been to New Jersey," I reminded him. "A lot."

But he could not be dissuaded. "Then we'll go to Pennsylvania," he shouted, shifting into a higher gear as he gunned it through a yellow light onto Canal Street. "Or all the way to California!"

I was never going to make it to California, not in this car. Careening through the Holland Tunnel, assaulted by smoke and noise, imagining the river coursing along directly over my head, I had doubts about my ability to make it to Hoboken. All I could think was, I'm too old for this. Every doubt I'd ever had about my ability to keep up with Josh came rising up to meet me. I knew this was supposed to be fun. I had no doubt that Josh had gone to enormous lengths to create a wonderful experience for me. But I hated it. And I couldn't let it go on for one more minute longer than was necessary.

"Which way?" Josh called as we bombed

out of the tunnel.

"Pull over!" I shouted.

"Where?" He looked around, confused. There were only gas stations and warehouse buildings and lanes of highway leading west.

I knew that downtown Hoboken was off to the right. But there was no place to park on the street there to have even a minimal conversation. To the left was Jersey City, as mysterious to me as Calcutta.

"All right, just keep going," I said, pointing up ahead.

This route I could have driven in my sleep, and sometimes nearly had. It was the terrain that looked like the New Jersey of everyone's imagination: the arching roadways and flattened wastelands, the black metal towers and shells of ugly buildings. I knew each little cutoff and secret shortcut, directing Josh along the Pulaski Skyway and along Route 280, past the buildings of Newark and the highways to nowhere.

Finally, when we broke through to the green hills that hid the suburbs beyond the highway, Homewood among them, Josh seemed to relax.

"This is pretty," he shouted.

I nodded, steeling myself for what I knew I had to do.

"Are you okay?" he said.

I nodded again, but pointed at the sign for the next exit.

"We're going to get off here," I said.

He looked surprised. "Here?"

He must have assumed I needed a bathroom, or had an urgent need for water or tissues, as I directed him through the suburban streets, my mind racing through the possibilities of where we could sit without being harassed, where we could park without any of my Homewood acquaintances spotting us, where we could go to talk without making it harder than it was already sure to be. A parking lot seemed too cruel, an isolated road too romantic, and the idea of some anonymous suburban street — with the stay-at-home moms peeking at us through their windows and the joggers staring openly as they ran by — made me want to hurl myself onto the blacktop.

Finally, I directed him into the drive that led to an overblown restaurant, where Gary and I had gone a couple of times for our anniversary, that sat on the top of a cliff overlooking Manhattan. But first, before you got to the restaurant, there was a public park with parking spaces along a promenade with an amazing view of the city. It was here that my friend Lori and I had gone the day the World Trade Center towers were hit, watching in horror with hundreds of strangers as the buildings turned to columns of smoke.

I still saw the ghosts of the towers there on the horizon, a palpable absence from the otherwise glorious vista of the city that Josh and I had been deep inside just a short time ago.

"This is amazing," he said.

"I'm going to miss you so much," I blurted, blaming it on the missing towers, the reminder of pain I'd forgotten when I chose this place for its privacy, its beauty, its calm.

Inexplicably, he smiled. "That's what I wanted to talk to you about. See, it doesn't have to be such a bad thing, what happened with your job. Because now you're free. Free to come to Japan with me."

"Oh, Josh," I said, horrified at the direction he was taking the conversation, so different from the one I planned. "I can't go to Japan with you."

"Why not? You don't have your job tying you down now. You can write anywhere."

"It's not that, Josh."

This was it. Absolutely. This was the moment I would have to tell him how old I was.

"There are things about myself I haven't

316

told you," I began.

"I figured," he said, twisting in the car seat to face me directly. "I mean — are you married, Alice?"

"No!" I said, shocked at what he'd surmised. No, I shouldn't be shocked; it was a logical conclusion. And it wasn't all that far off.

"No," I said, more softly this time, but determined that full disclosure was the only path. "But I was. I'd already been separated for a year when I met you."

"Oh," he said, relief flooding his voice. "I started to think that it was obvious, when you'd disappear for days at a time and would never take me to your apartment." He laughed a little. "I was starting to think that you really had a husband stashed there and, like, five kids."

"Only one kid," I said.

Again, he looked stunned. "But how is that possible? All that time in the city, there wasn't any kid. Unless he was staying with his father or something, or some relative, but it doesn't make sense —"

I reached out and laid a finger on his lips. "My daughter is twenty-two years old."

He pulled back his head and looked at me quizzically, as if this were one of those riddles with an answer that should be obvious — The surgeon was the patient's mother! There was nothing to do now but tell him the punch line.

"And I'm not twenty-nine, Josh. I'm forty-four."

Everything seemed to stop then. The trees stopped waving in the breeze, the city skyline disappeared from view. Even the plane that was droning overhead in the pristine sky seemed to go silent.

Finally, Josh shook his head as if trying to clear it of a disturbing vision.

"That's not possible."

"It's possible," I said. "Not only possible, but true."

"Jesus, Alice!" he exploded. "It was all a lie from the very beginning!"

At that, he pushed open the door of the car and strode out across the parking lot onto the expanse of grass, heading toward the line of trees. I waited a moment, thinking he would surely circle back, but he kept going, fast disappearing, until I finally jumped out of the car and ran after him.

"Josh," I called. "Stop!"

He stopped walking, but he didn't turn around.

"I never lied," I panted when I finally caught up with him. "I just didn't tell the truth."

"But that first night at the bar, on New Year's Eve," he said, turning to face me. "You pretended right from the beginning to be young."

Was that right? I'd made myself *look* young, but from there, a lot of it was assumption. An assumption I'd actively encouraged.

"It was supposed to be just for fun," I said, my heart sinking at the memory.

"Fun for you. Without caring about how I'd feel."

"I did it before there *was* a you," I said. "Or at least before I had any idea we were going to get involved. The last thing I expected was that I was going to fall in love with you."

Josh looked at me. He looked at me hard.

"What did you say?" he said.

I felt the heat rise in my cheeks. I hadn't intended to say that. Hadn't known I was even thinking it. But now that I'd said everything else, why hide that?

"That's true too," I said. "I fell in love with you, even though it was supposed to be no commitment. I didn't want it to happen. But it did. I'm sorry."

Josh was staring at me with his mouth open. Then suddenly he spread his arms wide and threw his hands up and cried,

"But that's great! I love you, too! You wouldn't let me say it before, but it's true. I love you, Alice. I love you!"

I shook my head and took a step back, more stunned by his reaction than I would have been had he told me he never wanted to see me again.

"But you don't know me," I said. "Not the real me."

He reached out and ran his hands down the outsides of my arms, which I was holding stiffly at my sides. "Here you are," he said. "This is you, isn't it? You love me, and I love you. That's everything I need to know."

"Oh, come on, Josh!" I cried. "It's not that simple. Maybe in some ideal world our ages wouldn't matter, but the fact is, they do. Just because we love each other is not enough to make a relationship work."

He crossed his arms over his chest and stuck his chin into the air. He didn't look angry anymore, he didn't look hurt, but instead assumed an expression I'd come to recognize as determined.

"Why not?" he said, jutting his chin toward me. "It's enough for me."

"Well, for one thing, I can't pick up and go to Japan with you. I've got my house, I've got my daughter, I've got a life here

320

you don't know anything about."

"So I'll stay here," he said. "There are other gaming schools, or I can get a corporate job for a while —"

I reached out and gripped his forearm. "I'm not going to let you do that," I said. "I know how much you want this. You can't give it up for me."

"Then we'll fly back and forth," he said. "We'll do a long-distance thing until we can live in the same place again."

"And then what?" I burst out. "What is our future really, Josh? You're young. Eventually you're going to want marriage, a family —"

"So we'll get married." He grinned.

I couldn't let myself take that in, was already shaking my head no. "I can't have any more children, Josh. I tried for years after my daughter was born. It's not possible for me."

"So we'll adopt!" he said, moving to embrace me.

But more quickly, I stepped away again.

"No," I said. "I don't want a baby at this point in my life, Josh. And that's a huge difference between us. That option is out for me because I want it to be. But for you, it's all ahead."

"That's not important," he said, trying to

get close again. "I don't care about babies. I just want you."

I held up my hands to make him stop, to let him know I was serious about drawing this line.

"I'm not going to let you make that decision at this point in your life," I said. "In five years or ten years or twenty years, you may very well change your mind. And you have to leave yourself that freedom."

Josh was silent for an uncomfortably long time, and then he said, in a voice so quiet I almost didn't hear him, "I thought you said you loved me."

I knew what I had to say next, but I needed to postpone saying it, to savor what I suddenly knew was the last moment of my youth, of my own real youth and innocence. All of it, the clothes, the makeup, the pretending to be young, the job, even this relationship, had been not the calculated ploy of a mature woman but a girlish game.

And then, by getting younger, I had grown up, somehow. I had become my real adult self. The person who now took Josh's hand in my own.

"I do love you," I told him. "That's why I have to say good-bye."

CHAPTER 21

"It's so romantic!" Maggie said, actually clasping her hands near her heart. "It's like one of those old Bette Davis movies, or *A Farewell to Arms.*"

"I never read *A Farewell to Arms,*" I said glumly.

"Neither did I," said Maggie, "but it's that whole 'We love each other but we can never be together' kind of thing. You know what I mean."

"I can't believe you're going all gooey on me," I said. "I expected you to tell me that I'm doing the right thing, that it's time to stop playing with my boy toy and get on with my grown-up life."

"Yeah," said Maggie, "I might have said that, but that was before I realized this was really *love.*"

She started blinking hard and took a quick swallow of her wine. We were sitting outside at a sidewalk café near her loft. It was a warm, glistening day, and at first I thought the sun was in Maggie's eyes. But then I looked closer.

"Are you . . . crying?" I asked, aghast. Maggie hated to cry. Over the years, I'd seen her break her arm, get reamed out by her parents, lose lovers, have her artwork dismissed by the critics as trash — and never come close to shedding a tear. And now her eyes were brimming because of something *I* felt.

"No, it's just . . ." She swiped at her eye, succeeding only in smearing her mascara. "Okay, I am, all right? I don't know what's wrong with me. I've just been a little emotional lately."

My heart quickened. "You're pregnant!" I cried.

"What? No. I'm definitely not."

"How do you know? It's only been a week since the insemination."

"I haven't taken a test or anything, but I'm just sure I'm not. I don't feel it. In fact, I think I might be coming down with something. I've been really tired and weepy. I cried last night at a cell phone commercial."

It sounded like pregnancy to me. In fact, the more I looked at her, the more pregnant Maggie looked, even at this early date. Her angles had softened, her skin looked pinker, even her hair was refusing to spike, instead curling gently around her face.

"So have you heard from the adoption agency?" I asked.

"Yes," she said, suddenly animated, grabbing my hand. "That's *my* news. I didn't want to tell you over the phone. I'm officially on the waiting list for a child."

"Oh, Maggie, that's wonderful! Any word on when a baby might be available?"

"That's still all up in the air," Maggie said, her whole being alight. "It could be years, it could be tomorrow. But I'm definitely going to be a mom."

"I'm so happy for you," I said, standing up to enfold her in a hug. "I can't wait to see you with your child."

For the first time in that awful week, my mood lifted with joy for Maggie and excitement about going into her future with her. Sitting back in my chair, looking around the café and at the crowded sidewalk beyond, I was surprised to see how many babies had suddenly appeared, snuggled against the chests of their skinny-again young moms.

"Since when did this get to be a family neighborhood?" I asked Maggie.

She looked around. "Isn't it weird? For years I never saw a kid down here, and now they seem to be everywhere. I thought maybe it was just me, noticing it for the first time now that I'm going to have one of my own."

"It looks like you're going to have a lot of company," I said. "That's great."

"What about you?" said Maggie. "Why won't you even *consider* having another baby, if you're so crazy about this guy? We could go to China together, raise the girls to be best friends. Hey, the next apartment that opens up in my building, I'll rent it to you and Josh and the baby, and we'll all be young parents together."

"What about Diana?" I said, amused at Maggie's communal vision, one that had thrilled me in my early years of motherhood and that Maggie, at that point in our lives, had found pedestrian beyond belief.

"Well," Maggie said, "she'd be in there somewhere too."

"I'm sure she'd get along well with Josh as her stepfather. They probably like the same music. And they could play video games together."

"Gary's hygienist sweetie isn't all that much older than Josh," Maggie pointed out.

"She's in her thirties," I said. "And besides, you know it's different when the genders are reversed."

"It shouldn't be." Maggie frowned.

"Of course not. But it is. And the guy can have kids at whatever age he wants."

"So can you, within reason," Maggie said. "If you adopt."

"But I've done all that, I've lived that entire lifetime," I said. "I can't start all over and put myself on hold for the sake of my child."

"You wouldn't be a stay-at-home mom this time," said Maggie. "You'd keep working, just like I'm going to do."

I sighed. It was never that simple; you were never that thoroughly in control. But neither could you fully explain that to someone before they actually had a child of their own.

"Maybe," I said. "I could rock the cradle with my foot while I typed on my laptop."

"Exactly!" cried Maggie, as if this were a eureka moment. "I plan to let my child work in the studio right beside me. I'm going to get her her own little easel and paintbrushes, and just let her create."

"Great," I said. "What if she paints on the walls?"

"That would be cool! I think if you give kids freedom, they become truly creative beings. I plan to offer guidance but basically let my daughter make her own choices."

All *right*! A lot of moms-to-be held this kind of theory, I reminded myself; I had too. But once they started dealing with a real live crayon-scribbling, milk-spilling, book-ripping child, they usually changed their thinking. Maggie would have to go through that kind of progression in her parenting style herself — or else decide she could cope with the consequences.

"Things have been a little better with Diana," I said, deciding it was time to shift the subject. "She's trying harder to chip in around the house, and seems to have dropped the teenage attitude."

"That's good. Did you tell her what happened with Josh?"

I shook my head, hard. "She doesn't know that there was a Josh, and she never will. At this point, there's no reason at all for me to tell her about him or about my whole age charade."

"Why not?" said Maggie. "I would think she'd find it amusing."

"No," I said firmly. "There are things you don't tell your kids. You don't talk about your sex life. You don't dump your emotional problems on them. And I'm definitely not going to confess I was leading this double life that required I pretend that she

328

didn't even exist."

"When you put it that way," Maggie said, "I see your point."

"It doesn't matter now anyway," I said. "I'm right back where I started, and I just need to pick up my life as if this whole stupid escapade hadn't happened."

It took me a minute to realize Maggie was staring at me with a look of incredulity on her newly pink face.

"Don't be ridiculous," she said. "You are absolutely not right back where you started. You're writing a book now, correct?"

"True," I conceded. Without a job or a boyfriend, I had plenty of time and energy to write, spinning out pages upon pages every day and into the night. "But it's a book I started before."

"But now you have the confidence and the experience to finish it," she said. "Plus the contacts to get it published."

"You mean Gentility Press?" I grunted. "I doubt they're ever going to want to hear from me again."

"See, you can't get discouraged so easily. Plus, you've always had the tenacity to keep going after something you wanted. I remember how long and hard you tried to have another baby after Diana. That's been a real inspiration to me."

"Aw," I said, realizing for the first time that my persistence in trying to get pregnant was something I might apply to my professional life. "Thanks."

"I think Mrs. Whitney might be interested to hear your side of the story after all," Maggie said. "And I bet Josh would be open to hearing from you again too."

On this I had to firmly disagree. "We were going to break up, one way or another, when he left for Tokyo next week," I told her. "I just made it easier on him."

"What about on yourself?" Maggie said.

"What about it?"

"Did you make it easier on yourself? I thought you were going to put yourself first from now on. Or maybe that's what you were doing. Maybe you broke up with him because you were afraid that if he got to know the real you, however willing he was, he wouldn't love you anymore."

"Ouch," I said.

"BLT, baby."

Suddenly she sniffed at the warm spring air, her lip curling and her face turning from pink to an unflattering shade of green.

"Oh, my God," she said. "What's that horrible smell?"

I sniffed. "I think it's broiled chicken."

She moaned and looked as if she was going to be sick. "Don't say that," she said. "I don't know what's wrong with me, but even hearing that word makes me gag."

"What word?" I said, puzzled. "Chick—?"

She leaped from her seat and rushed inside the restaurant, presumably toward the ladies' room.

If she hadn't left so precipitously, I would have set her straight on a little matter, too. But she'd find out the truth for herself soon enough. It always revealed itself, in the end. BLT, baby, right back atcha.

I was spending so much time writing that by the end of the weekend I had finished enough pages to send to Mrs. Whitney, via what I knew was the e-mail address she personally checked, with a letter explaining my side of why I'd left Gentility. I didn't blame Teri or anyone but myself. I said it was wrong for me to mislead everyone. But I also pointed out that I was a deep admirer of her and her publishing company, that I'd tried to get a job as my middle-aged self and been turned down, and I believed that my actions had just been an attempt to find a creative solution to the problem of age discrimination that plagued the American workplace.

I was tempted, once I sent this missive off, to devote the rest of my time to praying for a positive outcome, but I knew that if I didn't keep working, I'd end up obsessively cleaning the house and cooking and gardening and undermine any progress I'd made with getting Diana to pitch in.

And she had started pitching in. Occasionally. Sloppily. But still. My part of the deal was to retreat to the garden or my bedroom with my laptop, working ahead on my book and letting her take over.

As the days ticked by, I thought constantly about Josh. Now he's boxing up his apartment. He's probably packing his suitcase. Now he's probably heading to his parents' place, where I knew he planned to spend the last few days before he left. I'd had his departure date and time, his airline, even his flight number, committed to memory for weeks.

He was on my mind so incessantly that the afternoon I came home from the supermarket and Diana met me at the front door and said, "You missed a call," I thought immediately that it had been from Josh. The next day was the day he was supposed to leave, I knew. Maybe he just had to talk with me before he went. Maybe I'd even call him back, to say good-bye. Maybe . . .

Diana was talking, interrupting my reverie. It hadn't, it seemed, been Josh who'd called after all. Diana was saying something about Lindsay.

"Wait a minute," I said. "Lindsay? You must have gotten that wrong."

Diana smiled. "Oh, I didn't get it wrong. Lindsay, the editor you used to work with."

I felt the heat rise to my cheeks, the grocery bag slip in my hands. "Am I supposed to call her back?"

"She was about to leave the office. But she asked me to tell you that she wants to buy your book."

Diana took me out to dinner that night to celebrate. When I protested that she couldn't afford to do that, she winked and said, "Dad gave me some money."

After our meal, she ordered us a bottle of expensive champagne and raised her glass to me.

"To my mom," she said. "The youngest-looking woman in the room."

I felt myself blush. "Except for you," I pointed out.

"Yes, but I really *am* young," Diana said. "Whereas you, you're in your forties, but anybody would believe you were, I don't know, twenty-seven, twenty-eight — certainly under thirty."

My cheeks were really burning now, but Diana was smiling so innocently I thought she might just be reacting to the way I looked in the candlelight.

"It's just that it's so dark in here," I said, making myself laugh.

"I don't know about that," said Diana. "Even in, say, the kind of fluorescent lights they have in an office, or in a gym, someone might think you were a lot younger."

I froze. Obviously, I was busted.

"Lindsay," I breathed.

"That's right, Mom," Diana said, the corners of her mouth twitching. "Really: Krav Maga classes?"

"She told you about that?"

Diana nodded. "Martini bars? A boyfriend named Josh who designs video games?"

That was when my hand jerked out, involuntarily, and I knocked over my champagne glass.

"Oh, my God. She told you everything."

"She couldn't believe you hadn't told me yourself! Why *didn't* you tell me?"

I tried to smile, but could manage to lift only one side of my mouth. Briefly. "Embarrassed?" I said. "Afraid it would make you hate me?"

"I could never hate you!" Diana cried,

scooting over next to me on the banquette. "You're my mom! I think that's the most awesome thing you've ever done!"

"Really?"

"Are you kidding? It's inspirational! It makes me want to go out there and do something crazy too."

"I hope not too crazy."

"Let it go, Mom. I mean, try something different, take some chances. Like I've been thinking. I know I'm one semester away from finishing my art history degree, but after my experience in Africa, I think I want to be a nurse."

"That's great," I told her. "You should go for it."

"You really think so? It would mean almost starting all over again, taking all these science and math classes and spending a lot more time in school."

"But if that's what you want to do, it's worth it."

"So you don't mind having to pay for the extra years of college it's going to take to get my nursing degree? I can go straight back to NYU, but a lot of my credits aren't going to count in the nursing school."

"Diana," I said gently. "You're going to have to talk to your dad about that. I can help you, of course, but the way my alimony is structured, I don't have enough money to support myself and pay all your expenses at school. Whatever advance they give me for the novel will probably just make it possible for me to finish writing it. Unless . . ."

Again, I hesitated, not sure whether I was prepared to go forward.

"Unless what?" Diana pressed.

"Unless I sold the house," I said. "And I'm sure you wouldn't want me to do that."

"Why not?" Diana asked, looking honestly stumped.

"It's your childhood home," I pointed out. "You've always said I could never sell that house, that you wanted to bring your own children there for holidays, maybe even take it over one day."

"That's not important anymore," Diana said. "Once fall comes, I'll be back in school, and after I graduate, I hope to go back to Africa or South Asia or somewhere like that."

My only child, planning to spend her life halfway around the world. There was no reason, then, that I had to keep sitting in New Jersey.

"I thought you were the one who said you wanted to hold on to that house forever," Diana said.

"I did feel that way," I admitted. "And I

love that house. But especially without you there, it wouldn't feel like my home anymore. I mean, not the home of the person I've become."

"Because of this guy?" Diana asked. "Do you think if you sold the house you'd move in with him?"

I shook my head. "We broke up."

"But what happened? Lindsay said you two were like totally in love."

"Oh, I don't know . . . ," I began, prevaricating again.

And then I'd just had it. I'd had it with myself, still dodging, still denying, still telling lies when the truth was arrayed around me, clear as my upturned champagne glass.

"I was," I told my daughter. "I was . . . I mean, I am in love with him. But I broke up with him because he's so much younger than me. We want such different things out of life, it would never work out."

"What different things do you want?" Diana asked me, deadpan.

I tried to think. There was Japan. But Josh was going to Japan because he wanted to follow his passion rather than do what was expected of him, and I wanted that for myself now too. And I guessed he was more infatuated with fast convertibles than I was. But other than that, on an everyday basis, we seemed to want just about exactly the same things.

"It's not now I'm thinking of," I told Diana. "Now we agree on nearly everything — I mean, everything important. But eventually he's going to want kids, a house, all those normal grown-up things, and I've already done that. And then it will be a disaster."

Diana shook her head and narrowed her eyes the way she did when she wanted to convey that she thought I'd said something especially idiotic.

"I don't get it," she said. "You love him, you get along great, but you're breaking up with him because you might disagree about something ten years from now?"

"Not about something," I said. "About the most important thing there is — children. I don't want him to give that up for me. And I don't want to get into a relationship that either forces him into a huge sacrifice or leaves me alone and heartbroken in five or ten years."

"Oh, so you'll just leave yourself alone and heartbroken now," Diana said. "Mom, this doesn't make sense. I mean, it sounds really noble, but you have to be with him or not be with him because of what's happening now, not what you think *might* happen ten years from now! Who knows? You might meet somebody else, some old dude whose kids are also grown up. Or maybe you'll change your mind and decide you want a baby after all. Or maybe he'll get killed in a plane crash tomorrow —"

I groaned aloud. "I wish you hadn't said that."

"I didn't mean really," she said, horrified. "It was just a way of saying life is unpredictable —"

"I know, I know," I assured her. "It's just that he's leaving on a plane for Japan tomorrow morning."

"So this is your last chance to see whether you might go forward."

Imagining it — all of it: his plane crashing, my rushing to see him one more time, our lurching forward into an unknown future — I knew for certain what I had to do. I had to take the chance that I could make a relationship with Josh. However slim the odds for success, they were better than what I had now: the absolute and unbearable certainty that I would never be with him again.

CHAPTER 22

If Josh had still been in Brooklyn, I would have gone directly to his place from my dinner with Diana. But he was, I knew, somewhere in the wilds of Connecticut with his family, and would be traveling to Newark Airport by himself on the day's first train.

When I got home, I went straight to bed, setting my alarm for five, intending to go immediately to sleep. But there was a phone message from Maggie, asking me to call her, no matter how late I got in.

I guessed what she was going to tell me as soon as I heard her message, had guessed it two weeks ago, at the sidewalk café. And indeed, as soon as she lifted the phone, without even saying hello because she knew that the only person calling at midnight would be me, she said, "I'm pregnant."

"That's awesome!" I cried.

"You know what," said Maggie. "For once, that word actually fits."

"When?" I asked.

She chuckled. "That's one of the beauties of insemination: no guessing about the date. January twenty-ninth."

"I'm so happy for you."

"There's more," Maggie said. "The adoption agency called. They have a baby for me. Well, not precisely a baby: she's nearly two. But I can pick her up in September."

Oh, my God. Not one baby but two. "What are you going to do?" I asked Maggie. All her dreams had been about being the single mom of a single child, not of shepherding an entire brood.

"I said yes, absolutely," Maggie said. "I didn't dare to hope for two, considering how difficult it seemed to get just one. But I'm thrilled."

"I'll help you," I said. "Diana will help you. She's planning to be at NYU again in the fall. And Maggie, Gentility wants my novel."

"Whoopie!" Maggie cried. "That's *your* baby! So are you rich?"

"Knowing Gentility, it will be a modest advance. I didn't actually talk to Lindsay. Diana took the call."

"Uh-oh."

"Big uh-oh. Lindsay totally spilled the beans. Diana knows everything."

341

"Even about the boy?"

"Especially about the boy. She thinks I should go to the airport to see him tomorrow."

"I think so too," said Maggie.

"I think so too," I agreed. "So I've got to go to sleep so I don't look a hundred and three tomorrow morning."

But I couldn't fall asleep, not for long, anyway. I set my alarm for five, but I got up before it rang, showering and dressing and putting my makeup on carefully. I was almost unbearably nervous, but I didn't want to spend hours hanging around at the airport before he even got there, so I made myself wait.

As I waited, though, all sorts of terrible possibilities passed through my mind. What if he'd decided to leave early for Tokyo, or from an airport closer to home, now that he thought I wouldn't be there? What if his family came with him? What if he was so angry at me that he refused to even talk to me once I got there?

Any of those things could happen, along with a whole host of dire possibilities I hadn't even thought of, but I couldn't let that stop me. This was it, my final chance.

In the car, to keep my mind off what might happen with Josh, I called Lindsay on my cell. She loved my book, she told me immediately, and she was so sorry for being angry with me about Thad. I'd been right about him all along, he was a total jerk — it turned out that on that business trip to California he'd slept with like three other women. And she hadn't even seriously *considered* having sex with that creepy guy from the club!

She was beginning to think now that maybe I'd been right about everything — that it was the perfect time for her to be out seeing the world, doing adventurous things. My daughter was so lucky to have a wise mom like me.

"She doesn't always see it that way," I laughed. "Plus, I realize now that what happened to me when I was in my twenties doesn't have much to do with what's going to happen to you or my daughter."

"But we can learn something from your experience; we just don't want to," Lindsay said. "We see all the shit you go through — putting up with asshole husbands and bratty kids, losing your careers, getting cellulite — and we need to believe that's not going to happen to us. Because we're *different*."

"I guess we need to do the same thing to you," I told her. "We're so threatened by how gorgeous and skinny and sexy you are, we need to believe you're immature and incompetent to make ourselves feel better."

"But when I believed you were my age," Lindsay said, "I thought we were so much alike."

"We are alike," I said. "The only real difference is our ages."

It turned out that Mrs. Whitney was sympathetic to my explanation of why I'd sidestepped the age issue at work. But more importantly, she'd loved my book. She thought it would appeal to both younger women and older women, and she knew Lindsay was the perfect person to edit it.

"That doesn't mean Thad and Teri are going to be involved with it, too?" I asked, suddenly alarmed.

Lindsay laughed. "One of the women Thad slept with in California was an author, and she threatened him with a sexual harassment suit. He's gone. And when Mrs. Whitney insisted on going ahead with your classics ideas even after you left, Teri quit. She's going to stay home with her kids."

"God," I said. "Maybe I could even come back to work for Gentility."

"Don't you dare," Lindsay said. "You've got a book to finish."

Signs for the airport appeared, and promising Lindsay that we'd talk again soon, I hung up and maneuvered toward the parking lot closest to Josh's airline. I figured I'd arrived about the same time he would, and I hoped to spot him standing on line, wait until he was ready to head to the gate, and talk to him then. My intention wasn't to stop him from leaving; just to see him, to talk to him, before he did.

But he wasn't waiting on line. He wasn't in the bookstore. He wasn't drinking a cappuccino or eating a Krispy Kreme.

His flight was still not for over two hours, I knew. Maybe he was still en route to the airport, his train somehow slower than my car. I should station myself at the door, wait for him to show up.

But what if he was already here? If he'd already gone through security and passport control, and was inside waiting for his flight to leave? What if he was, in effect, already gone?

He wasn't gone, I reminded myself firmly. His flight didn't leave until eleven-something. And until then, he was somewhere very close.

I had been hoping not to have to call his cell phone. I didn't want to give him a chance to reject me by phone before I could even get close enough to see his face, to touch his arm.

But now it was my only hope. I dialed, and he picked up on the first ring.

"Thank God," I said. "Where are you?"

"I'm at the airport. Where are you?"

"I'm at the airport, too." I looked around. "I don't see you."

He laughed. "I hate you for making me laugh. I'm already through security."

My heart dropped. "I have to talk with you."

He didn't say anything for a long moment, and then, "You broke up with me two weeks ago, Alice. You told me you didn't want to see me again, ever. What are you going to say now, as I'm about to step on the plane, that would make any difference?"

"I want to explain," I said. "I want to tell you the truth. Before you leave, and I never get the chance."

He hesitated. "I thought you already told me the truth."

"I did," I promised. "But there's more."

While I waited for him, standing there staring at the open space beside the security machines, I tried to think of something I could say, something I could do, that would make this easier for both of us. But then I realized if there were a simple approach to this relationship, I would have figured it out by now.

Then I saw his face, serious as he approached the exit, then breaking into a smile as he caught sight of me. He tried to make himself look somber again, but he couldn't do it.

He walked right up to me and took me in his arms. I hugged him back hard to let him know how I felt, before my words could screw everything up. When we finally moved apart, he smiled a little and said, "So what's this other truth that you have to tell me? You're a hit woman for the Mafia? A Middle Eastern spy?"

"Nothing that dramatic," I assured him. "I just realize now that I shouldn't have broken up with you that day. I wasn't really trying to protect you, I was trying to protect myself."

"From what, Alice? You know how much I love you, how much I want to be with you. I told you I didn't care about your age, any of that —"

I put my finger to his lips to stop him. "I was trying to protect myself from the pain of losing you."

He shook his head as if he didn't understand. "But you weren't losing me. It was exactly the opposite."

"From losing you, ever," I said. "I figured if I dumped you now, you wouldn't be able to dump me later."

Josh just looked at me. Finally he said, "That's really screwed up."

"I know," I said. "I know. I'm embarrassed to even tell you. But I had to see you, and I didn't want to lie about why. I don't want to lie about anything, ever again."

"You really hurt me that day," he said, "in the park."

"I'm so sorry," I said, moving to put my arms around him. "Do you think you can forgive me?"

He pulled away. "I don't know," he said, refusing to meet my eye. "I don't know if I can trust you again."

"You can trust me," I assured him, "from this moment onward."

He took a deep sigh and looked toward the ceiling, out the long window where the planes were lined up. "But this is the moment I'm leaving," he said. "We're not even going to be together."

One option occurred to me as a serious possibility for the first time. "Maybe I could go to Japan," I said impulsively. "Not this minute, but once you got settled. For a while, I mean. I've talked to my daughter about selling the house. And she's going to school in the fall."

But Josh was already shaking his head. "I

don't know," he said again. "I'm going to need time to think about it. To think about everything."

I hung my head. "So that's it, then," I said. "You're leaving, and we're not going to be together anymore."

"I don't know, Alice!" he cried, flinging his hands out in exasperation. "Maybe if we're ever going to be together, you're going to have to just let whatever's happening at that moment happen and not try to nail down what's going to happen next."

He picked up his pack then and started walking backward. Instinctively, I took a step toward him, but he held up both hands to warn me off. I stopped. But I thought that any second he would stop too, move toward me again, take me in his arms and at least let me feel certain that he still loved me.

Instead he turned around and walked away from me. When he laid his pack on the belt to go through security, I called his name. There was no one else around, and I knew he heard me, but he didn't turn around. Instead, he walked through the metal archway, held up his arms as if he were under arrest while the agent ran the metal wand over his body, and walked off down the causeway into his future, without even a backward glance.

And I did the only thing that, under the circumstances, I could do: I let it happen.

CHAPTER 23

The next New Year's Eve, it was Maggie who wanted to stay home and me who campaigned for us to go out. Last New Year's Eve had been the start of a whole new life for me, and I was almost superstitious about wanting to celebrate the holiday again. Josh had e-mailed me that New Year's was the biggest holiday of the year in Japan, where days' worth of rituals symbolized the making of a fresh start for the incoming year. That seemed right to me. Come and visit, Josh urged. Then you could experience this with me. And we could see what kind of fresh start we might want to make together.

I was tempted. All through last summer, I hadn't heard anything from Josh. But then he'd begun e-mailing, first just to let me know where he was, and that he was doing all right. Then, slowly, we began writing about what had happened between us, and how we each felt about it. And then we moved on to how we were each feeling about our lives now. It was partly the shelter of the e-mail that made me feel freer, as if Josh and I lived only as minds, as spirits, our bodily existence immaterial. And it was partly that I felt, with him, completely known in a physical way — sexually, yes, but also as a human being, all artifice stripped away. There was no point any longer in trying to hide anything from him.

I loved him, he loved me, that was certain. But could we be in love again? I knew we wouldn't be able to answer that question until we got to know each other all over again, in the flesh, as our real selves, with the same depth and passion we'd brought to reconnecting on the virtual plane. And that required time, and proximity, and so was going to have to wait, and might never happen.

In the meantime, it had started to snow, the fat white flakes that had eluded us all through the balmy December and into a springlike Christmas Day now falling fast and hard. A dusting had been predicted, but this, I saw, gazing out the window at the Lower East Side street from where I sat at my computer — I had sold my house and moved into an apartment in Maggie's building — was beginning to look like a blizzard.

It was just as well, then, that Maggie had insisted we celebrate the holiday at home. Her reason had not been the blizzard but her pregnancy and her reluctance to leave Edie, her nearly-two-year-old daughter who'd come from China just three months before. Diana had offered to babysit, but Maggie had said no, Diana should go out with her friends. Besides, Maggie felt she spent enough time away from Edie when she was working — she'd moved her studio and her enormous sculptures with it to a separate space on another floor — and she wanted the little girl to feel as secure as possible before the baby came.

The truth was that Maggie needed to be home with Edie more than Edie needed her to be home. Edie seemed as comfortable with Diana, who'd been babysitting and living most of the time in Maggie's loft, as she was with Maggie. It was Maggie who relished every moment with her little girl.

I heard a key turn in the lock and swung around to see Diana, who'd been upstairs at Maggie's most of the day.

"Maggie asked me to check on dinner," Diana said. "She wants to know whether there's anything you need, whether she can help in any way. Plus, she said to tell you she's starving."

Pregnancy had brought on a fierce appetite in Maggie, and her lifelong boyish figure had ballooned so that now she resembled one of her sculpted fertility goddesses.

"Tell her I'll be up in about half an hour," I said. "She can get the table ready if she wants."

Diana rolled her eyes. "We tried that," she said. "Everything we set out, Edie pulled down. She was running around up there brandishing a butter knife."

I laughed. Edie was adorable, but a handful. It seemed to take the energies of all three of us — me, Maggie, and Diana — to keep up with the toddler. Leaving the building — and worse, climbing back up the five flights of stairs — was like a military operation that required at least three able-bodied adults.

"Was I like that?" Diana asked me. "I mean, I love Edie, but she's so much work! I don't know what we're going to do when the baby comes."

"Maggie may end up wanting to move to the suburbs yet," I said.

In fact, Maggie had briefly considered buying my house in the suburbs when she found out she'd be having an instant family. But then we both decided that, however lovely it was, that house came with too much freight, and it would be better for us individually and for our friendship to leave it behind.

"She still swears she won't, but we'll see," said Diana, letting herself back out of the apartment. "In the meantime, do what you can to hurry that dinner. When I left to come down here, I saw her heading for the ice cream."

I had been writing, something I did every day now, even Sunday, even Christmas, even New Year's Eve. My first book would be out in time for Mother's Day, and I was starting on something new, already under contract with Gentility. Sighing deeply — I put my work away only with reluctance — I saved the file and got up to check on dinner.

I'd taken over the lease on this apartment at the beginning of September, just before Maggie went to China to get Edie, another time of the year that was prime for fresh starts. I'd moved in all my favorite things from home, finding I could not bear, as I had claimed I would, to get rid of everything. The apartment looked warm and cozy, full of my kilims and hooked rugs, with my cross-stitched bedspread on the bed and my copper pots hanging from the wall in the tiny kitchen. It felt like home, more like home even than the house had felt in those final months, the only thing I really hated to leave in the end my beloved garden. This, I thought now with satisfaction, was exactly where I wanted to be.

I removed the vat of spaghetti sauce made according to my grandmother's secret recipe from where it had been simmering in the oven and put on a huge pot of water to boil. Better to cook the pasta down here, where the boiling water would pose no danger for Edie. I spread oil and chopped garlic on the Italian bread that I'd walked all the way to Little Italy, to one of the few remaining authentic bakeries, to buy, and then wrapped it in foil and popped it in the oven. I took the salad out of the refrigerator and mixed the vinaigrette.

Now all I had to do was wait.

I wandered back to the window, gazing out on the snowy city. So quiet, so beautiful, with the fresh white coating hiding all the grime. It felt almost like being in the country, without the isolation that I realized now was so depressing, once Diana got too old to spend every waking hour wrapped around my body. I'd been so lonely then, I realized, even before Gary left, even before Diana left, so alone by myself, waiting in vain for them to pay attention to me.

Sitting at my desk, I was about to turn off my computer when I decided to check my e-mail one more time. There were two new messages. The first was a brief Happy New Year's wish from Lindsay, who'd gotten a job with the French office of a big publishing house and moved to Paris, leaving my book to an even younger editor who was nevertheless amazingly astute — another reminder to me never to judge a person solely on the basis of her age. Smiling with delight at picturing Lindsay sipping champagne on the Left Bank with her new French boyfriend, whom she was already proclaiming was "the one," I quickly tapped good New Year's wishes back to her.

The second message was a letter from Josh. It was early morning on New Year's Day in Japan — I'd become accustomed to calculating the time difference, with Tokyo thirteen hours ahead — and so now Josh and I were living in different years.

"Consider this my *nengajo* to you," he wrote,

> . . . my New Year's card. Everyone sends them here. There were no parties last night. New Year's Eve is considered a solemn occasion, marked by the eating of

357

soba noodles and the ringing of the temple bells — 108 times to dispel the 108 earthly desires that cause suffering. Right now, I can only think of one, and that's to see you. There will be nowhere to go and nothing to do for the next few days but eat dried cuttlefish (a New Year's delicacy) and go to temple and think of you.

I've been reading, obviously, about the Japanese New Year traditions, and here's one I think you'll be interested in: Hatsu-Yume, which means First Dream. The theory is that the first dream you have in January signifies the kind of year you will have. So last night and this morning, all I dreamed about was you. Do you think this dream could come true?

I typed a one-word answer: Yes.

We had finished eating and had pushed our chairs back from the table, relishing the feeling of fullness. Edie had fallen asleep on my lap, and her warm body, heavy with sleep, made me feel as if I might drift off myself.

"I'll put her down," Diana said. But she didn't move.

"Wait," said Maggie. "I don't want to risk waking her up."

"Yes, leave her," I said.

I was enjoying the feeling of being pinned beneath this sweet girl, the absolute surrender of it. This was something I hadn't really appreciated about having a small child until I'd passed through it: how much time you were forced to do nothing but sit, holding the child as she ate or slept, watching closely as she played. So many hours spent in a world pleasurably constricted to two, much like the early days of love.

"I could fall asleep right now," said Maggie. "But then I know in the middle of the night this baby is going to wake me up and I won't be able to go back to sleep. This morning, I had just drifted off again when Edie woke up and started calling, Mama, Mama." It sounded as if she was complaining, but she had a big grin on her face.

"Well," Diana said, shifting in her seat. "I told my friends I'd meet them at this club."

"And I've got to go to bed," said Maggie.

"Wait, wait!" I said. "It's not even close to midnight yet."

"I'm never going to make it to midnight," said Maggie.

"Neither am I," said Diana.

"Well, at least we have to make our wishes," I said. "Our New Year's wishes."

Maggie rolled her eyes. "Haven't you learned your lesson on that one?"

"No," I said. "Actually, I think that worked out rather well in the end. Come on, Diana, you always liked this. What do you want to happen this year?"

"I want . . ." Diana looked up at Maggie's tin ceiling. "I want to get laid."

Maggie burst out laughing, but I, despite my best efforts, knew I looked shocked.

"Come on, Mom, don't get all moral on me. I know all about you and your little boy toy."

"I'm not being moral," I said, but I heard the priggishness in my voice. "It's just that I only ever hear you talk about nursing, and Africa, and wanting to make a difference in the world."

"Well, I want those things," said Diana, "but I want a little action too. No, I'm lying. What I really want is to fall in love. Stars in the sky, the earth moving — that's what I want this year."

Now that she said it, I realized, it sounded good. I'd had it myself the year before, without even wishing for it, and it *had* been good. Better than good. I wanted my daughter to be as happy.

"Okay," Maggie said, "if we must, I'm going to wish for a healthy baby and an easy delivery." She put her hand on her stomach. "Ouch, he's kicking me."

"He?" said Diana. "Are you telling us something?"

"No," said Maggie, who'd had all the prenatal tests but had resolutely refused to learn the baby's sex. "I still don't know. But my current vibe is a 'he.'"

She put her hand on her stomach again. "Ow," she said. "He's going crazy tonight."

"Oh, my God," I said, suddenly alarmed. "You don't think this could be it, do you?"

I was going to be Maggie's labor coach, and I knew from experience — Diana was born on Thanksgiving — that holidays, when the hospitals were low on staff, could be a scary time to give birth. And then there were the added complications of Diana going out and so not being there to take care of Edie, and the impossibility of getting a cab on New Year's Eve, in a snowstorm, no less.

"No," said Maggie. "I don't think so. The doctor said the baby's still up under my chin. I'm just tired, is all."

She worked herself to her feet and stretched, her belly and breasts enormous beneath a purple stretch velvet turtleneck that matched her chaise.

"I'll take Edie now," said Diana, standing too.

"Wait!" I said. "You haven't heard my wish."

They both looked at me.

"What is it, Mom?" Diana asked finally.

But I had to tell them the Bottom Line Truth: "I haven't made up my mind yet."

After Edie was tucked in her crib, after Diana and I cleaned up and left Maggie to sleep, after Diana went to meet her friends, I decided to go out for a walk. The snow was still falling, the powder covering the sidewalks and streets so lightly it seemed like a dusting of sugar, sweetening the world.

The snow had kept most people inside, so that instead of a holiday this felt like a night quieter than most others. My thought was that I would go down to the restaurant where Maggie and I had gone last year and drink a glass of champagne, but then it was so beautiful outside, I decided to just keep walking. Wearing corduroys and hiking boots, an old ski jacket and Maggie's leopard-skin hunting cap, I trooped through the fringes of Little Italy and the north end of Chinatown into Soho, where the sidewalks were cleared and the restaurants were full of people.

I thought again about stopping for a drink,

but again, kept walking. I turned south, thinking of how I'd borrowed Maggie's boots that night after my heels were killing me.

It was then that I remembered Madame Aurora. Was she still there? Still offering New Year's wishes? I tried to refocus, tried to think of what I'd wish for, how I'd answer Diana's question, what I might tell Madame Aurora if I laid down my money.

The first thing that had come to mind, back in Maggie's loft, was that I wished I could have Josh again, that we could be in love just like before, better than before, for always. But almost immediately, I questioned whether that was what I really wanted, whether that was what he would really want.

So what then, for myself: success for my books? Yes, I wished that. But now that I was actually writing, I saw that as something within my power, not something to pray to the heavens for when blowing out the candles on a cake or spying the first star.

What? Happiness for Diana? For Maggie? Yes, yes. But was that really my one true New Year's wish?

As I neared Madame Aurora's street, I considered whether I would go in and see the gypsy. Who knew, maybe there had been some power in going there after all, in stating my desire out loud. Something, somehow, that made it come true.

I shivered, despite myself. I didn't want to believe that. I didn't even want to think about putting myself in that position again. I'd walk down a different street. I didn't even want to see the fortune-teller's shop, didn't want to place myself within its force field.

But once I got to Madame Aurora's street, I couldn't resist turning down. I had to just know, had to just see, had to let myself feel again what I'd felt a year ago, before anything had happened, to try to judge how much of the power for change had come from within me, and how much from magic. I slowed my steps as I neared the storefront, my heart throbbing in my throat.

And then I stood, not believing what was in front of my eyes. There was no Madame Aurora's. Where the shop had been stood a shoe store, the window filled with pumps and boots and silver sneakers. I looked around, thinking I might have the wrong street, the wrong address. But no, this was it, everything else was right. But Madame Aurora's shop had vanished as thoroughly as Cinderella's coach.

I reeled blindly away and trudged forward

as if by rote, not focusing on anything around me or thinking about where I was going until I found myself in Tribeca, near the dock for the New Jersey–bound ferry. When I'd landed here last New Year's Eve, it had been so crowded with people, but now it seemed almost sleepy, a few stragglers ambling toward the tented dock where the boat was waiting, its lights beckoning.

Well, why not? The moon was full, the snow had stopped, and the Statue of Liberty glowed gorgeous in the distance. It could be the ride that I had dreamed of and hadn't really gotten the year before.

I paid my money and boarded the boat and headed directly for the deck upstairs. There were two other people out there, but I had no trouble claiming the perch at the front, exactly where I'd stood last year. Holding on as the engines roared to life, I thought that maybe this — this ride, this view — would inspire the wish that had been eluding me all night.

The boat pulled away from the dock, and I anticipated that, as had happened the year before, we would swing around once we'd cleared the shoreline. I held the railing and gazed at New Jersey, at the enormous clock on the dock there, the high-rises and the darkness beyond. That was my past, I thought, and any second now the boat will turn around and I'll be riding backward, but facing my future, the buildings of New York, my new home.

But the boat didn't turn around this time, and I found myself, once again, careening directly toward New Jersey. I caught my breath in dismay, thinking that maybe this was a sign that I was condemned never to escape, that New Jersey was indeed my inexorable fate. But then I looked back over my shoulder at the receding skyscrapers and realized that getting a different view was as easy as turning my head. If I stood just so, if I adjusted my angle a tiny bit, I could see both New Jersey and New York, both my past and my future, at the same time.

That's when my wish came, unbidden and impossible, to my mind: I wish, I thought, that my life would stay exactly as it is, right this minute, forever.

UP CLOSE AND PERSONAL
WITH THE AUTHOR

WHERE DID THE IDEA FOR *YOUNGER* COME FROM?

I wanted to write about what I saw as the war between younger and older women, and I came up with the idea to let that struggle play out within one person, my heroine Alice. My first notion of the book was very dark: I saw Alice as a rich and shallow woman on the brink of killing herself who decides to spend her last hour of life reading *Vogue* — and therein discovers a miracle-working plastic surgeon whom she gets to transform her into someone who looks young. But I had no interest in writing about the kind of woman who would do such a thing, however redeemed she may be by the end of the book. Then I spent a long time imagining that the fortune-teller, Madame Aurora, would magically transform Alice into a younger woman. And then finally I realized that Alice could simply pretend to be younger, that in fact her rejuvenation by act of will was more powerful than it could ever be by magic or surgery.

LET'S GO BACK TO THAT WAR BETWEEN YOUNGER AND OLDER WOMEN — WHAT'S THAT ALL ABOUT?

I believe all women are under a tremendous amount of pressure, imposed by time and age, to get all the pistons of their lives — relationships, babies, home, career — firing efficiently. Younger women seem to have a need to believe that it's going to be different for them than it was for the generation before them, that they'll have an easier time balancing work and motherhood, for instance, and that their own marriages will stay as hot as their bodies. And older women, of course, have some need to see them fail, to prove that they really couldn't have done it any better no matter how hard they might have tried. And of course both groups are raging against the same truth: That most women's lives demand considerably more compromise than men's lives do.

WHAT KINDS OF COMPROMISES?

The main one, of course, is the relatively

narrow window women have in which to have their children. Young women today are more aware of that than women now in their forties or fifties were; they know they really need to be having their children by age thirty-five, which doesn't leave them any time to fool around. But older women know how difficult it is to keep a career moving forward in high gear once you have kids, or to step off the career path for a few years and then hop back on. They know that devoting your life whole-heartedly to either children or a career can mean sacrificing the other, and that trying to do both often means constant compromise.

HOW HAS THIS PLAYED OUT IN YOUR LIFE AS A WRITER?

I have three children and I've always worked, but the biggest sacrifice I made when my children were younger was that I stopped writing fiction completely for ten years. I only had time to write purely for money — magazine articles and nonfiction books — and to be a mom. Then when my youngest child was five and started kindergarten, I felt ready to go back to working a longer day and was able to devote half my time to working on what became my first novel, *The Man I Should Have Married*. That book took a long time to write, mostly because I had no idea what I was doing, and I wasn't getting paid for those thousands of hours — and didn't know whether the book would ever be sold. But with my nonfiction career well established and my children more independent and those incredibly overwhelming years of pregnancy and babies behind me, I was able to take that professional risk.

IN WHAT WAYS ARE YOU LIKE ALICE, THE HEROINE OF *YOUNGER*?

I love my house; many writers, I've found, invest a lot of creative energy in their houses, maybe because they spend so much time there. And I have a daughter, my oldest child, who's the same age as Alice's daughter. Although I haven't lived Alice's life of being a full-time mom, I do relate very much to that feeling in your forties of wanting to live out your dreams before it's too late. For Alice, looking younger began as merely a means to reclaiming her old job as an editor. The corollary in my life was writing fiction, something I'd done in my early twenties and then given up for years.

WHY DID YOU MAKE ALICE'S FRIEND MAGGIE GAY?

370

She didn't start out being gay, but I always wanted her to be someone who'd lived independently, who'd never wanted to get married and have kids, and her being a lesbian explained all that very neatly. Also, Maggie is the opposite of Alice in that she's never tried to fit in or be conventional in any way. But the fact that the two have stayed best friends all these years is a testament both to Alice's constancy and her willingness to step outside the box.

WHAT DOES ALICE LEARN FROM BECOMING YOUNGER?

In some ways, she learns that she is who she is, regardless of age. Being younger doesn't automatically make you braver or wilder or more independent. In the same vein, she realizes that if she wants to change those aspects of herself, she's going to have to put a lot of hard work into it, work she avoided because it was too difficult the first time around. She really grows up from this second chance at youth.

WOULD YOU BECOME YOUNGER THE WAY ALICE DID IF YOU HAD THE CHANCE?

What woman wouldn't look fifteen or

371

twenty years younger if she could? The trick is owning your hard-won experience and life and getting the respect of someone older while also enjoying the fruits of looking like a babe — and it doesn't usually work like that, as Alice found out when Teri didn't take her seriously at work. I'd love to have the option of looking younger when it suited my purposes, but I don't have that kind of face or body. I have friends who do, though, women in their forties with kids in high school who can pass for being in their mid-twenties. It's amazing. But I don't think I'd like to go back to that stage of life of being confused about love, of having to prove myself all the time. That's not fun for anyone.

DO YOU BELIEVE IN HAPPY ENDINGS?

Although I know it's not very cool, I do believe in happy endings. I need to believe in at least the possibility of a happy ending, in a story as well as in life. All of my books have a fairy-tale aspect to them, which reflects my earliest reading love along with some underlying wish I have about how things will work out in real life. I continue to believe in magic, in hope, in change, in true love. And any of those things, or all of them together, can lead to a happy ending.

ABOUT THE AUTHOR

Pamela Redmond is the *New York Times* bestselling author of more than twenty works of fiction and nonfiction, including *Younger, How Not to Act Old,* and *30 Things Every Woman Should Have & Should Know.* She started publishing novels, cofounded the world's largest baby name website *Nameberry,* got divorced, moved from New Jersey to Los Angeles, and changed her name, all after the age of fifty. The mother of three and grandmother of one, Redmond's website is at PamelaRedmond.com.

The employees of Thorndike Press hope you have enjoyed this Large Print book. All our Thorndike, Wheeler, and Kennebec Large Print titles are designed for easy reading, and all our books are made to last. Other Thorndike Press Large Print books are available at your library, through selected bookstores, or directly from us.

For information about titles, please call:
(800) 223-1244

or visit our website at:
gale.com/thorndike

To share your comments, please write:

Publisher
Thorndike Press
10 Water St., Suite 310
Waterville, ME 04901